MW00748019

Even Such Is Time

By Elizabeth Bartel

Copyright © 2002 by Elizabeth Bartel. All rights reserved.

No part of this publication may be reproduced, stored in a retrieval system, or transmitted, in any form or by any means, electronic, mechanical, photocopying, recording, or otherwise, without the written prior permission of the author.

This novel is a work of fiction. The names, characters and events are the product of the author's imagination. Any resemblance to real events or actual persons is entirely coincidental.

National Library of Canada Cataloguing in Publication

Bartel, Elizabeth
    Even such is time / Elizabeth Bartel.
ISBN 1-55369-685-9
    I. Title.
PS8553.A77174E8 2002   C813'.6   C2002-902926-0
PR9199.4.B367E8 2002

In bringing this book to birth, I am indebted and everlastingly grateful to my editor, Wendy Dyck for challenging me to write a truer, finer story; to all my friends and especially the women of the Comox Valley's University Women's Book Club who read and cheered me on. I thank my children for allowing me to be their mother, and lastly, I dedicate this book to my husband Dennis, who believed in me and did not leave during some trying times.

Even such is time, which takes in trust
Our youth, our joys and all we have,
And pays us but with age and dust,
Who in the dark and silent grave,
When we have wandered all our ways,
Shuts up the story of our days;
And from which earth and grave and dust
The Lord shall raise me up I trust.

Sir Walter Raleigh

Prologue

Here she comes. Lily. A figure in dark green - or is it black? Slipping and sliding in the icy ruts of the driveway, the prairie sky behind her streaked rose and violet with the morning rays of the sun. On each side of her, young Manitoba maples march along like scrawny sentinels, bare branches laced against the April sky.

Lily. I get up from my chair behind the Boston fern and go to the big doors, ready to push the buzzer and let her in. Through the glass she smiles with those perfect teeth all the young people seem to have nowadays. This is not quite the Lily I remember, of course - a small girl with her father's brown eyes and her mother's high cheekbones. Last night her voice on the telephone had sounded quite grown up.

"Anna? Anna Heppner?"

What to say? It was a voice I couldn't place, smooth and professional with a big city confidence.

"So who is this?" I finally asked, clearing my throat, the black receiver clutched tightly against my ear. I thought it might be a pollster doing a survey. Last week there was one, asking endless questions - what kind of cake-mix did I use? Had I used cake-mix in the last week? The last month? The last year? I finally hung up on that girl. It's not polite but I lost patience. After all, I'm eighty years old and should be allowed a few lapses.

"Is this Anna Heppner?" The voice was more urgent.

"I was Anna Heppner before I married. Who is this?"

A crank phone call, I thought, wait until I tell Conrad.

Even though he is retired and somewhat forgetful, my brother would put a stop to this. I would tell him tomorrow when he came for his daily visit.

"My name is Lily Heppner," she had said slowly as if I might not understand her. Deaf and dumb besides old, she probably thought.

"I'm Lily. Remember now?" There was a little laugh. "I believe I'm related to you."

"Oh, oh, yes," I stuttered. "Lily? Felix's Lily? Of course, that Lily...how are you? It's been some time. Where are you calling from? It's nice to hear - how is Alice, your mother?" Suddenly I was breathless. My heart fluttered in my throat. I had to sit down.

"I've come to see my father's grave," she said abruptly. "I've come to find out, to ask...what really happened, you know about the accident?" The voice of the woman on the telephone paused before going on uncertainly. "My mother gave me your address, your phone number. She says you always kept a journal." Her voice rose at the end of the sentence so that it was half question, half statement. I smiled grimly into the telephone. My journal. Why had I ever confided that to Alice? Not even Conrad knew I kept a journal.

It was my father who had encouraged me. "Someday you will be glad," he said. "You will surprise yourself." That had been years ago, the first one begun when I was a bare fifteen and left home to work for the Strachans in the city. Now the journals, one for each year, gather dust. They are stacked on a shelf of the linen closet in this retirement home where I now live.

I will have to read through them before I let anyone see, especially Lily. I remember only my rage and grief. Those memories pierce me still. What have I written about that terrible quarrel between my brothers? And what of the accident itself and after that? Can I bear to go over all those old wounds? What has Alice told Lily, who will want to know everything? She is my dead brother's daughter after all, and has a right to know.

But she has come, sweet Lily, after these many years, come to the place where she was born, the daughter I never had. Lily, Felix's Lily. I pressed the buzzer to let her in.

I had always hoped, always wondered, if anyone would come.

Chapter One

"Dearest child, we'll not forget what you are giving up," my father said, his eyes watering in the glare of noonday sun.

I paid no attention to his words. Please let me not have to go, I prayed. A swirl of dust eddied above the cinders of the station platform. Grit stung in my eyes.

My father looked towards the red brick schoolhouse across the street. "You're only fifteen. I hoped so much to keep you in school, Anna. You are such a fine scholar. I fear I have failed you now. If only times were better."

I looked once more at the high school surrounded by empty playing fields. The students would be at their desks now, opening text books, their new pen nibs poised above clean white foolscap, the whole room pervaded by the sharp metallic smell of fresh ink, the woodiness of pencil shavings, the dust-bane the janitor used to sweep the wooden floors.

"No, no, Papa. Don't blame yourself," I tried to sound reassuring, but I could not meet his eyes. I looked at the steep roof of the station and its drab red walls, at the galvanized milk cans in the baggage cart. Finally my eyes came to rest on the station agent, leaning casually against the canvas mailbags, his C.P.R. badge glinting in the light. I was glad he could not understand our German conversation.

"Can you forgive us, Anna? Your mama, especially?" my father said, his voice gruff. "She has her pride, and our Reise Schult, our debts to the Canadian Pacific, haunts her."

"Could they send us back as Mama keeps saying?"

My father smiled faintly. "I don't believe so, not now, but

9

she will be more at ease when we are no longer beholden to them." My father's voice trailed off.

"Papa, Papa. It's alright. I understand." I thought of my mother stirring plum preserves on the stove in our steamy kitchen a few miles away, her mouth a thin straight line. She had been brusque when we said goodbye as if this was just an ordinary leave taking. "Be good," she'd said and kissed me, hard.

The approaching train's whistle interrupted my thoughts as it sounded at the crossing on the outskirts of town. Sudden tears made the white petunias in the station window boxes blur, softened the bright colours worn by the station agent's wife who stood over the flowers with a watering can. Across from the main tracks a steady stream of grain poured from the elevator into a waiting rail car. Fine dust rose high into the air in a golden haze.

"If it's too hard, Anna, and you can't stand it, you have only to write and come home." My father raised his voice to be heard above the thunderous approach of the train. He reached down to put an arm around me as the train slowed to a halt with a noisy hiss and puff.

The conductor swung down from the coach, a small stool in hand, its carpeting of dark wine and olive green worn down by the feet of many travellers. He placed it below the steps of the coach, took a whiskbroom from the back pocket of his dark blue trousers, bent down and brushed the fading nap briskly like a fastidious housewife.

Then he straightened. "Five minute stop. All aboard for Raulston, Calgary, Vancouver," he called.

"Good evening," my father greeted the conductor, switching to English. My father handed over my bag to the conductor who tucked it under one arm and handed me up the steps of the coach with the other.

I was the only traveller to board. In the coach there were not many passengers; one or two raised curious eyes at the rush of different air and a new face, then satisfied, their heads disappeared again behind the high backs of their seats.

The train juddered slightly back and forth as if uncertain which way it would go. I sat down with an abrupt thump into the worn plush of an empty seat as the train drew away from the station platform. Smoke from the engine blew past the window and obscured the last view of my father.

"Well, young lady?" The conductor stopped beside me, his bright eyes twinkling, and took the ticket I held out.

"Next stop, Carville," he called out and thumped the back of each empty seat as he moved forward. Little clouds of dust rose with each thump. By the time he reached the end of the coach the train had gathered speed.

The coach was overheated. Sweat quickly gathered at the back of my neck. I smelled coal smoke, stale tobacco, discarded wax paper sandwich wrappers. I unbuttoned my new jacket.

So like my mother, I thought as the stubbled fields passed by the window of the train. She might be driven to send me away to work in another woman's house but she would make sure that I went looking presentable. She'd ripped apart her one and only suit, the one she had brought with her from the good years in Russia and altered it so that it would fit me.

"Our seamstress always came to sew for us in the spring - at Pentecost," she had told me, her voice soft and sad with remembering, as she worried the aging seams of the skirt with a razor blade. The jacket required little alteration. "My sister and I had these identical suits made. They were the latest fashion from Berlin that year. Navy blue with a pin stripe. We wore them for the first time to church in Schoenwese. Your father was there, home from the university for the summer holidays."

She stood up to shake out the bits of thread and dust, turned the skirt inside out, and then sat down at the sewing machine. "I won't bother with basting," she said as the needle flashed up and down along the new seam, her foot moving purposefully on the treadle. "Once I am done with this it might be too fine for a house-maid," she smiled, teasing me a little. "Of course it never hurts to look your best, does it? You might meet a handsome young man at the Madchenheim."

At the thought of whom I might meet at the Madchenheim - of whatever gender - I flushed uneasily. The Madchenheim was a place for Mennonite girls who worked in the city.

I was suddenly struck by the thought of how the girls at the Madchenheim might laugh at my mother's efforts at stylishness. In the old brown suitcase at my feet, lay a nightgown with an embroidered yoke, salvaged from the last of the pillowcases that my mother had brought with her from the old country as part of her dowry. I was wearing the white blouse she had trimmed with lace and under my skirt, peach silk panties swished between my thighs. My mother had not said where she had found the silk.

Four hours later, the train, shedding soot and cinders, drew in under a smudged glass roof. As I stood dazed and bewildered on the station platform, a lady, tall and slender in a blue tweed suit came towards me. "Good afternoon. I'm Mrs. Strachan. You must be Anna," she said with an English accent. Circles of rouge blazed on her thin cheeks.

I held out my hand. I had been taught it was polite to shake hands.

She ignored it. "Welcome to Raulston. My car is waiting just outside. How was your trip?" She did not wait for my reply but led me away through the doors into the station. I followed wordlessly.

"Your trunks will be delivered," she said above the sound of her heels clicking on the smooth marble floor of the station. The sound of her clipped English words tended to disappear into the cavernous dome of the station. It reminded me of the grand railroad station in Kiev that we passed through on our way to Canada.

"The ladies'?" Mrs. Strachan looked at me and raised her eyebrows in question.

I nodded. Mrs Strachan turned and I followed her into the station rest room where dark wood panelled the walls. Small amber lights glowed in candle brackets over each writing desk. Through a further door, white tiles gleamed in the lavatory. Mrs. Strachan pointed to a cubicle and disappeared into the adjoining one. There was the rush of water in the silence. When I emerged from the cubicle I caught sight of my reflection in the mirror above the pedestal sinks. I saw my dark brown, almost black eyes, dark curls escaping from under my hat, my full red lips.

Beside me, Mrs. Strachan patted the waves in her hair and composedly snapped open her bag and took out a gold compact. It was as if she brought frightened country girls to this station restroom every day. She brushed a powder puff over her nose and cheeks, never once looking at me, but only at her reflection in the mirror. I looked again into the mirror at Mrs. Strachan and then at myself. Suddenly I looked terrible. I was short and frumpy with fat cheeks, fat eyes, fat hair. Everything about me screamed immigrant. And my suit - I had been so proud of my suit. Somehow I knew it was all wrong but I didn't know exactly why. Mrs. Strachan snapped shut her compact and I followed her out of the rest room, through the station and out into the busy street.

She stopped beside an expensive-looking grey car parked at the curb. "Climb in," she said, gesturing toward the passenger side. I did as I was bid. In the car's grey mohair softness I stared at the mahogany dashboard, at its gauges and dials. "McLaughlin-Buick" it read in flowing silver script. Mrs. Strachan fitted the key into the ignition and I heard the lazy purr of a powerful engine. She shifted gears and grasped the wheel as we moved off.

I tried to settle into the seat. What would my mother make of this, she who had boasted of my grandfather's imported German automobiles before the Great War in Russia? Here in Canada my father always threw her a warning glance when she spoke of those times. It made him uneasy. "We will not boast about the past. We're immigrants. These people here might take offense." My mother had remained silent about automobiles after that. "Your father is too modest," I heard her fume once in exasperation, "He cares nothing for machinery, always the helpless scholar."

Mrs. Strachan drove slowly, at first beside a boulevard along which grew a double row of trees. Fallen leaves lay thick along the curb. Between the trees, bright orange streetcars, their bells clanging, rattled by, both coming and going along the tracks.

"This is the so-called downtown. King Street," Mrs Strachan said and braked at a traffic light. In one shop window a mannequin stood in a long fur coat, flowered silk at her throat, a grey handbag at her feet. In the next window, gold watches glittered on dark velvet and in another, china bowls and plates and silver teapots multiplied themselves in a mirrored wall. We passed the flashing marquee of a theatre. Playbills advertised Greta Garbo in a film called Ninotchka. Russian, I thought. I had heard of Greta Garbo, a Swedish actress. My father admired her. What if it should so happen that my father would come for me one day in a grey Mclaughlin-Buick and take me to see Greta Garbo in Ninotchka before he took me home for a holiday?

"You're quite young to be so far away from home," Mrs. Strachan said, breaking into my reverie. She looked sideways at me, as if she was not sure I would do. "You will have much to learn. I insist on a well-run household."

I came back to reality and stared down at my hands. I wondered if she was seriously thinking of sending me back before I even got out of her car. I was too shy to tell her how good I was with bread and noodles. It would sound like boasting. I could have told her that I liked to clean and dust nice furniture, wax floors, that I really wanted to please her, but I said nothing.

The car continued on, crossed a bridge spanning a sluggish river. Iron girders threw black lace shadows before us. Along the river's edge trees stood shedding yellow leaves. We crossed another bridge, this time with no girders. Nearby, children played ball on an asphalt playground beside a tall schoolhouse of weathered brick.

"Our cathedral, where we attend mass and sometimes evensong," Mrs. Strachan pointed, a note of pride in her voice.

I saw a large grey stone church standing on a corner, shrubbery tucked neatly around its foundations. One tall wooden door stood half-open but no light shone behind the stained glass windows. I could not see the top of the spire from the car window. St. Luke's Cathedral, I read on a modest board facing the road and below that, Anglican Church of Canada. A carillon rang out just as we passed, as if to greet us. I had not thought of the Strachans as being religious. Were English people religious?

The car stopped at last on a quiet street before a two-storey white house, surrounded by elm and oak trees. Juniper and Spiraea grew under the downstairs windows. Mrs. Strachan did not speak as she drew up on the side driveway. She seemed tired and out of sorts now, and climbed wearily out of the car and led the way to the side door. "Bring your bag," she said and ushered me through the door and up three steps into the kitchen. I looked around. White, everything white, so different from our kitchen at home: white stove, white sink, white counters, and a white electric refrigerator. I looked down at a tiled floor that was white and black and smooth as glass.

"The servants stairs are here, Anna." I could see a long flight that led up into the darkness. "Your room is right at the top. Everything you need is there. For your supper there are sandwiches left over from lunch in the fridge. Your bathroom is down that way in the basement. In the morning the judge will show you how he wants his breakfast. Set your clock for six a.m. Later in the morning I will explain your other duties." Twice she cleared her throat, as if reinforcing who she was - Mrs. Strachan - and who I was - Anna, the new maid.

"That will be all now," she said as if she was reading instructions from a book. "I hope you will be happy here." She turned and disappeared through a doorway.

And that was the end of it. I heard her footsteps recede, then silence. Alone in a strange house, I jumped as the motor of the white refrigerator jolted into action. I thought of my father. I will not cry, I vowed. I must remember why I am here. Suitcase in hand I stumbled up first one flight of unfamiliar stairs and then another and found the one lone room at the top of this alien house. Against the far wall was a narrow bed covered by a dark wool blanket instead of the old-fashioned comforter of my mother's making. Turned down over the blanket was a stark white sheet and one thin white pillow. My eyes smarted with tears as I thought of my mother's fat pillows stuffed with goose down.

It was just getting dark. In this house I was high, high, up in the sky. From the little round window of my room I looked out over the treetops. Beyond the houses on the other side of the street, the trees along the river bank stood stripped of their leaves so that I could see the last rays of the sun glinting on a gunmetal coil of water that was the river. From this distance it looked frozen in place. Nothing moved, waiting. My new life had begun.

In the weeks that followed, I would wake each morning to the buzzing of the Big Ben alarm clock that I had placed on the floor by my bed. The dark grey uniform and black stockings that Mrs. Strachan had provided lay on a chair. I scooped them up and hurried down the long flight of stairs in my petticoat. It was quite safe to go half-dressed - who was there to see me? No one else used these stairs to the basement bathroom. In the darkness, for often I did not bother with the light switch on the first landing, I longed for a dressing gown of blue flannel, or the newest thing, chenille, which I had seen in the Eaton's catalogue at home. After I had washed and dressed, it was time to bring up Mrs. Strachan's tray that I had set out the night before.

She was very particular. The china cup and saucer banded with pale green and gold must be placed just so on the embroidered linen, with the matching sugar bowl and the milk jug. When I placed the tray beside Mrs. Strachan's bed she was often awake, but we did not speak except for my whispered good morning. Heavy satin drapes, a pale green that matched the china on the tray, kept out the morning light.

My feet made no sound on the thick India carpet which Mrs. Strachan had brought with her from England along with the mahogany bureau, the chest of drawers, the triple mirror above the dressing table and the satin covered chaise longue. "My pieces," she called the furniture, "family pieces, quite good pieces, handed down to me." Later in the morning, I would Hoover the carpet and arrange the bottles of scent on the glass top of the dressing table. Before I left the room, I would dust the bowed fronts of the bureaus and the night table and straighten the matching satin spread that covered the bed.

But before that there was the judge's breakfast to deal with: toast in a silver toast rack, strong black tea in a brown pot, Dundee Marmalade in a crystal jar and the Raulston Herald folded beside his plate.

"Well, Anna, is it?" the judge asked on the first morning. "Where are you from?" Although his voice was kind he did not wait for an answer; his eyes returned to the newspaper. The smell of his shaving soap mingled with the smell of toast, and later, when he lit a cigarette, the smell of fresh tobacco. From his full head of grey hair - which must have once been dark, for his heavy brows remained so - to the intense blue eyes behind his glasses, the judge radiated well-being. His shoulders were at ease in a tweed jacket; gold cuff links gleamed at his wrists. His flannel covered legs stretched out under the table, polished shoes resting confidently on the oriental carpet.

He presided in the Law Courts building on Broad Street just across from the domed Legislative buildings. I imagined the judge in black robes as he pronounced sentence on the law-breakers that came before him. Did he listen more closely there than he did here to me?

Before the judge went to his duties I would hear him trudge up the stairs to greet his wife in her room where I imagined him kissing her smooth, scented cheek. Shortly after I would hear the front door close behind him. Then I knew Mrs. Strachan would get up. I pictured her putting on her silk blouse and English woollen skirt with matching cardigan, leaning over the dressing table to powder her nose and rouge her cheeks, and then bending to lace up her fine leather oxfords.

On most fine days she took Fletcher, her French poodle, for a walk. When I first came, I could not imagine how anyone could lavish so much attention on a dog. Through the window above the kitchen sink I would watch as Mrs. Strachan, with Fletcher trailing behind, headed towards the dusty willows along the riverbank. It was as close as Mrs. Strachan could get to the green English park she so longed for.

When she returned she came into the kitchen to prepare the menus for that day. In the weeks that followed I learned how to cook in the English way: bland Yorkshire puddings, buttery short bread, junket. Mrs. Strachan shuddered at the mere mention of garlic and did not care for my preference for aniseed or fresh dill.

In the afternoons, Mrs. Strachan would often play bridge. On those days I wore a black uniform with a white apron and a starched white frill of muslin perched precariously on top of my unruly head of hair. When I came into the room with the tea tray the ladies would put down their cards to light their cigarettes. Each of them had a different brand: red Turrets, white Buckinghams, green Export A.

"A small slam! I should have bid it. Oh, silly me," said Mrs Hawkins as she blew smoke out of the small crimson circle of her mouth.

"Oh this old thing? I got it at the Bay,"

"You've heard? They're breaking up. She's keeping the house in Riverview."

I heard only scraps of seemingly disjointed conversation while I served cucumber sandwiches from a silver platter. Fingers with painted nails reached for an olive, a stick of celery. Mrs. Strachan lifted an eyebrow, a signal to me to bring more hot water for the teapot. Only Mrs. Strachan acknowledged my presence; to the others I was invisible.

It was different when the judge entertained. In his library, the well-fed bodies of his guests filled the leather armchairs, which I dusted each morning. They were mostly lawyers and politicians who looked much like the judge in their dark suits and ties. I sensed the power straining behind their buttoned vests, the tight shirt collars. I had seen their faces on the front page of the Raulston Herald and the Tribune. They spoke like well-bred Englishmen - so different from the broken English of my father and his friends.

Professor Hadfield huffed and puffed. "Anarchy is what it is. Pure and simple. Bloody Socialists. Farmers marching to Ottawa," he would bluster.

"What we need is another war." Colonel Douglas was a military man. He would twirl the blue globe beside him on its stand, as if he was about to decide where it might begin. "Teach the young ones a thing or two. Like the 1919 Strike, we'd soon see." The judge would say nothing but poured more whiskey into their heavy glasses.

Doctor Silvers smiled a lot and always tried to catch my eye as I passed him to fetch more ice. I would flush and look away, unaccountably embarrassed by his glance.

After I had served and cleaned up the supper dishes, I was free to go to my room and read or write letters, but most nights, at least at first, my eyes would not stay open for more than a few minutes and I would be asleep by the time my head touched the pillow.

In the middle of that first November at the Strachans my father wrote to thank me for the money order I had sent at the end of October. "Dearest Anna, we are so grateful." I could see my father bending over the letter, guiding the pen to form the narrow German script. I remembered the Academy where he had been the headmaster. I would have been a student there, I mused, if war and revolution had not intervened, changed everything in our lives. We would all still be there - my father leading his scholarly life, my mother as the headmaster's wife, lording it over the other wives at the school, and we children looking forward to holidays on the Black Sea.

I read further. "Mama's been to the doctor. The weather continues dry and cold. Your brother Conrad is fine and working hard in school. He sends regards. Felix has tamed a wild crow."

I smiled at the thought of my younger brother; he so loved animals. But what was that about my mother being sick? I read again. My mother was never sick; never went to the doctor but relied on her own remedies: enemas, mustard plasters, bottles of Alpenkrauter for women's ailments.

All through the morning, waxing floors and polishing silver I kept my mind on my work. But in the afternoon as I bent over the laundry tub in the basement, my father's words suddenly came back to me. I stopped squeezing suds through Mrs. Strachan's silk underwear. What if my mother was really ill? Who would take care of my father and the boys? I draped Mrs. Strachan's sheer stockings over the line, and then gathered up the judge's clean shirts, dampened and ready for ironing, into the basket. I lifted the basket to my hip and climbed up through the gloom of the stairs and into the bright kitchen.

I set up the ironing board so I could see into the dining room and the sunroom beyond where the light filtered through the greenery of the ferns. Momentarily the worry about my mother receded. The gaudy colours of the Ladies Own magazines, lying open on the chintz cushions of the wicker settee beckoned. How I loved Mrs. Strachan's house and all her things!

But then I felt shame. How could I forget my mother? Back and forth, back and forth, went my thoughts, just like the iron sliding over the judge's shirts. I had been seduced by Mrs. Strachan's crystal bowls and pitchers. How could I forget my mother and the crowded spaces of the two small rooms where she struggled to keep things nice? Where the finest object was a Spruch, hanging on the wall above our round oak table. "The Lord is my strength," it read in ornate script, with stylised flowers embroidered on fine linen. I hung the last of the judge's shirts on a hanger, ready to go upstairs. I thought of my mother in her tiny kitchen ironing my father's shirts. I was torn between two different worlds and yet, freshly ironed; my father's shirts and the judge's smelled exactly the same.

The doorbell rang; I could see Mrs. Strachan standing on the other side of the glass, her arms full of packages. I turned the brass latch to let her in. She handed me her several parcels. "I forgot my key, Anna." She looked around at her surroundings, checking to see what I had done. She peered into the dining room where I had laid the table for dinner with the linen place mats and gold-rimmed china. The aroma of roast beef mingled with the smell of the fresh ironing reached us from the kitchen.

Mrs. Strachan removed her furs, retrieved her parcels and turned to go up the stairs. The seams of her stockings were no longer straight. She must have had a trying day.

"So how is everything, Anna?" she asked, pausing briefly on the landing. "Have you heard from your family? Are they well? Your mother?"

I took a breath, wanting to tell her about my letter. Then I held back. "They're fine, thank you, Mrs. Strachan," I said.

Mrs. Strachan nodded and continued up the stairs. I retreated to the kitchen.

What had I been thinking? Mrs. Strachan did not really care how my mother was. She could not possibly understand. If Mrs. Strachan ailed she could always afford to pay a visit to Dr. Silvers. I opened the oven door to baste the roast. I thought of my father, how he would always end his letters with good wishes for the Strachans. "Give them our regards," he would write. The Strachans did not care about my father, either. No matter what, rain or shine, the judge would get his salary. What did he know about poor farmers, anyway?

That evening after cleaning up the kitchen, instead of hurrying up the back stairs as I usually did, I went into the judge's library looking for a book to read. When I had first come to work for her, Mrs. Strachan had instructed me on how to dust the books. She had noticed how I revered them and invited me to borrow one whenever I wished. In that instance she was generous and I tried to show my appreciation by taking special care of those I borrowed - no dog-eared pages, no coffee spills.

I heard the front door close on the judge and then the engine of the Buick cough into life.

"I just thought I'd look for another book to read before bed," I said to Mrs. Strachan who had wandered into the library from the sunroom where she had been reading.

"Yes, definitely, Anna. You should be reading more," she said now from behind me, her eye running over the rows and rows of books on the shelves. She seemed strangely sociable. It did not happen often. "So good for you, Anna," she continued. "It improves the mind, I'm sure."

I thought of how often at the end of a long day, my eyes would want to close as soon as I fell into bed. Still, when I had a mystery novel by Agatha Christie, I would finish it in one night and wake up in the morning bleary-eyed but happy.

She went on. "My governess despaired of me, you know. I'm afraid some of the judge's books are beyond me, rather heavy-going." She laughed in a sort of apology.

I reached for a book. "Oh yes, of course, that's John Buchan's Thirty-nine Steps," she said peering over my shoulder. She took it and opened it at the title page. "Autographed, too. You should read this, Anna. He's the judge's uncle. Imagine. It's a very well thought of book, too. There's talk he might become the Governor General of Canada. Astonishing for a minister's son, really, to become a Governor General," she mused and handed it back to me. "I really must read it sometime. After all, an uncle as a Governor General in the family."

I kept silent about my own uncles even though my mother had told me how important they were; I knew Mrs. Strachan would not be impressed. One uncle was an Elteste of the largest Mennonite church in all of Russia, another a manufacturer of farm equipment that before the revolution had been exported to America. And then there was my black-sheep uncle - a worldly boyar fallen from true Mennonite ways, who rode his fine horse across his broad estates along the Dnieper river. But my uncles lived in a part of the world where no Union Jack had ever flown and therefore they meant nothing to Mrs. Strachan.

Still she lingered. I was ready to take my book and go, but it seemed Mrs. Strachan was not finished with me. There was more. What was it she couldn't bring herself to tell me? She picked up an atlas that lay on the desk and absent-mindedly riffled through its pages. "My ancestors came with the Hudson's Bay Company to live among savages. You know Anna, when I first came to Canada as a young girl like you..." Mrs. Strachan paused as if she had forgotten what she meant to say. She turned her tall thin body and stared out of the library window into the darkness. Snowflakes drifted and eddied under the streetlight. She sighed.

"I've been here over twenty years," she went on at last. "This is such exile for me. When the judge retires we'll go home."

Was Mrs. Strachan then an immigrant, too? She was obviously homesick and as lonely as I was. My feelings for her shifted in that moment and I came close to liking her, almost loving her.

She turned back to the table where the atlas lay and pointed with her finger to all the places marked in red on the map of the world. "The British Empire," she said, "on which the sun never sets and never will," as if that explained everything. I waited. I had learned all about the British Empire in geography class at the school in Hackett where a map of the world hung on the far wall below the portrait of King George the fifth, crowned and sceptred.

"Yes, take the book, take it," she said. "Take it to your room. I think it's all about British spies. If nothing else it will improve your English. Good night, Anna."

On my way up the back stairs to my bed, I remembered overhearing her say to the judge. "Anna! Babbling in German or whatever language she speaks. People will think we are harbouring a spy. These immigrants must realize they are now living in a democracy where we all speak English."

By the time I reached the top of the stairs, my blood was on the boil again. Was my English so terrible? I knew that Mrs. Strachan hated German. To her it was the language of the filthy Boche, those beasts who in the last war had thought nothing of spitting Belgian babies on their bayonets. As I undressed in my room I vowed never to tell her anything. Nothing. I would never tell her that I spoke Russian as well. As for the part about democracy, I wondered what Mrs. Strachan would make of what my mother said about it. My mother didn't believe that Poles and Galician and Bukovinians could ever understand democracy. How would they vote when they could barely read the name on a ballot? And whom would they vote for? "What they need is the murdered Czar alive and well and back on the throne," my mother often said. It came to me suddenly - Mrs. Strachan would probably agree with my mother, although she would never admit it. I smiled at the thought.

That night I dreamt of Mrs. Strachan and my mother meeting in the friendliest possible way. In the dream they were making noodles together. The thin dough as vast as several bedsheets was spread out over Mrs Strachan's smooth mahogany dining room table and draped over the chairs and the wicker settee in the sunroom. "Now it is dry enough," my mother said, a sharp knife in her hand. Then I realized she was preparing to cut the dough into the finest of noodles, right there on the perfect surface of Mrs. Strachan's beautiful table. "Mama, no, no," I screamed in my dream. Mrs. Strachan only nodded obediently.

The following morning I awoke feeling foggy and when I turned back the sheet to climb out of bed I was horrified to see a blood stain the size of my hand on Mrs. Strachan's white sheet. It was the first time I had had my monthlies since I left home. My mother had tucked a bag of clean cotton menstrual rags into my valise before I left home. "Wash them in a pail when you are alone," she whispered obliquely as if menstruating was a disgrace that she did not want to discuss.

Now here was this awful stain on Mrs. Strachan's white sheet. It had even soaked through to the mattress cover. I should have known, but with everything else going on, I had paid no attention, had not noticed how the time had gone by. I swept both sheet and cover from the bed and hurried with it down the back stairs to the basement. My mother had taught me about stains. I would soak and scrub, bleach if necessary. Mrs. Strachan need never know.

But later that morning her sharp eye noted the slight bulge under my uniform. "Anna, you should have told me," she said. "I have Kotex for you. There is a supply in your bathroom. Homemade pads fit so poorly; it's embarrassing for my lady guests. I like my girls to look nice." She turned back to her magazine as if menstruating was no big secret. I could have kissed her, but by now I knew better. A kiss from a maid? She would have died of shock.

Chapter Two

My feelings for Mrs. Strachan continued to blow hot and cold as the weeks passed.

"I can't figure her out," I wrote to my cousin Zena, who lived four hundred miles away in Millbach. Zena had been part of my life since I was born. With her older brother, her parents, and a contingent of several uncles and aunts, she had emigrated to Canada a few months before us. The Walls had settled in Millbach amongst Mennonites who had lived in Canada since 1874, and even though the Walls were also Mennonite, they did not fit in, according to Zena's letters. The earlier immigrants saw them as too "worldly."

"Mama says I should try to fit in, but I don't know," Zena had written in one of her first letters. "Andrew says to ignore them but he will be gone to the university in Winnipeg by next year." Zena's brother Andrew had always been ambitious and cared little what others thought and Zena was much like her brother. Even when we were little Zena had been the one to climb up on her brother's big stallion without permission and ride him around the pasture. She was the one who talked back to the Russian kitchen maids when they scolded her for cutting haphazardly into a fresh pie. There had never been a time when I hadn't feared a little for Zena's spirit of adventure. And now she alarmed me with her bold words about the boys in Millbach.

"The boys here are not much, one or two, maybe, but their mothers are on the alert and watching every move their sons make. I am not one of their own. They look down on my Slavic cheekbones, my slanted eyes. Ukrainian for sure, they whisper. They can't understand how I came to be in the Wall family, but it's none of their business."

It was no big secret. We all knew that Zena's parents were not her real parents. Zena had been adopted soon after her birth. But her story was never discussed publicly.

"I wish you were not so far away," I wrote, now. "My diary is a comfort but I worry about, well, for instance, what if I should drop dead and Mrs. Strachan discovers it? She'll read all the awful things I've written about her." Automatically I put my hand over what I had written, just as if Mrs. Strachan might be already peering over my shoulder as I wrote. "I must tell you about this coming Thursday," I went on to Zena. "I will finally go to the Madchenheim. The housemother there phoned Mrs. Strachan to see if I had been sick because she had not yet seen me there. So this week I will be allowed to go. I will tell you all about it." I put down my pen for a moment, then picked it up again. I could hear the shunting of the trains in the rail yards far away across the city. It was a lonesome sound. "How far apart we are now. Please write soon." I wrote, put down my pen for the last time, folded the letter to fit into the stamped envelope already addressed to Miss Zena Wall, General Delivery, Millbach, Manitoba. Zena was an erratic correspondent. Sometimes she answered right away, but often I would write several times before I got a reply. That was how it was with Zena. Sometimes I waited so long for her to reply I began to wonder - had she run away, or got sick and died? Or did I only have the address wrong?

The next day was Sunday but it was not my Sunday off. In the afternoon I took Fletcher for a walk down Harkness Avenue across River Street and then along the curving drive of Durham Crescent that led to College Road. It was a pretty street with an early snow lightly dusting the grass on the boulevard down the centre of the street. Further down along the river, the oak trees that had been old when the Indians still roamed these banks raised tortured branches to a grim November sky. A narrow channel of water, barely moving, ran down the middle of the river. Soon it would be completely frozen over. Fletcher and I walked further, as far as College Road where the street broadened. I stared at the grand homes there, even larger and finer than the judge's. I slowed so that Fletcher could sniff and mark a wrought iron fence while I peered over a bristling hedge and wondered how it felt to live in a house like that with a big glassed-in porch. High up just beneath the eaves was a tiny window. That would be my room, the maid's room. How had it come about that some were millionaires and some, like me, were maids? Who could answer me that?

Fletcher pulled on his leash and we turned for home.

When we got back to the house, Mrs. Strachan was sitting alone in the sunroom. "I'll have my tea early, Anna," she said and went back to her magazine. When I brought in the tea tray, she smiled and turned from the window through which she was watching two chickadees fighting over the crumbs I had put out for the birds that morning. She seemed in a mellow mood. I dared a question and asked her who lived in those grand houses on the Crescent. She sniffed disdainfully, and picked up the teapot to pour herself a cup of tea. "Railroad barons and grain buyers. Speculators. Not our kind at all." Apparently there were people richer than Mrs. Strachan and the judge.

I took Fletcher down to the basement laundry tub to give him a good scrub after his walk. Fletcher lived inside the Strachan house like a person. So English a thing. What would my mother say to that? She believed dogs belonged in the barn. She would have been shocked to see Fletcher among the sheets and eiderdown on Mrs. Strachan's bed, eating from her china dinner plate when she set it down beside her chair. Fletcher caused a lot of extra work for me but I had grown to love him in spite of that, although for a long time I could not admit it. Loving a dog as if it was a child seemed against what I had been taught.

All that week I eagerly awaited my first visit to the Madchenheim. The night before, I was hardly able to decide what to wear: the green and blue print or my black skirt and white blouse. It hardly made a difference; my winter coat covered everything anyway.

By the afternoon a thaw was melting the snow as I walked to the streetcar stop by Caledonia Curling Rink. Through the windows of the rink I could see the men. Brightly coloured badges festooned their sweaters. Brooms aloft, they ran up and down the long narrow sheets of ice, but their shouts of "Sweep, sweep!" in this first game of the season were no affair of mine.

The streetcar appeared on the bridge, it poised for an instant then seemed to hurtle down the incline towards me, its bright orange sides spattered with muddy slush. It squealed to a stop and the doors clanged open. I climbed aboard and dropped my ticket into the holder, accepting a transfer slip from the conductor's hand. At this time of day it was almost empty. It started with a jerk and I sat down abruptly in the first empty seat, clutching my handbag and braced myself against the swaying motion of the car. I stared out of the grimy window and wondered about the Madchenheim and the housemother there who was waiting to meet me. Her name was Miss Fast. I had never met her although I knew my father thought highly of her. She had been a matron at the *Krankenhaus* in Nicolaipol before the revolution. My mother did not hold her in such high esteem, but differences of that nature were often the case between my parents. "She has only a diploma from that sanatarium in Germany," my mother had scoffed when she heard who it was that had been appointed by the church to administer the Madchenheim. In spite of what my mother thought, I hoped Miss Fast would be friendly.

The car rocketed past the railroad station where I had first arrived. Now, just as then, people milled about on the sidewalk. Pale sunlight flashed on the row of brass doors as they opened and closed.

The car slowed. Ahead loomed the huge pillars of the Bank of Montreal. The statue of the Unknown Soldier in his helmet and puttees, rifle held high, stood on a plinth above the traffic, his stone mouth open in a silent shout. At his feet a policeman in a shaggy buffalo coat waved us forward. Electric sparks crackled overhead as the car turned on its track into the deep curve of Main Street. As we passed the limestone pile that was the Grain Exchange, the conductor called out the stops: Banning, Argyll, William Avenue. We stopped before the ornamental brick of the City Hall.

"Princess Street," called the conductor. Past the city Hall I could just see several blocks of Chinatown, a strange other world with black spidery characters in vermilion and gold on the street signs and in the store windows and restaurants. An old man with a pigtail hanging down his back stood on the steps of a laundry, partly enveloped by clouds of steam shooting out of the side window of the building behind him, the foundation of which looked ready to sink further into the ground.

Burnett, Logan, Pacific, the conductor called. The car swooped into the subterranean gloom under the tracks of the C.P.R. main line and then up the other side. I blinked in the sudden glare. We had reached the North End - that section of Raulston that Mrs. Strachan so disapproved of. "Sauerkraut in open barrels right out on the street," she had sniffed disdainfully to her guests as if she could still smell it. "In summer on our way to the beach we have to roll up the car windows."

The judge was not worried about his wife's sensitive nose. "It's those communists meeting at the labour temple nearby we should be worrying about," he said. "They could strike again. This time it could be worse. If it was up to me I'd send them all back where they came from."

What was the judge afraid of? I wondered as the streetcar stopped to let on more passengers. Two women boarded, shluffed down the aisle of the car in their shin-high boots. They wore heavy coats and cotton stockings, their heads wrapped in green and red kerchiefs. More immigrants, I thought, and by their conversation, Ukrainians or Poles. They seated themselves across from me. A small boy accompanied them, holding fast to the hand of the biggest woman. One of his mittens hung from a string escaping from the sleeve of an outgrown jacket. I looked away and down towards the river. It was very low and not quite frozen over. Sewage steamed from a pipe near the bridge where the ice had not yet formed. The boy reminded me of my brother Felix.

"Selkirk Avenue," the conductor called. I had reached my stop. The conductor rang his bell as I stepped down. The car shot off like a bright orange rocket and was soon out of sight.

The Madchenheim was two blocks from the streetcar stop and one block past the bakery, I had been told. I began to walk slowly along the street. The smell of fresh bread came from an open door. Through a large window I could see golden braided rolls dusted with poppy seed and long loaves of crusty pumpernickel rye bread. A dark-eyed woman in a tall baker's hat beckoned to me from behind the counter. I smiled but walked on, passing a butcher shop where shiny coils of garlic sausage hung against white tile walls. Then came a picket fence behind which stood a small house, like a child's drawing, painted white with bright green trim. It had a small porch leading to a door in the middle and narrow windows on each side. It was comforting to see red geraniums on the windowsill inside below a frill of white curtain. But this was not the Madchenheim. A tall man with a beard and burning eyes, his coat tails flapping hurried along the street like a whirlwind. I paused before the door of what must be a store - it had no sign but only numbers nailed on the brown imitation brick above the door. On the other side of the grimy window among old kettles and crockery, dusty encyclopedias spilled from a cardboard carton. A snow white cat slept on an old khaki army coat, its one tarnished brass button hanging by a thread. Old newspapers and a few dusty leaves had gathered under the window ledge and against the door that looked as if it had not been opened for a long time, despite the presence of the sleeping cat inside.

Then there it was: 615 Selkirk Avenue. A tall three-storey house with narrow white siding halfway up and then dark brown cedar shingles to the eaves. The windows shone cleanly in the sunlight. It looked very reassuring and not at all a place to fear. There was a cement walk between a border of what had probably been marigolds or petunias but were now frozen clumps of brown. I climbed the wide steps and stepped on to a straw mat that covered the grey painted floor of the porch. I hesitated before a brass bell set into the door.

The door opened wide before I could ring. "Welcome, here," a woman said in familiar German. Her white hair was swept up behind her narrow head and fastened with a black velvet bow. She wore a dark blue dress with a white lace collar.

"You must be Anna. I have been watching for you." She ushered me in, took my coat and gloves, then took me gently by the arm and looked into my eyes. "I'm Miss Fast. Be at home, here. This place is for you."

I soaked up her warm words and manner.

"My, my, you do look like a Heppner, with those eyes -

your father's eyes. I remember him well from the Academy. I was housemother there, while he was headmaster, though that seems a long time ago, now. So much has happened since then." Her blue eyes looked weepy behind her rimless eyeglasses.

There was the smell of cinnamon buns and coffee brewing. Mennonite cleanliness surrounded me, waxed linoleum and freshly starched and ironed curtains. I laughed in relief. There was nothing to be afraid of. I was so glad to finally be here.

"Let's go into the dining room, Anna," Miss Fast offered. "The other girls are all waiting to meet you."

I heard laughter from somewhere then footsteps coming down the stairs.

"This is Trudy," Miss Fast said. A tall blonde girl with her hair braided in a crown came forward. She wore a dark skirt and white blouse. "And this is Mariechen," Miss Fast said. Another girl, not quite so tall. I took a deep breath. I was glad I had worn my green dress and my good shoes. I wanted them to like me.

Miss Fast was still talking."... And there will be one or two more in a few minutes. Annaliese and Erika have just returned from shopping. Eaton's is so busy at this time of year. They will be down shortly." She led the way into the dining room at the back of the house.

It was a lovely room - almost as fine as Mrs. Strachan's with striped wallpaper and a plate rail running all the way around. "The Pennsylvania Mennonites sent the plates wrapped in several of their fine quilts," explained Miss Fast. She had noticed me admiring them. "I wrote and told them we had this empty rail and so they sent us these. Aren't they lovely? This home is one of their special projects."

Through the large window I could see a garden patch neatly dug up and folded away for the winter. Against the back fence stood a stunted crab-apple tree bare of leaves. A few shrivelled apples still clung to the crooked branches. I looked down at the white cloth on the table. A tall nickel-plated coffee pot stood ready on a trivet, steam drifting from its slender spout.

Several girls entered the room laughing and talking and crowded around the table. "Anna, please sit there." Miss Fast pointed to a chair. "We will leave a place for the Elteste for Faspah although we will not wait for him. He is visiting at the hospital this afternoon - I heard old Mrs. Reimer will not last the night. But the Elteste will be here in time for Andacht, I'm sure." Miss Fast sighed and shook her head. "Trudy? Will you bring the cream and then we will say grace."

We all bowed our heads. "Segne Vater diese Speise," I mumbled along with the others. Thank you, Father for this food and thank you, thank you for this place, I prayed in my heart. I could stand almost anything if I had this place to come to once a week.

Miss Fast poured the coffee and the platter of cinnamon buns was passed around.

"How do you like your place?" Trudy asked quietly so that the others who were talking about their recent purchases did not hear.

"It's alright, I guess," I said. "I haven't been there all that long." I bit into a piece of cheddar cheese to go along with a mouthful of cinnamon bun. I was hungry.

"You're lucky. I'm thinking of quitting my place," Trudy confided. "I've been there for almost year, but the woman is a bitch." I was shocked at Trudy's words. Bitch - wasn't that a female dog? "Miss Fast says she's going to put her on the Verboten list and never send another girl there."

"You mean you'd go home?"

"No, no. I can't do that." Trudy said. "My father depends on my earnings. I will have to stay for now," Trudy glanced quickly at the other girls around the table.

I did not know what to say in answer so I said nothing.

Trudy dropped her voice to a whisper. "How do you deal with delivery men?"

"Delivery men, deal with them? I open the door, take the parcel." I was wondering what Trudy could mean. Weren't deliverymen just that? It took me an instant to clue into what she meant. "Oh yes, Mrs. Strachan said not to have anything to do with them, I mean in that way."

"You're lucky. I've had to almost beat the egg man off with a stick." Trudy covered her mouth with her hand.

I looked at Trudy. She was really very attractive; with her huge blue eyes like jewels set far apart, lovely white teeth and red lips. I could see how deliverymen, any man, for that matter would be smitten by her. She gave off an air, an aura almost, which I could not name but only feel.

"I shouldn't be saying this, but I'll tell you, Anna" Trudy leaned towards me a little so she could speak directly into my ear. "Every time the butcher brings the meat, my mistress is at the door, putting on the charm as if I didn't know what she is really like when we are alone."

I thought of Mrs. Strachan, perfumed and powdered, who never even looked at a deliveryman for more than a few seconds. She suddenly seemed the soul of rectitude. Did she even have such feelings?

After Faspah was over and the dishes were cleared we arranged the chairs for Andacht. Church, I thought. I hadn't been since the beginning of September. Most of us did not get Sundays off. The Elteste arrived at the last minute and apologized profusely to Miss Fast. He was a spare man with pink cheeks, a handsome nose and kind eyes but slightly stooped as if he had been leaning over for too long, listening to confessions. He wore a dark clerical suit and spoke so softly that I had to lean forward to hear.

After a short devotional, we stood up to sing a hymn - our voices sounding thin and lonely without the tenor and bass of male voices. The afternoon and evening flew by. "Elteste Epp is very kind," Trudy said at my side. "He keeps his sermons short - only one Bible verse and no long rambling."

I nodded. We were all milling about in the hall finding our coats and bags.

"Wait until you hear the Deacon." Trudy lowered her voice so that only I could hear. "On and on he goes, as if we didn't already know everything he was going to say."

I laughed. I was glad Trudy was willing to trust me with her confidences. I longed to have at least one friend in this place.

"Which way do you go home?" Trudy asked.

"Harkness Street."

"We can take the same streetcar and I'll transfer at Osborne St. It's not much further that way."

"That's nice of you," I said. I was glad Trudy was willing to go out of her way so that we could share part of the long ride home.

We walked together in the dark down the street towards Main Street and our car-stop. "Did you know that the Elteste doesn't believe in hell?" she asked.

I looked around to see if anyone was near enough to hear her. I was uneasy talking about hell. We avoided such discussions in our family. My father and mother did not agree on questions of theology.

"I heard that it's caused him a lot of trouble with the conference," Trudy went on, not fazed by my silence. "But so what? I don't believe in hell either."

I did not reply. I hadn't really thought about hell much, at least not as place where people burned eternally. My father said hell was what people did to each other.

"Last year when my mother died, the Elteste was so kind. He took my hand, put his arm around me. My father hardly does that, and never says anything more than "Be a good girl now, remember who you are," and things like that. I guess he's feeling bad about my mother." Trudy's voice sounded unsteady. I could not see her face in the dark.

Oh dear. Trudy's mother had died? How terrible. It reminded me again of my own mother and what could be ailing her.

"What happened - was your mother sick?" I asked Trudy. She didn't reply. By then the streetcar had arrived and we climbed on. We rattled back along the way I had come earlier in the afternoon.

"As soon as my uncle sends word, my aunt will take us, me and my brothers, to Chilliwack," Trudy said, changing the subject, then reverting to it again, like a tongue groping for a recently extracted tooth. "We have to get away from here. My mother - you don't know? She took rat poison. Our crops failed again and she was going to have another baby. They said she was out of her mind. My father...my father, well, it was very bad." Trudy's voice trailed off. She looked down at me. I could see tears in her eyes. Furiously, she tried to wipe them away with her gloved hand, smiling apologetically.

"Here's your stop," Trudy said tightly. Her face closed up and she looked stern. She felt she had said too much, I could tell.

"I'll see you next Thursday," I said and lightly touched her hand before I moved down the aisle. "Bye, now," I called out as I stepped down. After the warmth and bright lights of the streetcar it was cold and dark outside.

That night back in my room I wrote to Zena. "I had my

Thursday off finally and went to the Madchenheim. I think I am going to like going there. The girls were very friendly. I met Trudy Klassen. She was full of jokes and funny stories, then suddenly very serious. I did not know what to make of her at first. She told about the terrible woman she was working for, who is impossible to satisfy. The woman sounded like another Mrs. Strachan, only worse. But Trudy made it into a big joke. We all had to laugh.

"Later that evening Trudy told me about her mother. It's terribly sad. I want to be a good friend to Trudy, but she will never take your place, Zena. I wish you and I were not so far apart with four hundred miles between us. Write soon. Your letters do mean a lot to me."

In the middle of December the Strachans decided they would let me go home a few days before Christmas and return on Boxing Day. That way I would be available for the big New Year's Eve party that the judge so loved to host.

On the night before I was to leave Mrs. Strachan suggested I accompany her to the Cathedral. It was more command than suggestion.

"I need to go once a year. It's Christmas. The judge is a stubborn Presbyterian. He won't set foot in an Anglican church," she huffed. "I won't change him now. So come along - it's not too cold to walk."

I was puzzled. Why me? Why not some of her fine friends? But I was also curious. I had never been in that cathedral although I passed it almost every day. Besides once Mrs. Strachan got something into her head it was best to go along with it. In the end she would always get her way.

Now she donned her black seal coat, tucked in a bright silk scarf smelling of flowers and pulled on fur-lined galoshes. I bundled up as well - only not so fine - and followed her out into the darkness. The light from the street lamps turned the drifting snowflakes into flitting, shimmering bits of light. When we reached the cathedral the huge doors stood open and organ music poured out into the night. Inside, an usher showed us to an empty pew. It was chilly and I kept my coat on. The space above my head seemed to go on and on. It felt strangely familiar.

Suddenly it came to me what this place reminded me of. It was Kiev and the triple golden domes of the basilica. How could I possibly have forgotten?

"I want you to not forget this," I heard my father saying. His strong hand had held mine as he led me through the huge doors. "This is Russia, too; not all blood and lice and brutality." Inside the basilica had been that same vast echoing space as here in this cathedral and it felt like the same stone underfoot. The long ago scene came vividly to mind: bearded priests, candlelight, clouds of incense, flowers with their sweetness fading to decay. I remembered looking over the heads of the kneeling worshippers to the gold encrusted altar and, against the dim walls, people on their knees kissing the feet of statues. "The communists are closing the churches, but what about these anguished Russian souls?" my father said, more to himself than to me. He picked me up and held me high. I was almost too big to lift but he wanted me to see. "Someday you will understand," he said.

Beside me now, Mrs. Strachan knelt on a padded stool, curiously fitted into the wooden pew in front of us. Was I supposed to do the same? The incense rose in clouds. A figure in gold raised his arms before the altar. I wondered if the God I prayed to every night could really be in a place like this. "All this popery," my mother would have said scathingly, "idolatry." She held staunchly to the traditions and faith of our Dutch Mennonite ancestors and was determined that her children would follow in her footsteps. A "Free Thinker," she called my father.

Mrs. Strachan reached for one of the worn blue books in the rack in front of us. I had not knelt but I supposed it was safe enough to pick up the book. Tentatively, I turned its thin worn pages. I was used to the German *Gesangbuch*, my mother had carried with her to church all the years of my childhood. Its pages were printed in a Gothic script without any musical notation and had endless verses from as far back as the 1500's when Mennonites were being persecuted by both Catholics and Protestants.

"The Lord be with you," intoned the gold-robed figure before the altar.

"And with you," whispered Mrs Strachan as she bowed her head.

Nervously, I flipped through the pages. Was I supposed to say something too?

"The Lord is near to all who call upon him," intoned the priest.

"Amen," said Mrs. Strachan along with the other congregants. "Amen," I said a little too late, my voice sounding strange. At least I could join in with that. I did believe that the Lord was near - in moments of temptation, sometimes uncomfortably near. I wondered if Mrs. Strachan truly believed in God. What could she possibly need Him for?

The next day I left for Hackett. On the train going home I burst into tears I could not explain even to myself. The other passengers looked up in surprise, then politely turned away.

By the time we reached Hackett I was calm. My brother Conrad met me at the station. In the fast-fading light I hardly recognized him.

"Conrad, it's so good to see you." I had to reach up to put my arms around him. He seemed so much bigger and broader than when I left three months ago.

"Anna, how are you?" His voice had deepened. It was a man who spoke to me. "Your bag? Is this all you have?"

My dear brother Conrad. How lonely I had really been. Tears sprang to my eyes again. We walked side by side along the platform that the agent had kept free of snow. I looked at the dark building behind us and further away to the looming grain elevators black against the sky.

"I was just now thinking of what it was like when we first came to Hackett. Remember that, Conrad? The station hasn't changed, but the train was different, it had wooden seats. Now they are upholstered with that faded plush."

I let go the handle of my bag. Conrad smiled and shook his head; then picked up my bag as though it were weightless.

"Remember the fields, then, Conrad, rippling green and gold and the blue sky? It rained that year." I turned my face to the dark sky. In the background the train chugged once, then again, and chuffed away with a ponderous even rhythm towards the south and the next station seven miles away.

"It was winter and dark, Anna," Conrad protested, "and I came alone."

"Oh, of course. Forgive me, Bruder Mein," I was quick with remorse. Of course, how could I have forgotten? Conrad caught Trachoma on the dreadful ship over and was quarantined in Quebec, left behind when the rest of the family had to travel on. It must have been awful for him. Mama had never forgiven herself for leaving Conrad to the mercy of those French doctors. I reached for his hand. I remembered all our immigrant fears.

Conrad piled my bag into the sleigh and I climbed in and covered myself with the worn familiar quilt we kept there. He removed the blanket from our horse, old Jake, who stamped his feet in anticipation. "Aaaah, heck! It wasn't so bad," Conrad said and climbed in beside me, "except for the stuff they dripped into my eyes. I hardly remember anything. It's funny, how you forget." Conrad was making light of his childhood experience as befitted any young man in his teens who had attained his full height and was almost ready to shave.

I laughed and patted his arm, "No, no, Conrad. You know it was a very long six months, now wasn't it? But what could they do with Mama expecting? After her experience during the war she could not bear to be away from Papa again. You understand that now, surely? And the people here in Hackett had a place for us."

Conrad shook the reins and we were off, the bells on the horse's bridle jingling in the near dark.

"I'll never forget the look on your face when you finally did arrive. You rushed into Mama's room to find her with Felix in her arms."

Conrad did not reply at first. He had never made casual conversation easily. "Oh, you know how kids are," he said finally. "I didn't have a clue. I thought people left their kids behind all the time," he said and slapped the reins once more. Jake picked up speed.

I thought of my own fears. I remembered clearly not wanting to let my father out of my sight - he had disappeared once before - in the first days and weeks after we arrived as immigrants, full of anxieties, not knowing the language and the ways of the country.

"I still think it would have been better if you had been told what was going on," I said and steadied myself against the side of the sleigh. "Eight-year olds are not stupid. I won't do that to my children."

Conrad was quiet. He kept his eyes on the twin tracks of the road ahead, trying to avoid the icy ruts. I looked around me at the emptiness, the lights of Hackett disappearing behind us.

"So, how is everybody? How is Papa? Where's Felix? I thought they might come along to town."

"Papa is writing an article for the Nordwesten. The editor has agreed to pay him by the word. Felix is off somewhere, setting rabbit snares, him and that mutt of his." Conrad shrugged.

"And Mama? How is she?"

"She's alright," he said. The runners of the sleigh scraped on gravel for an instant, making a harsh sound in the velvety dark. Thin clouds drifted across a sickle moon.

After that we were mostly silent. When we reached the farm Conrad said, "You go on in, Anna. I'll take care of Jake."

I carried my bag across the snow packed yard, opened the door and stood transfixed.

"Mama, but Mama?" I blurted out staring at her swollen belly. "Mama. You didn't tell me."

My mother pregnant? I swallowed. I was speechless.

I had heard my mother's voice, often enough, upon hearing about another woman's Schwangerschwaft. "Ach du Gott im Himmel! Not another child?" she would say indignantly, far too loudly for the other women who had gathered to chat for a few minutes at the church door on a Sunday morning. "Where are our good Russian doctors, when we need them?"

And now to confront this. This was my mother's "illness" which my father had alluded to in his letter, one she had no remedy for. After the first rush, I kept my eyes from her straining apron and stared instead at her swollen ankles. She wore a pair of my father's woollen socks.

"Come in out of the cold, Anna. Close the door," she said matter-of-factly.

I stepped into the kitchen and reached out to her. Awkwardly, she put her arms around me.

"I didn't want... I wanted to spare you," she whispered. I looked into her eyes and saw the misery there.

"Oh, Mama." Like a child, I put my head on her shoulder. What could I say? That I was glad? I couldn't say that. Or that I was sorry? No. And what could I say to my father? Wasn't he to blame for my mother's state? I heard Mrs. Strachan's voice. "Immigrants breeding, we'll be overrun."

My mother gave a final squeeze and held me at arm's length. She looked me up and down. "You're thinner," she said, brusque again. "What have they done to you? Your hair - when did you cut it?"

"Hey, Anna. You're here! How are you?" Felix appeared from behind my mother's distended figure. "What did you bring me?" My brother had been laughing at something or other and his eyes were merry. "Mama made Plumi Moos and Kringel especially for you," he said. I could see the bowl of thick fruit soup on the table beside a basket of freshly baked Kringel buns. "And there's farmer sausage and fried potatoes, too."

"Felix, Felix, I missed you so." I moved out of my mother's embrace and tousled his thick dark hair. "Where's Papa?" I asked.

"The boys are hungry." My mother handed me the knives and forks to set on the table.

I moved the plates around in order to make room for five of us and thought of Mrs. Strachan and her view of immigrants. She would ask about my family when I returned. I would not tell her. I thought of Mrs. Strachan's overflowing linen closets. So much there that could be used for a baby. The Strachan sheets and towels showing the least sign of wear were given to the Salvation Army. But I would have my pride, too. I would not ask Mrs. Strachan for anything.

"You are my good girl, Anna," my mother said as if reading my thoughts. "I don't know how we would manage without you." Her face flushed as she turned back to the stove and gave the dampers an unnecessary turn.

Oh God, I prayed, let Mrs. Strachan be in a good mood when I do ask.

"Leise rieselt Der Schnie," my brother Felix sang over and over again in his boy soprano. Through the window I could see precious few flakes of the snow he was singing about. "We made these Ketten Kleben at school," he said shyly, pointing to the front window festooned with green and red paper chains.

I hid away the gifts I had brought with me: a book for Conrad, a box of paints for Felix, a nightgown for my mother, and for my father, a pocket thesaurus. I had wrapped each gift in red tissue paper.

When my father arrived home I was shy with him. I hated what he and my mother had done in the dark of night. I could not meet his eyes. With another baby, I thought, I would have to work for the Strachans forever. On this Weinacht's Abendt, this most holy, joyous time of the whole year I wished myself away from here, anywhere but here.

On Christmas Eve we did not go to church. My mother's feet were so swollen that she could not put on her shoes. I thought of the smell of oranges and peanuts in the crowded church. The singing.

Instead we exchanged gifts. Felix had made me a tiny leather change purse, stitched with black thread. "How clever of you, Felix," I said warmly.

Conrad looked embarrassed when I thanked him for his gift - a small photo album. On the first page he had fixed a picture of our family standing at the corner of our house just before I went away for the first time. It showed Felix smiling happily. Conrad's hair had lifted in a gust of wind. My mother stared straight at the camera, her face stern. I was wearing the suit my mother had made of which I had been so proud and frowning against the bright light. My father's shadow showed in the foreground where he had stood to take the picture. Now he handed me the camera he had used that day.

"It should be yours now. You can always send us pictures," he said.

I began to cry and reached out my arms.

"Never mind, never mind," he said softly and wrapped his arms around me. I could feel his heart beating, his voice resonating in his singer's broad chest against my cheek and I forgot all about the bad feelings I had harboured earlier.

The next day we had our Christmas dinner and the smell of roasting goose filled our tiny rooms. Peanut shells drifted on the floor and my mother did not bother to sweep them up immediately. We played Knips Brat. Conrad won of course. My father read a funny story from one of our favourites in Tyl Ulenspiegal. The hours flew by.

Conrad took me back to the train on Boxing Day. He was very quiet. "I'll be fourteen in a month. I can quit school. Go to Alberta. Maybe work on a ranch." He looked out over the bare fields, his voice confident.

"But Conrad. What about Papa? He'll want you to stay in school. Stays in school, please, please stay in school. You must realize how important it is."

Where I might once have cajoled and persuaded a younger Conrad, now my words seemed to fall on deaf ears. I could do nothing. And there were so much more than Conrad's schooling to worry about at home.

Chapter Three

I was relieved to go back to Raulston and the Strachans. I would not have to watch how my mother moved awkwardly about doing her daily chores in the tiny rooms of our house. I had become properly spoiled, accustomed to running water while she had to deal with a barrel of melting snow beside the cook stove. By this time I was used to a flush toilet and had forgotten how cold the seat of an outhouse could be. Once on the train I turned my thoughts towards the electric lights and the furnace heat of the Strachan house.

Fletcher welcomed me back with slurpy licks of his tongue. Everything seemed to need cleaning. As I scoured and scrubbed, the anger and disappointment of my Christmas visit to Hackett slowly dissipated. I belonged here now, preparing for the judge's New Year's Eve party, more than I did on the farm in Hackett.

There was a letter from Zena waiting for me, filled with details about her upcoming Christmas holidays, wishing me a happy 1931. The Walls had gathered at the Siemens house for the festivities. Mrs. Siemens had been a Wall before she married and her husband was the editor of the Millbach Post. Zena went on to tell me about the start-up of practice for the spring play. Zena would like that, she was good at make-believe. She never wrote much about school and I wondered what she was studying besides the boy playing opposite her in the love scene. But then there were the nightly skating parties. Maybe she was keen about the boy who she described whirling her about on the rink in the cold night air. She didn't really say, but his name had come up in previous letters. When I read about the skating, I could hear the sound their skates made on the ice, the waltz tune issuing scratchily from the skating shack. I missed skating behind the schoolhouse in Hackett. The teacher, who lived nearby in the teacherage, had always flooded a small section of the schoolyard for skating and hockey. Here in Raulston there was a skating rink near the Strachan's house for neighbourhood children, but I was not free to go there, even if I had a pair of skates. Mrs. Strachan would never allow it, not even on a Thursday night. Too late, she would have said. I want you hard at work in the morning, she would have meant. I hadn't bothered to even ask for permission.

"Happy 1931 to you, too," I wrote to Zena in reply. My letters must seem boring, compared to hers. "After I've finished my work I read. I'm reading through Mrs. Strachan's old Chatelaines. They go back at least ten years with the same advertising for Ipana toothpaste and the same stories, 'Can this marriage be saved?' That kind of stuff." Would Zena make fun of my taste in literature? "I've ordered a Butterick pattern with a skirt cut on the bias. Mrs. Strachan gave me a dress length of moire for Christmas. I love it. It is dark, dark red, the colour of wine, with marks like the grain in a piece of wood. It shimmers in the light." Zena and I both loved clothes.

I had reached the bottom of my page; it was late and I was tired. "I'll write more next time. Much love. Write soon," I sealed the envelope quickly, stamped it and laid it aside for mailing early in the morning. I put my head down on the desk. I had managed to fill the page. Now it was too late even for a postscript. I had not told her about my mother having a baby sometime soon; too late to tell her now. And too late to tell her about the other letter I'd received.

The letter had tumbled through the letter slot this morning, arriving innocently enough among the other Strachan mail - letters from England, a bank statement addressed to the judge, an Eaton's flyer scattered on the sombre Turkish carpet before the front door. Mrs Strachan had been out for her walk and not there to intercept it and hand it on to me at her convenience as she did with my other mail, so it was truly mine alone.

The letter lay on my desk now, beside the dark blue fountain pen my father had given me when I graduated from

Grade eight with the highest marks in the class. The plain white envelope was not so different from ones that Zena used or my father for that matter. But this neatly printed address was in an unfamiliar hand. The return address was General Delivery, Hackett, Saskatchewan.

I removed the single sheet of paper from the envelope as if it were fragile. "Dear Anna," I read for the tenth time since that morning. It was written in such lovely script - foreign looking almost, as if the writer had gone to school somewhere other than Canada. "I heard that you were home briefly for the holidays but I missed seeing you in church on Weinacht's Abend, so I greet you now with the Season's Best Wishes and a Happy New Year." I skimmed over the next few lines; I already knew them by heart. "Your brother tells me you are liking it in Raulston. I hope to visit there, soon. There is not much to do here on the farm; my parents say they can manage on their own. My job cutting brush in the relief camp is on again, off again but I'd like to earn more money. I'm ready to ride the rails to B.C. and see if I can find work at one of the fish canneries on the coast, but now my cousin in Raulston has been taken ill. My aunt needs a hand with their boarding house, so I will be in Raulston, at least briefly. Maybe we can meet and talk over old times. I hope to hear from you. Sincerely, Henry Redekop."

Meet? Talk over old times? What old times? I hardly knew Henry Redekop. Well, enough to say hello. I knew he was the only son of our neighbour to the north of us. I had heard his mother call him Heine after the German poet. He was older than I and had already graduated from the Gymnasium in Germany by the time his family settled in Canada. I remembered him vaguely as a young man in denim overalls, with smooth cheeks and clear hazel eyes, his fine hair combed back from a high forehead. What I remembered more clearly was his deft movements. I had once watched as he took apart and reassembled a cream separator. He had sung in the choir - a tenor. Now I looked once more at his signature. Could you tell what kind of a man he might be by his signature? It did have a certain flourish. Henry Redekop.

That night I found it hard to go to sleep. Henry Redekop. Of all things! I would answer his letter tomorrow. No, I would wait a few days before writing. Maybe wait and talk it over with Trudy. No point in making him think I was lonely.

"What should I do?" I asked Trudy the next time we met. The winter of 1931 dragged on endlessly, the way a prairie winter tends to do. We were at the library and I had to whisper loudly over the sizzle and pop of the radiators. Trudy closed the book she was looking at. "Oh heavens, write back!" One or two grey heads, bent over the foreign language newspapers, were raised for a moment. The eyes looked at us accusingly. Trudy had spoken in German. I hated it when she did that. Did she want everybody in the world to know that we were immigrants? She lowered her voice. "Why not? What are you waiting for?" she said in English.

"I don't know what to say," I whispered. The heads returned to their reading.

That night I decided I would try to write a reply. I filled my fountain pen, tucked in the lined sheet underneath the clean white page so that my writing would not wander up or down, the way Zena's hasty scribbles tended to do. "Dear Henry. It's very cold. How was it where you are? Cold, too?" I paused. What to write next? Usually my thoughts would outrun my pen. What if I wrote all the wrong things? "I hope you have a warm place to sleep. Do they feed you well? I've heard about those camp cooks." I read over what I had written; it sounded stilted. "At the Madchenheim we have begun Catechism classes," I wrote, but I did not go into details. It sounded pious. I wanted to stroke it out and begin again. I thought of the Elteste who asked us the questions, his voice so gentle, his long fingers with their well-tended nails on the open Bible, tissue thin gilt-edged pages bound in leather, lying on the white linen cloth of the table around which we sat quietly, obediently. Miss Fast would just barely have closed the front door on the Elteste, and we were racing up the stairs to the bathroom, their good-byes still ringing in our ears. By the time we reached the upstairs hall our decorum had spent itself and we bent over in a burst of giggles. I did not know what got into us at such times, why we were helpless with laughter, what was so funny. I could not convey to Henry how Trudy would poke me in the shins with one foot under the table when the Elteste smilingly asked us to name the three persons of the Trinity. "Watch out! The Holy

Ghost will come upon you, Anna!" Trudy would whisper. She made fun of everything, even something as sacred and impossible to understand as the Trinity. I had poked her back and looked away.

Later on that same evening at the Madchenheim the Elteste had taken me aside and asked if I was ready for baptism during the upcoming Pentecost Sunday. I shook my head and he did not press me. "I will not be baptized this year," I added in my letter to Henry. I began a new paragraph. "I like to listen to the radio. Mrs. Strachan lets me take the kitchen radio up to my room at night. Do you have a radio? Isn't Jack Benny funny?" I wanted Henry to know I was no *Dummbkopf.*

I did not go home for Easter. Mrs. Strachan did not invite me to go with her to the Lenten services. I wondered why but I had other things to think about and didn't really care, one way or the other. On my Thursdays at the Madchenheim, after the dull rote of the catechism class, we girls continued in our fits of laughter. The few hours of freedom at the Madchenheim would go to our heads but underlying all this was a knowledge never spoken out loud: we were like indentured servants of old; the money we earned and sent home to our families was what kept them off the dreaded relief.

I had received a second letter from Henry before I finally wrote to Zena. "I had a letter from Henry Redekop, a neighbour of ours on the farm. His family emigrated from Germany. He went to school there." I wanted her to be impressed.

"Henry was to come to Raulston but has since had to change his plans," I wrote. "He is up north cutting brush. He wants to meet me. I don't know when that will be. I am so glad winter is nearly over. The sun feels hot when it shines through the window. Outside the puddles still freeze over at night and the wind is cold."

I laid down my pen and opened the little round holes in my storm window. The air did smell different. It was what the judge called Bonspeil weather, a slight hint of balminess in the still frigid air. I felt it in my bones, the sudden letting go of winter, the promise of spring.

I paused over my letter, scribbled on a piece of scrap paper, little story book houses with a walk to the front door and smoke spiralling from the chimney. Was this what was meant by writer's block? I yawned. It was getting late. I had not had much sleep the night before because of the judge's party.

"The judge had a party," I finally wrote to Zena. "He does this every year - entertains his fellow curlers. I have to wear my black uniform then and serve hot canapés and cheese and fancy crackers. The judge pours whiskey with a lavish hand." It had made me uneasy at the time. Should I tell Zena about the other event that night? "From what I overheard the judge's rink won some big trophy." I had been offering the tray around when one of the men put his hand where it shouldn't be and pinched me. I had been shocked and quite surprised and without a second thought I had slapped him.

"One of the judge's friends was rude to me," I wrote to Zena. "I slapped him good and proper. You'd have laughed if you had seen his face."

The judge had seen what happened. "Don't touch Anna, Kenneth. She doesn't like it," the judge had said sternly to his fellow-curler, who looked dumbfounded. His face turned a flaming red. The little immigrant girl, to have the nerve to slap him? Those who stood nearby turned away as if they hadn't seen or heard. I left the room and didn't come back to clean up until they had all gone.

"That won't happen again, Anna," the judge had said the next morning when I was serving him breakfast.

I turned back to Zena's letter. "That was enough excitement for one night. Now Mrs. Strachan is having the whole upstairs redecorated - new wallpaper, new curtains, new rugs. Spring fever, she calls it."

In the middle of April my father wrote. "You have a baby sister. A fine girl, the mid-wife says. She has reddish fuzz on her head. She looks at me with her big eyes, as if she knows all secrets of the universe. We have named her Elene in memory of your great-aunt Elene. Mama sends her love. Everything is fine." I sighed. Was it with relief, was it with joy? Perhaps a bit of both. Ever since Christmas I had been waiting, hoping for the best, fearing the worst. But my mother was fine, after all. And the baby? I had a sister now.

"We have a new baby at home," I said to Mrs. Strachan. She looked surprised.

"Well! Well! Would you like to go home? I suppose we could spare for a few days," she said, her voice unusually gentle.

I shook my head. "Mama says no. She can manage."

"Well, what about taking your holidays earlier in June before we go to the beach?" I agreed.

In the next letter my father wrote, "Thank you for the money-order. We are looking forward to a crop this year. It looks like rain, today."

I thought of the poor sprouts of wheat that would barely turn green before they dried up and blew away. Please God, make it rain. If only He would. Oh God, I'll promise anything. I'll never wish for anything. Not even for the beautiful pearls that lay on blue velvet in the window at People's Jewellers.

But it didn't rain. When I went home in June, the land on both sides of the railroad allowance stretched away into hills and valleys of dry soil with dust dervishes moving the soil endlessly from place to place. The air was full of grit. Dry. Dry, dry. Against the far horizon, dark clouds mocked but it was not rain they promised. Each telegraph pole along the right-of- way was buried knee deep in fine dust. The only green was the weeds growing in the ditches. Had it ever been green? I tried to go back in my mind to the time when we first came here. I seemed to remember a greener land. I must have imagined it. Now everywhere I looked it was different shades of grey.

At home I looked into the baby blue eyes of my sister. She stared back. "Hello, Elene." I murmured. She kicked one bare foot and waved a fist. I smiled at her and picked her up in my arms. She smelled like a baby, soft and damp and sweet with mother's milk. It would be a while before we could be friends.

"She's a good child," my mother said. "Hardly any trouble at all." My mother was making the best of things just as she had said she would.

But I was constantly thinking of Henry and when we would finally meet. I held Elene and rocked her to and fro. She gurgled and dribbled, her diaper suspiciously damp. I brushed my cheek against the top of her head. I wanted to whisper into her tiny ear about Henry. Would she be my own true sister one day, one who would share my joys and sorrows?

Henry had done what so many others were doing - hopped a freight to the west. "I'm sorry about June. I don't know where I'll be so I can't give you an address. What with the drought, it's all I can do. Wish me luck, anyway," he wrote in his last letter.

After that I did not hear from him all summer except for the odd postcard showing totem poles, fishing boats or snow covered mountains, on the back of which were a few lines of Henry's now familiar script. "I have so much to tell you, Anna. I am with my cousin." On another he wrote, "I am helping to clear land. We are black with soot from the fires. Huge stumps are everywhere." And yet another. "It rains here a lot. Everything grows so fast. How would you like to live on Vancouver Island?" I thought about what he really meant by that. I put all of his postcards and letters in an empty box, which had contained chocolates and still smelled of them. After each card arrived I went down to Mrs. Strachan's atlas and looked up the places on a map of western Canada. "I hope to be back home at harvest time," he wrote on the last card to arrive.

"He's coming home," I told Trudy.

"Are you excited?" Trudy asked with a smile. Trudy had several boyfriends. "Life is short, Anna," she would laugh when I wondered how she would ever make up her mind between them. "Seize the day, is what my father always says." I could not be so flippant about it.

I decided I did not want to meet with Henry for our first time at the Madchenheim. I thought of the sharp eyes of Miss Fast and the speculative gaze of the girls who might be there. Would Henry pass the test? And in that painfully clean front room with its starched doilies on the back of every chair? No, it would not do. I wanted a more romantic place.

"Meet me by the statue," I wrote, "by the front door of Eaton's. From there we can go wherever - the park, the library."

Trudy and I had met at the statue once or twice before. A likeness of Mr. Eaton, founder of the store, had towered over us in all his glory, every bronze fold of suit and tie revealed, the watch chain across the ample chest. He sat on his chair, protected by swags of dark blue velvet rope - Trudy said it was so we should not be tempted to climb into his bronze lap. I imagined I could feel his gaze as he stared out over the heads of shoppers on the first floor of the store.

That Thursday I dressed with care. I wore my best black skirt and white blouse under my coat and my first pair of real silk stockings. I walked the few blocks to my usual stop and caught my streetcar; I did not want to be late. Rather me waiting for Henry than the other way around.

Through the window of the streetcar I could see across the railroad yards to the empty wasteland along the riverbank. A freight train slowed, staying even with us as it pulled into the yards. Hoboes, looking like tattered scarecrows, dropped off one by one from the rail car on which they had been riding and tumbled and slid down the embankment, waving to their comrades already seated around several smouldering campfires. Would Henry look like one of those men? Suddenly I was afraid.

I thought of the few times a tramp had reached the Strachan back door. Harkness Street was too far away from the railroad tracks for that to happen often. The last time had been a few weeks ago. I had heard the knock and when I opened the door, I was face to face with one. I could have touched his unshaven cheek. He had smiled as he asked for work, any little job. I looked down at his torn laces in worn-out boots, not knowing what to say. Then Mrs. Strachan appeared at my shoulder to see who was at the door and promptly sent him away. "Next time just send them away, Anna. There's a soup kitchen down on Main Street for people like that," she had said.

Now I wondered where the soup kitchen was. But thoughts of Henry distracted me. In just a few minutes - a half an hour at the most - I would see Henry, look into his face. My stomach lurched. At that moment the streetcar conductor called my stop and I disembarked and crossed the street with a stream of pedestrians hurrying to the doors of Eaton's. I wanted to be the first to reach our meeting place. I wanted time to compose myself. I came through the revolving door and was greeted by the mix of my favourite smells - perfume, fur coats and rich chocolate. I reached the statue and surveyed the crowd. Nobody waited by the velvet ropes. I fixed my eyes on a display of watches gleaming behind the glass of the jewellery counter.

"Anna?" I felt a tap on my arm and turned. All the images of him that I had pictured before this meeting disappeared. Here was no boy in overalls. Henry did not look like a farmer at all in his white shirt and dark suit, and not the least like one of those men who had come begging at our door. His nose was still like a knife blade, as I had remembered it, his fair hair still brushed away from a high forehead. He resembled his father.

"Henry? How are you?" I blurted. I had wanted to greet him in my purest German but in the excitement I had slipped into Low Platte.

He took my hand. "How are you, Anna?" he said in English with a German accent. "I thought we might go for a walk in that little park on the corner. I noticed it and would like to have a closer look. It's just two o'clock. Later we can go for coffee."

"Bitte, yes, Bitte," I said. "Please." I reverted to English, but my voice did not sound like mine. I had to clear the frog from my throat.

"Or have you shopping to do?" he asked. I looked into his hazel eyes. He was only a few inches taller than I was and very thin. He reminded me of my father with his *Heiflichkeit*, his old world manners.

"No, no, not today. Not really." My voice stuttered and stumbled but then it regained itself. "A walk to the park and coffee later sounds fine."

"How is your family?" asked Henry, pushing on the revolving doors.

"Oh fine, fine. Thank you. And yours?" I answered as soon we were through the door and into the busy street.

"My parents are fine," Henry said. "They send greetings." Without further speech, we walked together along St. Mary's Street until we reached the park. A gravel path led to an empty bench set beside an historic gate.

"Indian summer," I said and turned my face to the sun, "I wonder why they call it that?" My cheeks felt flushed, whether from the sun shining on my face or Henry's nearness I wasn't sure.

He did not reply but got up, with hands in his pockets, to read the marker posted nearby. "This is the gate of an old fort. Did you know that?" he said and sat down again. "A Hudson's

Bay Trading post. And not so long ago as time goes - a hundred years."

"Indians bringing furs to trade for guns and blankets." I tried to imagine what it must have been like - smoke from their campfires, the rank smell of muskrat pelts. It all seemed like another world. "Trudy and I have come here once in while. But we don't come at night. Miss Fast has warned us. It's not safe at night."

"Oh, because of the hoboes down there?" Henry asked.

I nodded. Smoke from the bonfires along the riverbank drifted towards us. I watched a leaf come drifting down. Sodden heaps of them already lay against the old stonewalls of the fort. An old cannon was mounted beside the gate. It looked ridiculously small. How could such a weapon win the day? But there it was. The British had conquered once again. The red white and blue of the Union Jack fluttered on a flagpole above us.

Henry put his arm along the back of the bench behind me but he did not touch me. He kept his eyes on the distant figures on the riverbank. I followed his gaze.

"But why is it? How can it be?" I asked before I could stop myself. "Miss Fast remembers the Bolshevik robber bands from the old days. What if there was a revolution here like in Russia?"

"I don't think so. No, no, not likely. Not here." Henry shook his head. "That could have been me a few weeks ago." He pointed to the distant bonfires. "The police kick them, kicked us off with baseball bats."

He looked into my eyes with a grim smile and leaned forward, his elbows on his knees. "In Germany it would not be so. There would be work for all... something. But here? Revolution? You having such thoughts. You are your father's daughter, alright." Henry straightened up and leaned back against the bench, his shoulder just touching mine.

I thought of the Strachan's history books. "Did you know they had a strike here, once? People got killed. That was long before we came." I said and moved a little closer so we would not be overheard.

There was silence. "If it would only rain..." I said at last and looked out over the park. That was usually a safe topic - the weather. The lawn behind the bench was green from regular watering. I tried to remember what rain, real rain felt like - the sound of it - rain glistening on the leaves of Virginia creeper nearby, red as blood against the stone walls.

Henry's arm stretched along the back of the bench again. I leaned my head back, almost touching his hand.

"I'll have to go soon," I said. The sun was losing its warmth.

"Shall we go for coffee?" He stood up.

I picked up my handbag from the bench. There was a sudden chill as we passed under the gatehouse. Then we were out into the sunlight again, away from the rude multi-coloured graffiti on the uneven stone, the litter of dried leaves and old newspapers caught at the base of the walls.

"Will you go back to B.C.?" I did not ask him what he had meant by his question on the post card. "Is it better than here?"

"No, no, Niemals, never. I'm a prairie person, Nicht war?" The smile had reached his eyes. "But I will have to go where there is work - what with the drought and the price of grain."

I nodded. It was almost impossible to carry on a conversation with the noise of the traffic. We stood for a moment opposite the city hall, all its flags aflutter. The Unknown Soldier, rifle in hand loomed over us on his pediment as we waited for the light to change.

We passed the cathedral and the old cemetery with its blackened tilting headstones behind a wrought iron fence. Finally, we came abreast of the big show windows of Eaton's and Henry followed me through the revolving doors.

"I love Eaton's," I said.

"We go upstairs to the Grill?

"The Grill," I said and stepped on the escalator as it moved slowly upward to the second floor. I stared at the counters piled high with yarn in crimson and royal blue, dark brown, bright green. The escalator rose to the next floor and the smell of leather shoes and luggage. I smiled at Henry without speaking as we slowly ascended to the fourth floor. There was the familiar chill of the fish counter in the delicatessen. I could see pale transparent fillets displayed under glass. The next floor stretched out into what seemed like acres of rose-trimmed chinaware and silverware on white damask.

Henry was smiling now, too. How could we not be happy and forget the cares of the world with all these fine things to admire and dream over? We passed the floor where Indian and Turkish carpets hung, beautiful and intricate beyond words.

"You love all this?" Henry was watching me.

"Look, look," I said and pointed to the sheen of mahogany highboys, end tables, china cabinets. "I do love it. All these beautiful things."

I thought of the home I might have one day, a house like Mrs. Strachan's, where I would sit before a roaring fire with a black poodle leaning against my leg. In the kitchen there would be a Pyrex coffee percolator on the electric stove, and upstairs, a wide bed with snow white sheets and rose-shaded lamps.

We stepped off the escalator and Henry led me into the Grill Room. He ordered plum tarts and two cups of coffee for us, then looked at me across the table.

I looked down at the white cloth. I had been dreaming the impossible. What had I been thinking? Henry would never fit into those dreams.

"Anna, remember the Warkentin Verlobung. You wore a red velvet vest. I never forgot your dark eyes," he said and reached across the table for my hand. I thought of that engagement celebration, which now seemed like ages ago. I looked down at Henry's hand clasping one of mine, while with the other I picked at a tiny flaw in the tablecloth. Wait, I wanted to say. Wait. I'm not ready for this. All we had done so far was exchange a few letters.

"I've grown very fond of the dog, where I work," I said to change the subject. It was almost as if Henry had understood my unspoken words. He let go my hand. "His name is Fletcher," I said and put my hand down on my lap. "I never thought I'd love a dog."

Henry did not smile. "Not you, Anna? A fine Mennonite girl?" he said. His mouth looked stern. "Not you with English ways?" He stroked the fur hat that lay on the table beside him. It was Karakul, an old-fashioned fur hat exactly like my father's - distinguished looking. I had always admired it but seeing it now with Henry, it suddenly looked foreign.

I drew back. "What's wrong with English ways?" I asked.

We drank our coffee in silence.

"Delicious plum tart," I said.

"Not as good as your mother's," Henry said.

It was crowded on the streetcar on the way back to the Strachans. I held on to the strap above my head while shoppers around me clung to their bags and bundles. Beside me, a girl with well-plucked eyebrows and brightly rouged cheeks swayed back and forth on her high heels. Her marcelled waves shone like gold under the lights. She was extremely pretty. Was Henry watching her?

Finally, we reached my stop. It was an uncomfortably silent walk through the autumn darkness to the Strachan's brightly lit house.

Henry held my hand again as he said goodbye. Since we had left the grillroom he had been very quiet. I was not good at small talk. I thought of Trudy, or Zena for that matter, who could chatter endlessly. They would have both known exactly what to say.

"Thank you Henry, for this afternoon and everything," I said, at a loss for any words that would put us at ease. It was easier writing letters.

He bent forward a little, still holding my hand. Would he kiss me?

Fletcher barked just inside the side door.

"Goodbye," Henry said and let go of my hand. "Will you continue to write?"

"Oh yes, Henry. I surely will. And you too?" I asked.

Henry nodded, smiling.

I squeezed his hand and turned and hurried up the steps to the side door. Fletcher went into his usual frenzy of welcome and by the time I turned to wave goodbye, Henry had disappeared.

"Fletcher, oh, Fletcher," I bent down to hug him, surprised to find tears in my eyes.

"Is that you, Anna?" Mrs. Strachan called in her high-pitched English voice.

That night I wrote to Zena. "I went out with Henry. He took me to the Grill Room at Eaton's. He's very quiet." I sat for a while. Before I sealed the letter I added a postscript to Zena's letter. "I think Henry's really quite shy." What would come next? I squeezed my eyes shut in anticipation.

After that first meeting in the fall of 1931, Henry and I became easier with each other - both in our letters and when meeting. On my visits home he would often be there, putting in a crop for his father or helping neighbours with the haying or hauling water for the cattle.

The following summer on my visit home Henry came over and my mother treated him just as she would any neighbour dropping in. But she soon realized something more was going on.

"It's more than just letters, isn't it?" she finally asked me during my Christmas visit.

"It's nothing really, Mama," I said hoping to avoid further questions.

There was rain and the crops looked promising. My father walked about with his shoulders not quite so slumped. All that summer we lived in hope. Maybe this year there would be a crop.

In September I began to follow the crop reports in the judge's newspapers. "At least we can pay off the bill at Zimmermans and the taxes," my father wrote in his monthly letter. He sounded cheerful.

As for me, I felt the hardness of it all. Drought. Depression. My parents faced the daily struggle to keep disaster from the door. It strained the relationship between my mother and I and coloured my courtship with Henry. Only at the Strachans' was there a feeling of plenitude.

"Why don't we just go on relief?" I had once asked my father.

"Your mother would never hear of it," he said and shook his head. I never asked again.

Many people around Hackett had been leaving their drought-ridden fields for jobs in the canneries in southern Ontario or the strawberry fields of the Fraser Valley. "We might as well go, too. But where?" my mother said angrily, as one family after another piled their few belongings on the back of a truck and disappeared with a wave. My father said nothing.

Conrad was attending high school in Hackett and studying hard. Felix continued to live in a world of his own; sometimes he was an explorer leading an expedition across the Great Plains to the Cypress Hills, sometimes a Mountie chasing car thieves.

Then at Christmas my mother invited the Redekops for Christmas dinner. "After all, they are our neighbours," she said.

"You don't have to do that," I said. My mother and Mrs. Redekop had never been overly friendly with each other. The source of friction lay far back in the past, probably something that had happened in Russia. Lately, she had stopped saying anything nasty about the Redekops.

In June of my third year with the Strachans, the tone of the entries in my diary sharpened. "I should be glad of a job," I said to Trudy one Thursday as we sat in the park watching the ducks waddle back and forth in the mud. "But the Strachans - they make me sick with their high-handed ways."

Two days before we were to leave for the yearly trip to the lake I wrote to Henry. "I have to prepare for the trek to Willow Beach - pack the trunk of the Buick with groceries from the Piggly-Wiggly." I looked out of my attic window; it was a lovely evening. The day before it had even rained a little. Mosquitoes buzzed on the other side of the screen.

"There's only a gas station at the beach. It sells fish bait and tobacco, so we stock up in the city," I went on. "Mrs. Strachan loves it. To me the cottage always smells of mildew even on the hottest days," I complained. "The guests leave screen doors open and trail wet towels through the rooms. I'm the one who deals with the old stove and the rusty pump. Then they can't find their suntan oil or their poker chips. What's worse, I'm there until Labour Day. When will I see you again? With love, Anna."

I wanted to strike out that word "love." I looked at it written indelibly on the white notepaper. I was wary of expressing endearments yet I left it and sealed the letter before I could change my mind.

For Christmas that year of 1934 Henry gave me a watch. I didn't know how to thank him. Where had he found the money? "He must be getting serious," Trudy said. Henry's letters became more insistent, pressing, and in February of 1935 on Valentine's Day he proposed. He wanted to marry me. And soon.

"You don't owe the Strachans. They take you for granted," he wrote. "Marry me, Anna. What are you doing there with those stuck-up English? They don't really care about you. We could live on the farm. We've paid off our debts to the C.P.R. There's bound to be a good crop soon."

Did I want what Henry wanted? Did I want to live on a parched farm with him? I could not name what I wanted so I vacillated. "My father still needs me, Henry. I can't desert him." It was an excuse. I was afraid of accepting Henry's offer and afraid of refusing. What if I became on old maid working for the Strachans until they died? Then what?

"Think of Leona Penner," Henry wrote as if he sensed my indecision even though I had tried not to let it show.

I did think of Miss Penner, aged thirty-five, who was the president of the Women's Sewing Circle in Hackett. When the girls who frequented the Madchenheim returned from their semi-annual holidays in Hackett they laughed about Miss Penner, the lisle stockings sagging around her thin ankles. Miss Penner always apologized for every little thing. She wore her hair in a tight bun, rimless glasses on her thin sharp nose and stayed home and took care of her ailing parents.

In the maelstrom of Revolution her fiancé had been shot dead right before her eyes. "Leona is one of the despoiled," my mother had told me in a low voice, when at the age of twelve I asked what made Miss Penner tremble so. My mother had not elaborated then, and ever after I had been afraid to enquire further. No one I knew spoke of what had happened during those days of terror. Eventually I had learned to read the body language of women of my mother's generation who never spoke of rape aloud. It was almost as though they might be the ones at fault.

Two months later at Easter, Henry finally came to the Strachans house in Raulston to visit me. Before he was quite through the door Mrs. Strachan walked into the kitchen.

"So this is your young man?" She looked sharply at Henry standing on the back door mat. In his dark grey suit he could have been a bank manager or a schoolteacher. Her English voice sounded to me like a warning bell.

"Good morning, pleased to meet you," he said and bowed slightly, then held out his hand. Mrs. Strachan pretended not to see.

He quickly dropped his hand.

I flinched. Henry's German accent had betrayed him. I flushed with anger, unable to say a word. After Mrs. Strachan left the room Henry kissed me and put his arms around me. "Now, you see what I mean? You will marry me, now, Anna, won't you?"

I laid my head against his shoulder. What could I say if I did not say yes? I had terrible doubts. But if I said no, Henry would go away and never come back.

"Yes, you're saying yes, aren't you?" Henry held me away from him. He looked stern, like the judge, like my father the few times he had been angry with me.

I could say nothing else. I had to say yes. Finally I nodded.

Without another word Henry pulled me back into his arms. Was I now engaged? Is this how it felt? It was not a bit like I had read about in the Mrs. Strachan's magazines.

"I suppose he's going to give you a ring?" Mrs. Strachan asked after Henry left. Her voice was sour.

My cheeks went hot. "Henry has no money for a ring. It doesn't really matter," I said blithely. "We have time for all that." I had promised to marry Henry but had not said when. For days afterwards I went about the Strachan house in a daze. Henry's letters were full of his plans for our future.

In June there was a heat wave, one of those unseasonable spells with a strong hot wind. We were packing once again to go to Willow Beach. Mrs. Strachan wiped her brow as she came into the kitchen "Did you pack the Buckley's for the judge's cough?" she asked. "Thank heaven, it will be cool at the beach." She handed me a letter that had come in that morning's mail.

"Thank you, Mrs. Strachan." I pushed a big box of toilet paper, along the floor toward the back stairs, ready to load into the back seat of the car. Then I sat down on the stool beside the sink, turned on the cold tap and splashed water on my face. Without drying it, I opened the letter. It was from my father.

"Dear Anna. I have good news. We are Canadian citizens! Finally we have our citizenship papers, although Mama remains suspicious. She has no faith in the democratic process. I can vote now - for what that's worth."

We were Canadians! I slipped the folded letter into my apron pocket. It did mean something. What did it matter what the judge or Mrs. Strachan said or thought? Suddenly I didn't care. I could laugh at the judge's fishing efforts in his leaking boat, at Mrs. Strachan sitting in her rotting swing at Willow Beach, reading to improve her mind. I smiled to myself. Was Zena already a citizen? Or Henry? I had no way of knowing. A Canadian citizen!

My euphoria did not last. By the time the trunk of the car was loaded, the very idea of Willow Beach and the big lake made me sick to my stomach. Finally we were ready to leave, a panting Fletcher on my lap. The judge waved us off. He would come out on the train the following weekend.

It was hot in the car. I could feel the sweat dripping down my neck. Fletcher snuffled for fleas. Mrs. Strachan slowed for a railroad crossing, bumped over the single track and speeded up again. She slowed again and pressed the horn in warning to several cows grazing on the sparse grass along the side of the road. They hardly raised their heads. I wiped sweat from my face and looked over at Mrs. Strachan's neat hair and cool cheeks, her smooth hands on the wheel of the car. English women didn't seem to sweat.

She spoke above the sound of crunching gravel under the wheels. "Anna, these are such hard times. What if you do marry this poor boy and the babies come?"

I looked at the road unwinding before us. What did Mrs. Strachan know about babies? She had never had one. I knew how babies came. After all, I had watched animals on our farm, heard schoolboys tittering behind the barn although I had never really seen a live naked man. My mother had warned me about girls having to get married. I would rather die than shame my parents in that way.

"Henry has a farm... a place to live," I said and looked at Mrs. Strachan.

She did not meet my eyes but turned away to look out of her window. "Such poor land, this Palliser Triangle," she said and turned back to watch the road. "It should never have been ploughed up. A mistake. The government paid no attention to Palliser's advice."

I stared through the windshield at the land. What did Mrs. Strachan know about farming? This was rich land when it rained. All the farmers said that. But it did look bleak at this time of year. Cracks ran here and there on the bare ground like forked lightning. The land around us was exactly like the land around Hackett, like my father's farm, like Henry's. In the distance a grain elevator in drab red pointed an accusing finger to the cloudless sky. Water shimmered in the distance - a mirage. We passed a grey unpainted house and outbuildings. The house, behind the straggling Caragana windbreak looked ready to collapse in the next windstorm. In the ditches sow thistle grew rank and tall.

"It was the C.P.R. who wanted settlers here, in order to help pay for the railroad." The car swerved slightly in the loose gravel.

"You mean my father? And the other immigrants? Were they ever told about this Palliser?" I asked her.

"I don't suppose the C.P.R...." her voice trailed away. "The report was filed away in an archive somewhere. The judge knows all about it."

I almost choked. The C.P.R. - that faceless tyrant! I stared at the barbed wire fence that marched along beside us. My father and Henry held hostage by their debts to the C.P.R. I had always hated the C.P.R.

I did not know if it was the right decision, but I was choosing Henry and this land and suddenly, I was glad. I hated everything about the Strachans: the judge's professional kindness, Mrs Strachan's condescension. If I quit, she would just hire another girl to polish her mirrors, take care of her dog. The judge would remain unfailingly polite.

"I want something of my own, my own home, my own family," I said aloud above the sound of the wheels. "And Henry will give it to me. He loves me."

The first glimpse of the lake appeared suddenly out of the land itself, a shining body of blue water with its narrow green fringe of willow.

It was my last summer at Willow Beach. Henry came to get me at the end of July and by the end of August we were married. I had chosen. I would have to live with it.

Chapter Four

Six weeks after my marriage to Henry, my mother brought the news. "Anna. Good, good, you're at home," she called, sounding breathless as she hurried across the culvert towards me. "Where is everybody?" She looked towards the Redekop house.

I was in the Redekop garden. After a month I still felt like a guest in their house even though Henry and I shared a bed in one of its small upstairs rooms. Only a thin wall separated us from his parents' bedroom. At night when Henry reached for me I was sure I could hear his father rustle the pages of his Bible, his mother sigh into her pillow.

"Your Papa has a letter." My mother brandished the letter above her head. "It came this morning, by the mailman. Who will believe this? I can't. It's like a dream." My mother rushed towards me. "Albert Siemens writes. Gott im Himmel. I can't believe it yet. He wants Gerthe. He asks him..." She stopped for breath and looked down where I knelt among the dying foliage of the Redekop tomato plants.

"Gerthe is beside himself with it," my mother went on. "For weeks he did not dare to hope. But, now I can tell you, Anna. Oh, I have prayed and prayed. Get up from there, Anna. Why are you crouching so?" She did not wait for me to rise to my feet but moved back a few steps along the path towards the Redekop house.

"Ten years we have waited." My mother raised her arms again as if to embrace this dusty farmyard, the ramshackle barn, the unpainted house. "Now Gerthe will finally have his chance.

Editor of the Millbach News, your Papa. In Millbach, of all places. We will be near all our other friends. Sophie and Nicholas and all the others." She lowered her voice as if she did not wish to disturb the Redekops.

"You'll move away? To Millbach?" I quavered and sank back onto the dry earth. Grasshoppers sprang around me like catapults shot off at random. I held the few dusty tomatoes, just turning red, against my breast.

"Oh, Anna. It's not so far. Millbach. What's a few hundred miles," she said airily as if she travelled that distance often. I stood up and suddenly everything whirled around and blackened at the edges for a second. My face felt clammy. I groped to steady myself on the spade that stood stuck into the hard unwieldy ground of the potato patch.

She turned back to me. "You're pale. What's the matter?" She looked again towards the farmyard, empty in the September haze then her gaze returned to focus on me. "You're not...? Ach Du Lieber Gott, not that, Anna. I told you, told you. You have to get up and wash, douche yourself with vinegar water. Oh, Anna." She raised her hand almost as if she would strike down whomever, whatever stood in her way, then turned away to clutch at her head.

"But Mama. There was no place. The old people...and the lamp. I couldn't see to..." It was impossible to describe my misery.

She turned back to me and held out her hand. "Maybe it is not so. I hope it is not so. You know," she said, her wonderful news making her generous for the moment, "it could be this autumn heat wave."

I gulped down tears and looked away. On the other side of the barbed wire fence one of the Redekop cows munched dandelions and thistles. Crickets chirred in the weeds nearby.

I looked again at my mother. "Well, anyway you're married now. It's life," my mother said. She turned her back and tightened the kerchief around her head, giving it an extra tug. I followed her as she started down the path. I would not cry, I vowed silently. By the time we had reached the edge of the garden, her excitement for the glowing future was uppermost in her mind again.

"Sometimes I wondered if God.... I was so angry, so angry.

Now this. After our terrible times, after all that. I cried, I shook, I screamed. Then He promised me, He owed us, I said." She waved the letter against the dusty sky. "God listened after all."

God had relented. My mother suddenly looked much younger, her shoulders squared.

"But Mama, what if God doesn't listen? You said ..." I ventured, tears just below the surface, my cheeks burning.

"Said? What did I say? I did say. I did tell you." She did not look at me. "I hate this. This talk. At least you're married, Anna. That's what marriage comes down to in the end. And if you don't like it you have to pretend. Maybe you will, eventually. That's what my mother told me. That's what I tell you now. But you have to do your part. You have to douche."

I looked away. My wedding night had been a failure. Animals seemed to fare better. Did the female worry about pleasing her mate? The night following had been no better. Henry had barely given me time to pull up my nightgown before he was on top of me pushing into me. Afterwards he rolled over and without a word fell asleep. I lay beside him throbbing, the inside of my thighs raw and wet, my nightgown stained with blood. Every muscle in my body twitched. Where had the urgency gone? The lovely yearning that I had felt for Henry before? Did I even want again that pleasure which was so close to pain?

"Make the best of it," my mother said now.

I stared out over the ruined pasture and wished I was having a dream and would wake and find myself in my familiar attic bed at the Strachans.

"There are books, Mama. Mrs. Strachan tried to tell me. She was right. I should have listened to her." I put my hand on my mother's arm to detain her.

"Books! What do books know? What does a Mrs. Strachan know? She removed my hand from her arm. "What could a Mrs. Strachan know about it? From the very beginning she took advantage of you, a poor, young, innocent girl. You cared too much for her. What do rich Englander like that know about anything?"

My stomach tightened into a knot.

"You made your vows," my mother reminded me. "Remember the wedding, the white dress and you a bride?"

Yes, the white dress that my mother had fashioned so skilfully. It had lured me on. For this one day you will be queen, it had seemed to say. Like a child I had slid myself between its fitted seams. White for virginity. Purity. White, I thought now, so that virgin's blood could be witnessed.

And Henry? Solemn in a dark suit. Elteste Enns standing before us. What had been the words? Submit only unto him so long as ye both shall live. Henry taking my hand. When we turned, the faces of the people in the church, like puppets, row on row. Close by my father silent, eyes shining with unshed tears.

I had looked down at myself then, as slim as I would ever be, had wished that Mrs. Strachan could see me. But she had not come. Instead, a gift of silver flatware and a china dinner set for six came by express. It was the most expensive of all our wedding gifts.

Before the wedding my mother had baked and cooked for weeks. At the reception she had bustled to and fro like a small tugboat marshalling much larger vessels, her new shoes too tight, her corset straining under the navy blue dress, her hat firmly fixed on her head. She had made sure that the coffee was brewed, the ham sliced, the potato salad mixed, the pickle dishes full, before she allowed herself to sit down at the wedding table. Even then she had perched on the edge of her chair ready to leap up again, in case something had been forgotten. While Henry and I smiled and smiled and people came to shake our hands.

"Where's Papa? Why didn't he come?" I asked now, wondering if my father would remember his promise. Would he forget about all the years I had spent at the Strachans?

"He hasn't time now," my mother said briefly. "Regards to the Redekops," and then she moved away across the culvert and disappeared behind the windbreak between our two farms. She was deserting me, leaving me behind. Dust hung in the air like a haze. I tasted grit on my tongue. She had been angry. Well, I was angry too. I'd show her, show them all.

It took no time at all. My parents packed up their few belongings and were gone within a month. I went about my life like a mechanical doll. I was numb with shock for days, weeks.

I helped Henry's mother with the canning of tomatoes. I pickled beets and the few cucumbers she had kept alive with her dishwater. Henry was up before dawn, pitching sheaves and stooking for the farmers fortunate enough to harvest a crop. Finally the mailman brought a letter.

"We arrived in Millbach a week ago," my mother wrote. The letter was dated October 2nd. "All across the prairies the same, dust. But here in Millbach it is better. They've had plenty of rain. After so long it's so wonderful, to smell the green of things," my mother rambled on. "Albert and Katya came out to greet us at the printery. Papa and Albert almost fell into each other's arms, just like old times. Katya and I, well, we were never that close. Albert is still the dandy with his black moustache. And Katya still frowns like the stern school-mistress she was. Then there is her sister Hedwig, you remember her? You must remember her. She still flaunts herself for Albert to admire, as she always did. Now she does it behind a desk or before a linotype in the printery. Katya says nothing. Those two, they are still fighting over Albert. Your father forbids me to speak of it when I say Katya should just put her foot down for once. If Albert were my husband? Well, Gott Sei Dank, he's not."

I turned the page. My mother wrote on. "First thing, Albert showed off the printery. A big noisy press rattling, grease and ink, paper stacked in every corner, dusty windows, wires dangling. I could make no sense of it. This is a printery? This can show a profit? What would my father say? He knew about business, and manufacturing, too. He could have told us. Ach, if he were only here, what wouldn't I give?"

My mother had conveniently forgotten what an autocrat my grandfather actually had been. With death and an ocean now separating them, it most often fell to my father to remind her of that.

"But who will pay for setting words on paper?" my mother went on. "It seems a folly. But your Papa and Conrad already love it. They rise early in the mornings, hardly take the time to eat breakfast before they rush off to their work.

"Inside our house there are so many rooms. So much room! I've calcimined the walls white. All the woodwork and doors have been painted blue, a bright blue. I know they did this in the old country, too. Those superstitious Plain Brethren believe that that particular colour blue will keep away the Evil One. What nonsense! Your father says I better leave it, since we are only renting and we want to stay on good terms with our landlord. The floor heaves as if we are on the waves of a lake. The joists have given way, but I don't care. I am so glad there is an orchard with apple trees and several rows of raspberries. There's no barn, no cows, not even a pig. Now we live like city folk. I hope you are well. Our regards to the Redekops. As ever, Mama."

Her writing as it reached the bottom of the long page became more cramped and bled off the edge of the paper. She had underlined the 'well.' Was I well? Was she hoping that I had been mistaken? Or that I might miscarry? My mother had resorted to abortion during the famine in Russia although I was not certain how I had come to know that. All I could I remember was from long ago, in the days before we emigrated. My mother speaking almost in a whisper, saying to my younger aunts who stood by admiringly, "I told the doctor, no. Not this time. Not this one. This baby will be born in Canada." My mother had patted her belly and looked very pleased with herself. For the first time I had noticed that slight bulge. That had been my brother Felix.

Now I scanned my mother's letter again. Was I well? She would not want to hear how every morning I went out by the empty clothesline and retched up my breakfast. She had no use for weaknesses of that sort.

"Mit Kind," Henry's mother had whispered to Henry's father at the breakfast table after a week of such incidents. She was a thin, wiry woman who never wasted a word or a gesture.

Now I thrust my mother's letter between the pages of my diary and went down to the kitchen. I looked at the black iron cook-stove, the wood box beside it and the low washstand with its tin washbasin - the only place to wash. A roller towel hung just below the shaving mirror. It was a far cry from the luxury of Mrs. Strachan's kitchen and bathrooms. I thought of Mrs. Strachan's shining electric stove, the hot and cold taps in the white sink.

A dead chicken, fresh from Henry's chopping block, its wings still flapping slightly lay on the table ready for my knife. At Mrs. Strachan's, the butcher's boy delivered meat three times a week. It never dripped blood like this but came wrapped in brown paper ready to put into the refrigerator. I swallowed my nausea and set to work, plucking feathers, singing the naked carcass over an open flame, then removing liver, heart and entrails with one smooth motion of my hand just as my mother had taught me.

At supper the bile rose in my throat even as Henry's father praised the roast chicken. I could not eat what I had prepared. "So, your letter? How is your family?" Henry enquired politely as I began to clear away the greasy plates.

"Fine," I said and started to cry. His parents looked up, surprised as I rushed for the stairs. Im Andern Umshtanden, I heard them whispering to each other - allowances must be made, I was in the family way. Up in our room I sat on the bed and stared out of tiny window into the night. In the silence I could hear the rustling of newspapers, downstairs. They would be reading Der Bote by the light of the coal oil lamp.

Later, Henry came up with a glass of water for me. "There, there," he whispered and patted my shoulder. The words and the gesture reminded me of my father. Henry turned away with his face to the wall and I went to sleep somewhat comforted.

A week later my mother wrote again. "Sophie and Nicholas Wall and Zena live in Hunger Beware just outside town, a poor place with stony soil and stunted poplar bush. Not good farmland. The town fathers frown on the drifters and new immigrants that squat there, but Sophie and Nicholas are our dearest friends.

"It had been so long since we were together last and we had so much to tell each other. Sophie keeps telling her news bit by bit, always saving some for another time as if we will have all the time in the world. I have to tell everything at once, there will always be more. Nicholas gave us a basket of eggs. I did not want to take them because they are as poor as we are, maybe poorer. But still Nicholas laughs his hearty laugh, no different then when he was a rich Schonweser in Russia. Your fine Zena is now a clerk in the dry-goods department of Unger's store, where she's flirting with Ben, the one and only son. She says she is anxious to hear from you, sends greetings and says she'll write to you soon. I have not told her anything about you, except what a pretty bride you were and what a nice wedding we had.

With Sophie talking so much I have not even had a chance to describe your wedding dress."

What I hoped and prayed for was that my mother would not be discussing me all the time. It embarrassed me to death. What was she telling those people, the Walls, Sophie and Nicholas? And why did she tell me about Zena and her fine job and her rich boyfriend? Zena with the frizzy black hair and wild ways. She sounded the same as always. I longed to see her and yet I did not want her to see me like this.

I looked down at myself. My breasts hung full and heavy. My brain felt turgid, like corn syrup on a cold day. Write soon, my mother had written. I crumpled the letter in my fist. Henry's mother looked up from her knitting and I smoothed the letter out again. Henry's mother went on with her knitting as if she had not seen nor heard. I wondered how two mothers could be so different. Where my own mother had been made mutinous by hardship, Henry's mother had withdrawn into herself. She was as exiled in this terrible land as I was, yet even as my belly rounded with her grandchild we could not reach out to each other.

In her next letter my mother wrote, "Millbach is stretched out for almost a mile on both sides of a wide tree-lined street that follows a meandering creek. It looks a little like Schonwese only here everything is whitewashed cedar shingles instead of grey or red brick. There's a flour mill, a livery barn, a hotel, a Ford garage, a blacksmith shop, other stores, a post office and of course, Unger's big store.

"Across from us is the big white church. Everybody, the whole village goes to this Plain Brethren church. They are the ones in charge here in Millbach - those families who came fifty years ago. Even long ago in Russia the Plain Brethren thought us Schonweser too worldly. What will they think of us Schonweser now? Now we all must go to the Plain Brethren; there is no other church. The church is as plain as plain with square windows and plain glass. Inside are rows and rows of backless benches painted grey, as is the floor. Nothing like our beautiful Schonweser church in Russia, but surely God must come here, too. The Andacht is plain, plain and hours long. The Gesangbuch goes back to 1550. I know your father does not agree with their ways but he keeps silent. It's Albert who will get us into trouble. Albert does not go to church at all and watches from the side door of the printery office as we cross the street to enter the church on Sunday morning. Mr. Know-it-all I call him. Your father winces when I say that. Albert thinks he knows everything. Brags about finding God walking through the woods.

"Your Papa sends his regards. I hardly see him. Albert keeps him busy from morning until night. After Sunday dinner they go for long walks when the weather's nice. Just like the old days. Gerthe and Albert, they've found each other again. And the talk? They never stop. Please write Anna. Really, I must hear from you. Mama."

I read the letter again. My father sent regards. My father was too busy to write. My father had found his friend, again. Lucky father. I did not write. What had I to say?

Towards the end of October my mother wrote, "The weather continues sunny. A lovely St. Martin's summer. Our neighbour comes by often. Mrs. Peddlar-Braun, a big heavy woman, like a storm she is, fiery red hair piled in a knot on her head. Like everyone in Millbach, she speaks only Platte-Deutsch. So common. My Platte often fails me. Her three little girls tag along behind her. They want to make friends with Elene. Elene just stands there the whole time twisting her braids. Mrs. Peddlar-Braun brings English tracts to slap into my hand. This is the new religion from the States. I don't know what to make of it. What has possessed Mrs. Peddlar-Braun? She has been Plain Brethren forever. Why change now? I don't want to hear all this born again talk from her, but still, I have to tread carefully. Albert one day will say too much and the Plain Brethren will have had enough of him. Religion is serious here. Some things you just don't say aloud in Millbach."

I had to laugh. Poor Mama. Such a predicament. It was the first time in a long while I had felt like laughing. Millbach did not sound peaceful. A hotbed of opinion, more like. What would my mother do? She had never been one to tread carefully, no matter where she was. Would she have to choose sides? Plain Brethren or Mrs. Peddlar-Braun's newly adopted religion?

My mother wrote in the middle of December. "Katya had a terrible fight with her sister in front of everyone in the printery.

Hedwig has gone too far, prancing around, leading Albert on. I know Albert is no saint, but still. Mind you, I don't blame Katya for a minute. For how many years has she put up with Albert's philandering? Your father tells me to keep out of it, but this can't go on. People are talking about Albert and Hedwig telling each other secrets behind the big press, Albert and Hedwig, they are the talk of the town. They walk hand in hand along the creek path. And who spies on them? Albert's boy Ziggie, that's who, and our Felix with him. I can't ask Ziggie what he has seen, not about his own father. And Felix will say nothing. Don't tell the Redekops about this, Anna. They would be shocked. Keep it to yourself. Our regards to Henry and his parents, and please, please write, Anna. I must hear from you. Mama."

I put the letter away. I remembered a younger Hedwig eavesdropping on Katya and Albert in the summerhouse at our grandparents in Schonwese. It had seemed innocent enough then.

Soon my mother wrote again. By then, my silence must have told her that I was indeed pregnant. At least I didn't have to see the words on the paper and imagine my mother's face when she read them.

"We are well," she wrote. "Your father continues busy. Snow today. Sophie and her dog were here for tea. Sophie worries about Nicholas constantly. He was sawing firewood all afternoon and it's not the best for someone with bad lungs. He will end up in a sanatorium again."

It seemed to me there had never been a time when Sophie did not fret about Nicholas and his bad lungs. I had heard of it all my life, his delicate constitution, his years spent in a sanatorium in the mountains of southern Germany. I thought of Sophie now, with her little dog on a leash - Sophie would have a dog no matter how poor - walking home in the early winter dark. I suddenly missed Mrs Strachan's Fletcher. In the end he had become my dog as much as he was the Strachans'.

"It is nearly Christmas," my mother continued. "I'm baking Pfefferneus and Stollen. I wonder if Elene is too young for the Christmas doll I saw in Ungers. All lace and finery with eyes that open and close. She will be in Grade one next year. Too tall for her age and thin, thin. You were never like that."

I looked down at my thickening waist. Really, I must stop

this childish sulk and answer my mother's letters. I picked up my pen, and stared down at the blank sheet of paper.

"Dear Mama," I began and again put down the pen. My hand felt frozen. What was there to say? I was truly in Andere Umstandt - as the saying went - in another state.

By the end of December I still had not written. Another letter arrived from my mother.

"Zena has an engagement ring." My mother had not dated the letter. It must have been written around Christmas and delayed by the rush of holiday mail. "Sophie has seen it. A diamond. She says it's very fine. I have not seen it yet."

Why had Zena not written to tell me herself?

"The Plain Brethren frown on jewellery," my mother wrote, "even wedding rings, but Ben Unger has broken all the rules for Zena. And to think that Ben's great-great grandfather left the Schonweser because we were too worldly and founded the Plain Brethren! Now Zena will wear the diamond Ben has chosen for her. Our changeling, Zena has won Ben's heart - and all the young men of Millbach, I must say. I wish you could have been here for Christmas."

Ach, Mama, I thought. How you do go on about Zena. Are you jealous? Would you like to be young and beautiful again?

My mother went on. "The third day of Christmas we had a Verlaffness for Zena and Ben with wine and dancing. Never mind the Plain Brethren and what they might think.

"Elene had a recitation for the Christmas program, 'Es begab sich das Der Caesar Augustus.' She had all thirteen verses memorized and spoke in the purest German. I have been afraid that she would pick up the Platte accents from her little friends but so far so good. Your Christmas parcel is on the way. Frohliche Weinacht, Mama."

I got up to put more coal in the kitchen stove. Merry Christmas, indeed. I let the pages of the letter fall into the fire, but then I came to myself and snatched them back, just as they were about to burst into flames. Smouldered around the edges, they now had a black crepe border, the kind I had seen for funeral announcement. I was sick of myself, sick of feeling sorry for myself.

After months of absence - I had not been to church since my parents left - I had gone with Henry and his parents to the

Christmas Eve service at the church in Hackett. I had smelled the familiar Christmas scents of oranges and peanuts. The church was overheated and every bench packed full with sweaty human bodies. I hid myself away in the back of the church among the women with children. I needn't have; I could still button my coat over my changing shape. The choir sang Es ist Ein Ros Ersprungen. I thought of the baby Jesus and his mother, Mary. Why did we pay no attention to her except at Christmas? That is Catholic nonsense, my mother would have said. For her, Jesus was never a real baby. Was he for me?

Henry had surprised me with a gift: a fine pair of scissors, "from Solingen in Germany," he said proudly. I did not know what to say. I felt ashamed of my long sulk. It was our first Christmas together and I discovered I could be happy, after all. At the feast of Holy Three Kings in January I felt the first tiny flutter in my belly. Instinctively, my hand came to rest there. I no longer had the heart or the will to be angry with anyone.

My mother had included ten yards of flannel in the Christmas parcel she sent us. I sat down before the sewing machine and began to hem diapers. Over the top of the sewing machine, I looked out of the window. The fields lay bare in icy furrows. Deep in my heart everything was still the same, except everything was different. Now I could write my mother a letter. I laughed to myself. My mother didn't even know I had been trying to punish her. When Henry's mother saw me at the sewing machine, she smiled and without a word brought out several balls of soft white yarn she had stowed away somewhere. Later I cast on stitches for a tiny sweater on a pair of knitting needles and began to purl and plain.

"We are fine, Mama. Henry sends his regards as do the Redekops," I wrote at last, then paused. Should I tell her that Henry had gone at last to the municipal office and applied for relief? Would she write and tell me how we could have avoided that?

"I hope Papa is well."

My father had still not written. I wondered if he regretted his promise now. Now when I could do nothing for him. Now when it seemed he could do nothing for me.

"Give my regards to Zena when you see her."

I wrapped a blanket around my shoulders and walked out

to the mailbox on the road in the bright January sunlight. The constant wind had died in the freezing air. It was so cold the air burned in my lungs. I hurried back into the warmth of the house. The mailman would come by later in the day and take away my letter.

My mother wrote again towards the end of January. "King George the fifth has died. He looked so much like our dear dead Czar I could have cried. The Millbach News carried his picture on the front page. Gerthe wrote a fine editorial. Lauded the Mennonites of Millbach for being loyal subjects of the crown. Albert is never very diplomatic about such things.

"And Gott Im Himmel, what next? Albert talks of going back to Germany. I nearly swallowed my tongue I was that surprised, Anna. What is wrong with Canada, I ask you? Suddenly Albert wants to live in Germany. It is surely not the death of an old king that would raise such a fever in Albert, as Gerthe believes. I confess I have had a few sleepless nights. What will happen to us if Albert should continue this? To the Millbach News? Gerthe is a fine enough editor. And what about Conrad? He has finally stopped talking about working on a ranch in Alberta. I'm hoping things will calm down and we will hear no more about it. As ever, Mama."

"P.S.," she wrote in the margin, "Albert's desire to move back to Germany has more to do with Hedwig then he'd ever admit."

In early February a letter followed fast on the heels of the previous one. "Albert is determined." My mother wrote nothing about her neighbours, her tea drinking, her shopping at the store. "Impossible what Albert wants - for us to buy the Millbach News? With what I ask you? We have enough debt to choke a horse. But think of it, to own the Millbach News. At night I toss and turn. Your father groans, he says he has no head for business. What would my father say? I wish he was here to advise us. Gott Im Himmel. Pray for us. Mama."

It was the first time she had ever asked for my prayers.

"They're fine," I said when Henry asked after my parents. I would not burden Henry with such unsettling news.

In a P.S. my mother added, "The crows are back, snow is nearly gone. Spring cannot be far behind."

Then my mother fell silent. There were no more weekly

letters. After so much news, it was like a tap being turned off. What could be happening in Millbach?

By the end of March my dresses gaped at every seam. I waddled. Henry's mother dug into her old country chest and found a piece of brocade that had once graced the top of a parlour table of the kind we used to have in Russia.

"Dear Mama," I wrote, just after Easter, "I made myself a skirt and matching smock to wear to church. Henry says it looks very nice." I was lying. Henry had not really looked at me since I became so big.

Then a letter came addressed to Henry. It was in my father's handwriting. I held it gently. My father's hand had held it. Henry read the first part of the letter aloud to me. "As you may know, Albert Siemens has left Millbach. There has been great turmoil. For better or worse we now own the Millbach News. I tremble when I think of the debts we have assumed, but now we can offer you a position here at the printery in Millbach and hope you will consider it."

"They must come at once." I could hear my mother's voice. She would be hanging over my father's shoulder as he wrote.

Henry paused and looked up at me.

"It's true then?" I breathed to Henry on a rising note. "I didn't want to get your hopes up. Mama did write something but that was months ago. She didn't know where the money could be found. What else does he say?" I looked down at the page over the huge bulge of my belly.

Henry continued reading aloud. "You have excellent German and your skill with machinery would be a great help." In spite of himself, Henry looked pleased at my father's complimentary words. I tried to hide the smile forming on my lips. My father, ever the diplomat, sounded deferential enough to placate even Henry's prideful heart. Without further comment, Henry handed me the letter.

Millbach. To live in Millbach. The letters on the page wavered. In this offer to Henry my father had remembered.

"We'd be living close to your mother," Henry mused. "She'd know every penny I earned and how I spent it. I'd be their Sheck Bengal."

"Never just an errand boy, Henry. How can you even think that? They are not offering charity, Henry," I coaxed. "Papa's offering you a job. And even a house of our own. Here, do read it again more carefully." I handed back the letter. Please, please see this for what it is, our one big chance. Accept his offer Henry, I wanted to plead.

But I must not plead. Henry must think it had been his decision alone to accept my father's offer.

My baby stirred as if anxious to be on its way.

Our son surprised us by his early arrival two weeks before expected. The midwife who delivered him had pronounced him fit to travel, patting his well-padded bottom before she handed him to me. "But I'm not so sure about his mother," she had admonished me. Mine had been a painful labour and a rending birth, but it was the first and I had nothing to compare it with. But I overrode Henry's surprising solicitousness for my health, his mother's sudden protestations as she laid her cheek against the downy head of her first grandson.

And there had been another hurdle: Henry was concerned about his aging parents. But I was as ruthless as an Israelite woman determined to cross the Jordan after forty years in the wilderness. Although the invitation from my father had come to Henry I was sure it was meant as much for me and of course, for Harry, our son. We had a place to go and we would go there. I knew exactly how the children of Israel in the Old Testament story must have felt before they were admitted to the Promised Land. If his parents could not stay on the farm alone, why couldn't they go and live with Henry's sister who had a big rooming house in Raulston? His father could surely stoop to repairing window screens and leaking taps for his daughter, his mother could do her crocheting just as well beside the stove in her daughter's kitchen. I shrugged off the grief that they might feel at the loss of their farm - deep down I always remembered Mrs. Strachan's words, "that land should never have been ploughed." As my parents had left theirs to the coyotes and the Russian thistle, so too, could the Redekops. We knew what it was to give up home, and country, family and friends. Out of all this dying to would come something living. Out of giving up would come some getting.

Chapter Five

And so we came out of exile. Truly. But not to a strange land - coming to Millbach was like coming home to the village of my childhood. Sweaty and tired, Henry and I stepped down from a Grey Goose bus in Millbach with a newborn baby and little more than the clothes on our backs. The sky was clear. Lilacs bloomed in a tall hedge. We walked from the bus stop at the Fruit Store past the white school my mother had described to me, and the post office with its Union Jack fluttering in a slight breeze. I did not need directions to find our way. Strangers who had a familiar look, as if they shared the same blood, greeted us in Low German as we walked along a wooden sidewalk the short distance to the printery. Henry, carrying the baby, followed me along the path that led first to the side door of my father's office. Further on was the front door of my parents' living quarters where the window boxes set out with geraniums showed promise of an early flowering. It was as if I had been here before. I stopped by the open office door. I was home.

When Albert and Katya Siemens and their children left Millbach and immigrated to Germany, my parents had moved into the living quarters they left behind.

"Imagine, Anna! Katya, she left the piano. I can hardly believe it. Elene will take lessons of course and when Harry is old enough..." My mother could not contain her joy. "Ach Du Lieber. Think of it! Katya's dining room table. I always did admire it and those chairs with the tapestry. Also Albert's sofa in the study." My mother made a face at that - no one knew exactly where Albert and Hedwig had carried on their flirtation.

"They left the curtains, the rug in the living room, the refrigerator even!

"I mean, we did not have anything like that in the agreement, and Katya never said anything. Just went on with her packing. She probably couldn't sell it in such a short time. She packed and packed. So many books. Boxes and boxes. Well, you know. And all their paintings. Well, that's Albert for you. They never left a one. But I have to think Katya meant to be kind, don't you think, Anna and so... " My mother paused for breath. What the Siemens had left behind was a full two storey house built as an addition to the much older main building which housed the large press, several small presses, two linotypes and other printing equipment necessary for a newspaper and job printing business. There was a front office and in the back, my father's private office, with windows overlooking the side drive and the flowerbeds.

From there a door led to the front hallway of the house. A corridor led to a bedroom, a bathroom and a small study that held the famous sofa where it was rumoured that Hedwig and Albert amused themselves. The living and dining room windows faced south. The kitchen looked out over the back garden and further away one could see a grove of trees - oak trees, rare for this part of Manitoba. Willow and hazel bush marked where the creek meandered.

I did not envy my mother her house and garden; I had my own. On this July day, I stood outside my own back door in the early morning sunshine that was just beginning to touch the rows of blooming peas that my mother had planted and staked before we came. I put my hand against the grey cedar shingles of the house beside me. My new home was as different from the Strachan house with its carved lintels and barely trodden oriental carpets, as it was different from our flimsy homesteader's shack with its rough boards, smelling of dust and dashed hopes, barely tethered to the betraying land around it.

This house, which my parents had vacated only a few days before our arrival in Millbach, felt established, felt almost organic as if it had grown out of the soil along with the honeysuckle, Spiraea and gooseberry bushes surrounding it.

The tiny panes of glass in its deep-set windows had been hauled by oxcart by the settlers long ago. On this morning, they sparkled from my polishing. The past months of my mother's baking and scouring, the smell of her cinnamon buns and the soapsuds had not quite overcome the ancient smell of whitewashed walls, the iron hard water in the sink, the creosote that ran down the side of the chimney.

The thick walls of this house had been built by the settlers and let to us by a descendant, a man by the strange name of Machine Unger. I already felt a certain kinship to him. Surely somewhere in our family tree we had a common great-aunt or uncle. Deep in my heart I knew I had come home and I knew I would be happy here.

I looked with a possessive eye at the garden as the sun lit up the lilac bushes near the fence. Two robins fought over a worm. I heard a bugle and saw a cowherd coming down the village street. The cows ambled slowly before him on their way to the village pasture at the end of the street. He blew his horn again. I finished hanging out the freshly laundered diapers and then picked up the spade leaning against the fence and walked onto the road. I scooped up some of the fresh dung that had been deposited just minutes before and carried it back to the garden. It would fertilize the peony bushes that an old Unger granny had left behind when she died.

Henry had gone off to work in the printery at dawn. "I won't give your brother any reason to complain," he'd said more than once. I thought of Henry, his exacting fingers on the keyboard of the linotype. He had taken to his work immediately and I pictured him with his green eyeshade in place, leather apron tied around his waist to catch stray shards of lead that could sliver from the hot type into his lap.

The whistle on the flourmill across the wide street blew one long blast. It was seven o'clock. I straightened up from where I had been working the dung into the soil, and inhaled the perfume of the blossoms. I felt light as a butterfly. My body was my own again although fetal blood still seeped from me and if I moved too quickly I would break out into a sweat. It seemed to me that anything, anything was possible.

"Anna?" my mother called from the front gate. Startled, the robins flew to the lowest branches of the nearby maple.

"Here, Mama." I moved into the sunlight and waved a hand.

My mother came on like a ship in full sail and handed me a loaf of bread wrapped in white cloth. It was still warm from the oven. "Fresh this morning. I started the rising last night. How is Harold?"

"Thank you, Mama. And it's Harry for short, Mama. He's fine, slept right through the night. " I sounded more confident than I felt, although I had discovered that new babies were not as fragile as they looked.

"Harry. Harold. Why ever such an English name, Anna? Why not a good German name like Dietrich after my father?"

"He's Henry's son, too Mama. His name is Harold. Harry for short," I said stubbornly. I had known that living so close to my mother would have its advantages and disadvantages.

"What I really came for. Such news! Zena and Ben. You will never guess." My mother craned her neck to look over the hedge to the house next door where Mrs. Peddlar-Braun lived. Nothing stirred there, as yet. "Think of it! Zena and Ben. Married. They phoned from Redwin last night. Nicholas came to tell us."

"I knew that," I lied. Zena had seemed her usual self when she came for a quick hello last week on her lunch break from the store. Why had she not confided in me, her oldest and best friend? All she'd said when she came to ooh and aah over Harry was that she and Ben had plans. That was so like Zena, I had to remember that. We'll not let husbands and children come between us, we had always promised each other, but she could be secretive when it suited her and now she had kept her biggest secret from me.

"How did you guess? You knew all the time? Even Sophie had to admit she didn't know. Zena, that girl. So like her, though isn't it?" My mother was recovering from her surprise. I had not quite ruined the story for her.

"Who married them?" I would not let my mother see my hurt.

"Some outlandish priest in the North End of Redwin, among all those synagogues and orthodox domes. Zena among her own at last."

"Well, I don't blame Zena. She told me the Plain Brethren refused to marry them." I rewrapped the bread more firmly.

"No, no, Anna. That will not get Zena very far. I don't blame the Plain Brethren, even a Schonweser Elteste would object to Zena's infant baptism. Infant baptism will not do and Zena should be well aware of that. Sophie has been too soft-hearted with that girl."

"Well, infant baptism or not, it sure doesn't seem to matter with Ben." I said, still trying to hold my own against my mother. I knew how Zena felt. "It will be a big flare-up but soon the Omas and Opas will have something else to get excited about," she had said to me.

"First there was the engagement ring, then Zena's stubbornness about the baptism and now this. Ben thumbing his nose at his own people, his own Plain Brethren. Sophie says she is mortified beyond words but underneath I can feel it; she is actually quite relieved, if you want to know. The suspense is over. But there will be no big wedding now." My mother sighed and bent down to pull up a handful of weeds that had sprung up by the rain barrel near the door.

"They'll have a big party instead," I said. I wished Zena had confided more in me. I thought back to my own wedding. Tradition wasn't everything.

"I was so looking forward to a wedding," my mother said and brushed damp earth from her hands. "Of course it would have been hard financially for Nicholas. Such a proud man. That flock of hens and his wood-lot barely keep him and Sophie alive." My mother sniffed and dropped the weeds by the boot scraper to wilt and die in the sun.

"Zena knows what she's doing. She always had a mind of her own," I said.

"Yes, too much so. And wild to boot, Anna. That's the Russian in her. But why won't she submit to a proper baptism? I can just hear them going on about it. The Plain Brethren will hold it against the Shonweser forever. I feel to blame. We have to stand fast for our convictions, after all, be an example to the world.

"I always knew there would be trouble; Sophie rushing off with a newborn Zena, having her dipped by an Orthodox priest. And for what? To keep a promise to a servant girl who was as good as dead."

"But Mama, if Sophie promised her? A promise is a promise. Besides, I didn't know much more than an infant when I was baptized," I said. I felt worlds away from the silly ignorant girl I had been when I was baptized. I could speak from experience. I had married, borne a child. "I didn't really know much more than a baby, come to that. Tradition isn't everything."

I thought of my own baptism in the Hackett church a few weeks before I married. I had wanted to be baptized, wanted desperately to belong, if not to the God of Mrs. Strachan's world or the God who had brought my father to tears in that basilica, then at least to Henry's and my mother's stern God. Don't ever leave me, Lieber Heiland, I had prayed. In that moment an everlastingness surrounded me, a Presence impossible to describe. I would never forget the trickle of water that dripped from my bowed head down to the floor as I knelt before the officiating Elteste.

"Where would we be without tradition?" my mother said now, distressed by the attitude of the younger generation. "Look at Mrs. Peddlar-Braun. She'd be speaking in tongues if her husband hadn't put his foot down. Babbling away. Tradition's important enough. If Zena wants to get along in Millbach, she'll have to give a little, too, Nicht Wahr? Just marrying into the Unger family will not be enough."

"Who knows? It just might," I said flippantly, not looking at her but letting my eyes roam over the garden. I was daring to include myself in that generation. I wanted so much to best my mother. "It might well be, Zena can be very charming."

But she did not want to hear any more. For this once she would leave the field of battle with me having the last word. "I'll see the baby another time," she said turning to go. I watched her figure move quickly down the street until she disappeared into the tunnel of green that was the printery driveway.

And it just as well she didn't stop to see the baby. She would be have been sure to spot the rash that showed on Harry's plump belly just above his diaper and then I'd have never heard the end of it.

Zena had not noticed Harry's rash when she rushed over on

her lunch break the day after we arrived. I was so glad to see her I almost forgot that I had a baby. We hugged and cried and kissed.

"Isn't he darling?" She had picked Harry up as if he was made of thin glass and looked at me across the crib, the same Zena that I had always known. "I have so much to tell you," Zena said but then Harry began to fuss and I had to nurse him. So our talk had been postponed yet again.

"Come back soon, come when you can," I had called to her retreating back. The baby did not pay any attention to a clock, or allow for the long talk I had hoped for.

I went in to check on Harry now where he slept in his fine crib provided by my mother. Beside it stood my mother's other gifts: a matching chest of drawers, a rocking chair, a high chair. "Fit for a prince," my mother had boasted. Mrs. Peddlar-Braun's husband, the auctioneer, had brought them from an estate sale in Redwin.

"You know how it was when Felix and Elene were babies. We had so little," my mother had reminded me when I protested.

"Her gifts come with strings attached," Henry had warned me, but I shrugged him off.

Later that afternoon Sophie arrived bearing gifts for Harry. She had her dog, Mitzi with her, dancing at the end of the leash.

"Welcome here." I waved her to a garden bench close to the back door, sheltered from the street by a lilac bush. She sat down gratefully. "Would you like some tea?" I offered, ready to get up and go into the house.

"Sit, Mitzi." The little Pomeranian sat obediently on the ground beside Sophie's fine leather slippers. Sophie wore black as she always had. She looked cool in a skirt with tiny blue and white flowers, gathered around her tiny waist. She fanned herself with a wide brimmed straw hat. I looked down to see if my blouse was buttoned and I was not leaking milk. I felt sweaty and clumsy beside the elf-like Sophie.

"Thank you, that would be lovely. But no hurry."

"It seems like a dream now," I said, "this last year, Harry's birth. And now here we are."

"Nicholas and I have not forgotten you in all the excitement of Zena's marriage. Ach, Alles so Gut?"

"Harry's perfect, a very good baby," I said. With Sophie I could boast a little.

"Then you'll be wanting a few more like him, Nicht Wahr?" said Sophie looking sideways at me.

"Please, Sophie, not right away." I laughed to cover up my nervousness. "You know how my mother is about too many babies. Harry is enough right now. Last winter I thought bearing one child would be more than enough."

"Anna, I wished for a child with all my heart when I was like you. It was not to be. Those years. Such terrible things happened. Bolsheviks roaming the countryside. You knew I was one of the violated ones?" Her lovely eyelids drooped for an instant.

I shook my head. I had not known. Suddenly I understood a great many things about Sophie that had not been clear before - the shadow in her eyes when she looked upon a child, her seeming fragility. She had been raped and survived. I shook inside at the thought. What I had endured on my wedding night paled in comparison. I was still bleeding a little after Harry's birth. How much more would she have bled? It hurt me to think of Sophie's pain in that long ago war but it had not soured her. She was the kindest, most forgiving woman I knew and also the most fun. Not a bit like poor, dear Leona Penner of Hackett.

"And then Zena's mother took sick with Typhus. I nursed her day and might. She was dying and I promised to take her child. My Zena fell into these arms like a peach, a treasure." Sophie looked sad but only for an instant, then she brightened. "Goodness is never lost. It comes to those who love, not always right away, sometimes long after. I've always believed it."

"You're sure?" I asked. I wanted to believe her.

"Ja, ja. Nah Sicher, Sicher. Out of that awful time came my Zena. I do not have to bear the child for the child to be my own. And now that Zena is married, Nicholas and I can look forward to a grandchild or two."

"Zena? So soon? Not Zena, too? She's just married." I was horrified. Wouldn't Zena be the first to tell me about it?

"No, no. No. Zena won't have a baby until she's ready. You young people can plan these things nowadays." Sophie smiled again.

I looked down, embarrassed, wanting to confide in Sophie but not knowing how. Then I said in a rush, "Sophie, Sophie, I'm afraid. I'm so afraid. Tell me what to do. I'm nursing Harry, of course. Mama says it will help, you know...? I'll simply die if I have another baby so soon. I thought you might know what I could do? I mean Henry is not a patient man. I was married a few weeks and right away, right away, there I was, pregnant."

Sophie's sharp blue eyes looked into mine. "I'm sorry I cannot help you, Anna. You must talk to Zena. She will know." Sophie laid her hand with its birdlike fingers on my arm. "Promise me you will go to her...ask her?"

I was silent. I looked down at my feet. Then I nodded.

"Gut, gut. Now time for the presents," Sophie said when the silence became uncomfortable. She handed me several copies of the Hamburger Stern. "Here's some light reading for you. Marlena Dietrich is in the news again. And of course King Edward and Mrs. Simpson. The English will never put up with a divorced queen." Sophie laughed and took two gift-wrapped packages from her basket.

"Zena said I should bring this. She wanted to give it herself but what with the wedding and the honeymoon...also, and so on. But Harry will not care, will he? So I brought it."

I unwrapped a fine silver spoon with a curved handle engraved with Harry's name. Harold Gerthe. So fine - Zena was good with presents.

"Tell her Besten Dank. No, I'll tell her myself, when she gets back from the honeymoon," I said and opened the second gift. It was a blue satin bound baby book that Nicholas had inscribed with his elegant script. I riffled the pages. A place for the first photo, date of the first tooth, the first step, the first word.

Sophie laughed. "Zena said you'd like it. They have some really nice things in that store. If you can't find it anywhere, Ungers will have it."

"Besten Dank, Sophie." I leaned over to kiss her powdered cheek. "You are like my real aunt."

She smiled fondly. The gold filling in her front tooth caught the light. "You're family, like another daughter, Anna." She moved closer to give me a little hug.

"I must be on my way," she said and got up to go.

"Where will Ben and Zena live when they come home?" I asked as we walked down the path to the gate. "Zena said something about a house in the old orchard. Is that going to happen?"

"Oh, I think so. It will be very grand. No one will believe Zena has lived with us in a tar-paper shack for these last years." She smiled again, amusement in her voice, she who had been raised in a mansion. She patted my hand before she turned to go. "About that other. Now promise me you'll go?"

I nodded and then she was gone.

Later that night I stood at the bottom of our staircase and looked at the worn treads. Countless pairs of feet had hollowed them over the last fifty years.

"Come to bed," Henry said from the top of the stairs and turned to give me that certain look - a husband insisting on his marital rights. This was marriage, my marriage. I had made vows. Wives submit yourselves to your husbands, the Bible said.

I moved around the table away from the stairs. "I'll just put the milk in the cooler." I prayed that Harry who slept in an alcove just off our bedroom at the top of the stairs would wake and cry for my attention. I waited and I heard Henry pause as he looked down at his sleeping son before he went into our bedroom.

I wiped the balustrade with my apron, rung after rung as far as I could reach from the bottom of the stairs. I heard the water run upstairs in the bathroom. Henry would wash and brush his teeth before he got into bed. I waited. I looked at the steps again hoping Henry would fall asleep quickly. He had said he was tired.

I took a step, after all, they did not lead to a scaffold or a guillotine. How many settler wives had trod them, afraid to go up to an impatient husband's arms? I knew exactly how it went. First there would be Henry's urgency, then my submission and our clumsy coupling. I took another step and waited. How many unwanted pregnancies? The Bible said that children were a blessing from the Lord. Now I prayed only to be barren. Another step. How many women dead in childbirth? Liebster Heiland, I prayed when I got to the top of the stairs. Shoals of sperm seemed to swim toward me. Don't let this be the time I get pregnant, I prayed.

I paused beside Harry's crib. He was perfect. In the dark I could not see his lashes, the beautiful way they feathered on his cheeks. I pulled the quilted coverlet over him. There was no sound from the bedroom. A breeze fluttered the curtain at the window in the hallway. Through the half closed door I could see that the room was dark. Henry slept. Tomorrow, I told myself. Tomorrow I must go and ask Zena what to do, but now I was safe for one more night.

Zena. She would be wondering why she hadn't heard from me. Hadn't we been best friends forever? In spite of a baby and each with a husband, we did live just down the street from each other.

It was not distance that kept us apart and yet I kept putting it off and putting it off. I waited and waited until I knew I could wait no longer. By that time, Zena and Ben had moved into their nearly finished house. "We're living in a disaster area. Plaster and varnish all over," she said when I finally phoned her.

"I must come and see," I said. "How about day after tomorrow or maybe one day next week?" I said, stalling once more.

"No, that's too long. Tomorrow is perfect. Come tomorrow, if you can," she said. "Why are you so...Ben won't bite you know. Besides he'll be at work during the day. What is the matter with you, anyway, Anna?"

"Yes. Yes, I'll come. I'll leave Harry with my mother. Alright?"

"Whatever. With baby or without baby, you're coming then? It's about time," she said. Zena was not a baby gusher, I thought.

The next day I left Harry asleep in his pram in my mother's front hallway, saying to Elene, who sat at the piano in the living room practicing her scales, "I'll be back, I'm just going to Zena's. Here's his bottle if he cries."

I walked along the main street of Millbach. It was a lovely autumn day. Indian summer. There was a bustle of shoppers up and down the street. Cheerful people. Millbach was full of friendly souls, I thought. I smiled and said hello whenever I passed someone on the street. In Millbach everyone said hello.

I thought of the streets of Hackett, the feeling of desolation. Henry had received a letter from his parents only last week. Apparently nothing had changed there. It was enough to make me get down on knees. I was so thankful we were away from the blowing dust and the despair. I saw myself reflected in the glass at Unger's store. I looked fine, happy.

Here there had been a good harvest. There had never been the severe drought condition as in the prairie dust bowl of Saskatchewan. In this mix of dairy farms, market gardens and wood lots, the depression had never bit so deep. The farmers had finished with threshing although a slight haze of harvest still hung in the air. North of town black furrows gleamed as ploughs turned the rich valley soil while to the south where the land was stonier, black and white cows grazed in pastures among the golden drifts of poplar leaves.

Autumn, the way it was meant to be. It was the time of year I loved most with the apples picked, and the cellar shelves laden with canned corn and peas and when I brought up a few potatoes, the garden loam crumbled off easily in my fingers. A sure sign that they had been harvested at the right time. I knew what a squirrel must feel when she had her cache of acorns and nuts stashed away in the hollow trunk of a handy tree.

I rounded the corner and there was Zena's new house. It stood in the old orchard behind the big Unger house, the earth from the basement excavation roughly levelled around it. The old fruit trees with their crooked branches had survived the construction. Now they stood about every which way like sad victims after an earthquake. There would be no grass until next spring. I knocked on the big front door. It looked very solid, like a barrier.

"I've been meaning to come, Zena," I said without formal greetings when Zena opened the door. "I wanted to give you time to settle in."

"Come in, Anna. You're out of the breath." Zena ushered me into her front hall.

The house smelled new: new wood, drying plaster, paint and varnish. "I can live again. The painters just left," Zena said and took me by the arm. "Come on in, we can talk. Watch where you put your hand," she said as she led me down the hall. My feet sank into the thick pile of the carpet and I thought of

Mrs. Strachan's house, the vacuuming I had done every day, the waxing, the polishing.

In Zena's living room the curtains and upholstery smelled as if they had just been unpacked. She gestured to the sofa. "What was Mama hinting about? Secrets. You know my mother can't keep a secret. What is going on?" She sat down opposite me in the new armchair, the pleats of her red plaid skirt spread around her. "We'll look at the house, do the tour later. Now what's the matter?" She picked up some knitting from the table beside her chair, fingers busy even as she kept her eyes on me.

I did not know what to say next, although I had gone over it a hundred times before in my mind. How could I ask about something so intimate?

"Yes, the tour, by all means, you must show me everything. I can't wait," I stalled. "I've heard so much. I'm dying to see what you've done." I moved to the edge of the sofa and stopped speaking abruptly. It was now or never.

"Zena, I have to ask-"

"What, Anna?" I looked down at my lap and tried again. "I have to...your mother said, I should ask, I don't know..."

Zena remained quiet, her expression expectant.

"I have to know, Zena," I plunged in. "I mean, Henry won't stand for it much longer. What I can do?"

Zena put down her knitting and put her hand to her mouth. "You've been holding Henry off since Harry was born?" she asked incredulously.

"Well, not exactly - I am still nursing, but I couldn't stand it right now; another baby." It was out. All out. I had said it. I looked away my eyes on the French doors. I felt as if my words hung in the air between us like a curtain. Had I said too much? Too little? Would this spoil our friendship? "I don't want to be like those other immigrants, with one baby after another. Mrs. Strachan always talked about immigrants breeding like rabbits," I said, imitating Mrs. Strachan's English accent. I dared to look at Zena's face and to my surprise she was smiling. "Don't laugh, Zena. This is serious," I said indignantly. My voice shook.

"Oh, Anna, Anna. It's just the thought of Henry and you holding him off." Her mouth twitched. "Why didn't you say? You should have said. Poor Anna." Zena picked up her knitting again.

"My mother was no help with her vinegar douche." My eyes stung. I did not like to be reminded of those first months of married life.

"There's the drug store. French Safes," Zena said matter-of-factly, her fingers flying.

"You mean...?" My face burned. "Isn't that for soldiers? Henry would rather die than let that English druggist know what he does in our bed at night."

Zena's brow creased with a slight frown. "You can't go to the Millbach doctor - he's Catholic. You'll have to go to Redwin, Anna, like I did, and be fitted for a diaphragm. It's really nothing much, a little thing inside you, hardly bigger than a wedding band. I'll take you myself." She counted stitches with a polished index finger. Zena's diamond engagement ring flashed in the light.

My face had gone hot again at the very thought of someone poking around inside me. "Will Henry notice?"

Zena nodded. "You'll have to tell him." She began to purl. Zena knit the way Sophie had taught her, the old way, working the stitches with the tips of the fingers of her left hand. Mrs. Strachan had knit the English way, flinging the wool over the needle with her right hand.

"I don't know what to say. How will I tell him?" I moaned.

"For heaven's sake, Anna. What are you afraid of?" Zena asked impatiently.

I jumped as a log collapsed in the fireplace. Mrs. Peddlar Braun's predictions were wrong - Zena's fireplace did not smoke at all. "Henry and I don't talk about things like that. We never have." My eyes roved over the narrow windows on each side of the fireplace, then down to the built in shelves stacked with books. "How is it that you know all this, Zena?"

"I thought everybody knew. It's not the dark ages, after all. Women know, they just don't say."

"You mean Plain Brethren think sex is sin?"

"What? Sex?" Zena laughed, misunderstanding my question. "For them it's ordained. Be fruitful and multiply. But birth control? They don't say exactly. You know how Plain Brethren are - only men allowed at the brotherhood meetings. Women have no say." Zena put down her knitting and got up from her chair.

"Let's have a drink. You sit. I'll get it."

I sank back into the sofa. It felt as though I had just been released from dreadful torture. Zena would rescue me. I would be spared from further disaster. I heard the swish of a door.

"Prost," she said handing me a stemmed glass brimming with dark red wine and raising her own. "Here's to us."

"Oh Zena. In the middle of the day?" After two sips of Zena's plum brandy my head was in a whirl.

"Here's to us." She raised her glass again. "We won't wait for our menopause to enjoy married life."

I floated down the steps of Zena's house. On the street, a stout and purposeful Jacob Penner walked towards me. He was the Elteste of the Plain Brethren Church. I would not think of what lay below his belt, behind that sober serge and flannel, between the hairy flanks in long underwear. I raised my eyes to glance quickly at his shaven cheeks, the black hat fixed firmly on his big square head. I did not look directly into his eyes for fear that he would guess what Zena and I had been plotting. I was suspect. He would be sure to see that I was planning to go to Redwin to be fitted for that magical thing - a diaphragm. He nodded absentmindedly to me as we passed each other. I floated on. I thought of the stories I had heard. "He won't permit his wife to wear a wedding ring, although she yearns for one," Sophie had once told me.

Zena kept her promise and Henry never did have to go to the drugstore and be embarrassed by the English pharmacist. "It's for you to see to," he only said. We never discussed birth control again. I used my diaphragm religiously, I was far too fearful to be easily swept away by careless passion. And now I did what my mother had suggested at the beginning of my marriage, I pretended to enjoy sex, but it was never like the books described it - so powerful that I would give up everything I held most dear. Only when I sometimes woke from a dream, with my hand moist at the yearning between my legs could I imagine such a thing. Then my blood would boil up, my heart would pound until the storm in my body passed and I would be myself again.

In the fall of 1938 Henry began to come home with new

ideas. He seemed restless and he talked of following the Siemens to Germany. "I liked it in Germany, the schools. If it comes to that, I'm entitled, too. I have as much German blood as Albert," he said one night from his side of the bed. "German women are rewarded for bearing children. Hitler pays a baby bonus." He looked sharply at me.

I did not meet his eyes. Did Henry want another child?

I moved away from the bed and stood by the window looking out at the night. My stomach churned. Henry must have read the Hamburger Stern that came to my father's desk at the printery. It was full of such news items, illustrations of the Wehrmacht, the Hitler Jugend featured on its pages.

I ignored Henry's remark. "How many times have we been uprooted now? Too many times for me. We have a child now. We have a place here," I said from where I stood by the window. Could Henry make me go to Germany with him? "Don't you like it here?" I asked.

Henry half-sat up in bed. "At least there would be an end to your mother's hectoring," he said.

"Well, that? Yes. I know how you feel. She means well Henry," I moved closer to the bed and patted the quilt near his arm.

"Besides, the people here look down on us. Schonweser, Russlenda, they call us. New Brethren try to convert us as if we're some kind of heathen. In Germany, Hitler does not allow that." He lay down again, his sharp nose cast a shadow on the wall behind him.

"I know, I know, Henry," I said. I would soothe him into calm and sleep like a little child. "On Sunday morning I'm careful to speak Platte in the mothers' room at the church. I wish you could see me. You would be proud."

I did not tell Henry that I hardly spoke at all in that room. The women seemed to turn away both from my proper Deutsch and the English that Mrs. Strachan had so carefully instilled in me.

"And I don't like to complain, after all he is your brother, but Conrad is...well, difficult," he said.

"Conrad doesn't mean it, Henry. I know him so well. You take offence too easily." I finally got into bed. If I really wanted us to stay in Millbach I would have to placate this disgruntled unhappy man in the one way I knew. I got up again and went to my closet for my diaphragm.

It was the middle of November, when Millbach lay fallow between the autumn and true winter that Henry came home from work. He had teetered for weeks between staying or going to Germany as if it were as easy as a trip to Redwin while I kept myself busy canning the green tomatoes and wondering whether I could start the Christmas baking in the hope that we would be here to share it with our neighbours. I had not dared even to plan a January quilt.

"Hitler has annexed the Sudentenland and there is great unrest in Czechoslovakia," he said abruptly and spread butter on a fresh roll.

I had not heard the news.

"Germany is out of the question for now," Henry said. "Maybe later when things settle down. Your father persuaded me that it was poor timing."

And so the fate of lives and nations come to be decided.

"He also raised my salary," Henry added.

"Oh, Henry." My face must have showed my great relief.

"Try the jam, Henry. Your favourite, apricot." I moved the glass jar towards him. Be lavish Henry, I wanted to say. Spread both butter and jam for once. I sat down on the opposite side of the table and smiled.

Chapter Six

In December, my brother Conrad became engaged. On the Tuesday following the announcement, I went down to congratulate him.

Through the double front doors of the printery I could see my mother at the front desk, waiting on Mrs. Peddlar-Braun's husband who had come to order business cards and auction sale bills. Since business had become so brisk my mother worked behind the counter most afternoons. Today she wore a plain white blouse; pinned to the collar was her amethyst brooch that my father had given her on their wedding day. She looked as handsome behind the counter as Katya Siemens had. I knew she was displeased with my brother's engagement but would not let it show in public. At the moment she was all smiles, almost patting Mr. Braun's hand.

Beyond her, through another window I could see Henry busy at his linotype. Between the front office and the linotype room there was a thin wall and a door. It was just as well, I thought, for my mother's tongue was as sharp as ever - especially with Henry. I walked around the corner of the building along the path, the wall beside me reverberating with the rolling action of the big press churning out the Millbach News. Through the large window I could see my brother Felix in a striped pullover, feeding sheets of newsprint into the press. When he saw me he waved one hand then turned back to his work. Behind his head the big clock against the far wall of the pressroom said ten past three.

I reached the side door and entered the warm fug of my

94

father's office. Even after many months, Albert Siemens still haunted the place and I thought of him every time I came here to see my father. My eyes rested on the fading outdated maps Albert had left behind still pinned to the wall, their edges curling. Sepia tones of the once mighty Ottoman and Austrio-Hungarian empires. And then the map with which I was most familiar, the British, bright pink blotches like jam smeared on the face of a child.

Aside from Albert's ghostly presence, the rest of the Siemens had fallen out of our lives and it seemed, off the face of the earth. My father never spoke of Albert or his family, although I knew there would never be another friend like Albert Siemens for him. When he went to drink coffee at the Fruit Store or visited the post office, he walked alone. It seemed my father would remain a resident alien in Canada, a scholar with an ironic eye cast on the life around him but his roots in another soil.

Advertisers went to see Conrad, but preachers and politicians came to see my father, often sitting in the chair beside his desk. They were men who wanted their views made known in the editorial page of the Millbach News. Today the chair was empty. My father looked up, smiled over his glasses and put down his pen. He was in shirtsleeves, his coat draped over the chair behind him. The harsh light threw his face into relief. It showed lines that I had not seen before.

I perched on the corner of his desk. "Are you well, Papa?"

"Yes," he said, absentmindedly, reaching into his pocket for his cigarette pack. "How's young Harry?"

"Growing out of all his clothes. He's loving Tante Anna's kindergarten. Thank you for that."

My father smiled indulgently.

"I came to congratulate Conrad, Papa."

"Yes. Conrad. He's around here somewhere." My father leaned back in his chair. "We must hope the diplomats in Europe don't deny us the opportunity to celebrate Conrad's wedding." He raised his arms with both hands clasped behind his head. The swivel chair tilted precariously.

There was a knock and we both turned to see Conrad in the doorway.

I stood to greet my brother. "Hello Conrad," I said warmly.

"Congratulations. I just heard." I reached out to touch and feel the dark worsted sleeve of his suit. "You look splendid." Lately Conrad had begun to wear a suit and tie instead of work pants and the denim apron of a pressman. "I'm impressed. Nice cloth."

"Thank you Anna," he grinned at me and laid a sheaf of galley sheets on my father's desk, but my father had disappeared into the clamour of the shop for the moment, cigarette smoke trailing behind him. My brother and I stood alone in the office.

"Mama says you've set the wedding date for August. It will give us time to get acquainted with Nettie."

Conrad nodded, looking as pleased as he ever allowed himself to look. He threaded his fingers through the thick dark hair on his head.

"Nettie's shy. And you know Mama." He drummed his fingers on the desk. "There's not much I can do with Mama." He pulled a package of tobacco and papers from his shirt pocket and rolled a cigarette with long ink-stained fingers.

"Mama will calm down, Conrad. I'm sure she will. She had another bride picked out for you, but she'll get over it. You have a right to choose your own bride." I laughed as I patted his arm again. "Everything will be fine, you'll see."

"Well, I hope so. Nettie is used to Plain Brethren ways."

"I hope you'll be very happy, Conrad."

I buttoned up my coat, ready to leave the office. Marriage would soften Conrad, I was sure. The brother of my childhood would return. "Your Nettie's lovely. Such blonde hair," I said.

Conrad's shoulders relaxed. He struck a match to his cigarette, his blue eyes warmed and he smiled.

"No wonder Mama's a little jealous, having to give up her darling boy to another woman. And sooner than she thought," I teased.

Nettie truly was very pretty, young and fresh, with pale skin and sky blue eyes and the slender waist of youth. She seemed placid to me. She did not strive as we Heppners were inclined to. Conrad probably had enough ambition for them both.

Now he drew on his cigarette and looked pleased with himself. "Nettie's never met anyone like our driven Mama, Anna." He looked at me through the smoke. "It's not exactly easy for her. Nor has it been for Henry, I guess."

I was grateful for his recognition. At least Conrad understood. "Oh it's nothing, Conrad. I ignore her ranting. And where would we be if it wasn't for her drive?" I put on my gloves. "You must come for supper, soon."

"Right, Anna," Conrad said and stubbed out his cigarette. "I should get back to work."

I had my hand on the doorknob to leave, but then my father returned to the office. "Conrad has settled the date?" he asked, assuming his place behind the desk once again. "Pray, Anna, that there will not be another war. Conrad is of military age."

"Surely not, Papa." I said turning back into the room. "It can't happen. Not here in Canada." Suddenly I saw how old my father looked. "It's not fair. Why should it happen now?"

"Oh, Anna," he said tiredly. "We can't choose such things, which generation we will be born in." He gazed out of the window blind to the leafless shrubbery, the hard frozen ground, his thoughts on a past I could not see and did not know.

"Which generation would you choose, Papa?"

He didn't answer. I thought of the photograph on the piano in my parents' house. My parents before their marriage in 1911, my father in black and grey, sitting on a wrought iron chair, his hat on the table beside him, my mother in a white lawn dress her hand on his shoulder. It was their Verlaffness, their engagement. Beside the name of the photographer, a Gerhardt Rempel with a studio in Rosenthal, was the date 1910.

"I'm not sure. In my youth there was such ferment in Russia. A wonderful new world waiting to be born, I believed then." He threw up his hands. "Stillborn." He made a fist. "Anna, I would change the world for you. But I cannot."

"I know that, Papa," I said softly, then changed the subject. "Now you will have a house built for Conrad?"

My father nodded. "I promised him. Your mother thinks he's rushing into this marriage but he's worked hard and waited for this."

"Conrad deserves it." I said.

"Good. Well then, that's settled. I want to be fair." He looked at me, his thick brows drawn down for a moment above the almost Slavic tilt of his eyes, then reached for the galley sheets Conrad had left on his desk. I went out into the cold air and to the front door of the house to collect Harry.

It was four o'clock by now and my mother had come home to her kitchen to make coffee. When I mentioned what my father had said about a war, she dismissed it. "Pay no attention. Your Papa reads too much, thinks too much. Always he talks of war, spoiling the good times. It can't be true. Not here in Canada. The Indians are gone. Who would fight for the miles and miles of empty prairie?"

She shook her head as she filled the coffee pot with water. She was done talking about the war. Then her face lit up. "Come and tell me what you think," she said taking me by the hand and leading me down the hall to her bedroom. I could hear Harry and Elene playing the piano in the living room.

"How does it look?" my mother asked swinging the door open wide. "I was tired of Katya Siemen's roses." No trace of Katya or Albert Siemens remained in the newly decorated room. My mother ran her hand lovingly down the faint blue and silver stripes of the wallpaper; her fingers caressed the scattered sprays of daisies trailing narrow ribbons. "Do you like the bed-spread? And the rugs?"

"Fine, lovely, Mama." I nodded at the blue satin and chenille, the froth of white over the windows. "Almost bride-like, Nettie would like it," I said.

"Nettie can do her own. If war does come, God forbid, and money again becomes worthless, I won't have any of it lying around for my grandchildren to play with." She opened the closet door, removed a fur coat from its heavy wooden hangar, and held it out.

"Oh Mama, what have you been up to?"

The fur gave off the rich smell of well-tanned pelts. Mrs. Strachan's coat had smelled like that.

"I promised myself that one day I would have one, Anna. Here, try it on. Feel it. Isn't it grand?" Before I could put my arm into the satin lined sleeve, my mother had slipped it on and danced about like a ballerina, her right hand held high in the air. In the light, gold flashed on her finger.

"Let me see, Mama. A ring, too?" I reached for her hand. She held it out. The third finger of her right hand wore a red-gold band, wide and plain.

I turned it in the light.

"Like the one our calf swallowed?" I recalled the letter that came to me at the Strachans. My mother writing about the loss of her wedding band.

She nodded, laughing. "I vowed. Vowed, I would have another ring as fine. That stupid sucking calf. Lieber Gott, I was so angry." She laughed again.

"I didn't tell you in the letter, Anna because I was so ashamed but I can tell you now. I threw myself on the ground, I did. Pounded the earth with my fist. Screamed at the sky. 'God, You promised.' It was then I made the vow." Her eyes shone. Her cheeks were red. God had sent my mother prosperity at last. She had been vindicated.

I thought of how she would parade up and down the streets of Millbach in her new coat. She would not care what the people might say. There they are again, those Russlenda, they would whisper behind the curtains of their windows. The minute they have two cents to rub together they spend them. But would the people sheltered in this peaceful village ever know all that my mother had endured?

"I suppose Conrad falling in love with the rich Miss Unger was too much to ask." My mother shrugged. "But no, he picks Nettie Froese. They say she did not finish grade eight." She closed the closet door and stared out of the window for a moment at the early winter darkness.

"Ben's sister is too much for Conrad, Mama. He needs a soft, easy girl like Nettie, one who who'll look up to him and lavish praise on him. Ruth Unger is like Zena, headstrong, sure of herself. It flusters Conrad. He doesn't know what to do with a woman like that. You want him to be happy, don't you?"

Conrad had dealt with a strong woman all his life. I could understand why he might not choose to marry one.

"Never mind, Anna. I'll teach Nettie how we Russlenda do things." My mother's face brightened at the thought.

"I should be going to make supper for Henry," I said and turned down the hall to the living room. As I fitted Harry into his leggings, pulled on his toque and mitts, I thought of poor Nettie. From what I had heard so far she was in for a surprise.

All that winter and through the spring the headlines in the Redwin newspapers were tall and black. In spite of my wishful thinking the world slipped ever closer into war. Occasionally, when I passed my father's office windows I would see my father and Nicholas Wall, huddled together over the radio, their heads wreathed in clouds of tobacco smoke. If they looked up at all it was only to give me a distracted smile. They had a far-away look in their eyes, each with an ear tuned to the static on the short wave. But I was caught up in wedding preparations and did not pay as much attention as I should have.

Suddenly, it was the end of August. Conrad's wedding day dawned bright and warm. By one thirty, the sound of voices rose from the assembled guests inside the church. Surrounded by excited neighbourhood children, I stood with a fractious Harry beside me, on the stairs of the New Brethren Church.

My mother had persuaded my father to rent the New Brethren church for Conrad's wedding. It was one of several churches that had been built in the last few years, and the largest and most elaborate in Millbach. Her son's wedding could be held nowhere else, she said. This, despite her aversion to the New Brethren's theology of sin and salvation. Surprisingly, the New Brethren had voiced no objection to the importing of a Schonweser Elteste to perform the marriage service. They may have believed that our Elteste was lost and gone to hell with his 'soft on sin' preaching, but if my parents paid the steep rental, well, this too, could prove to be a mission field. Tracts could be left lying around where worldly guests might read them and be converted.

My mother stood at the top of the steps like a field marshal commanding her troops while my father waited at the back of the church until my mother was ready to accompany him down the aisle and sit at the front of the church just behind the bride and groom. There was no doubt about who was in charge nor had there ever been. My mother looked splendid in her deep purple finery, a purple rose on her brimmed hat. White gloves reached to her elbows and rhinestones glittered at her throat.

The bride's mother, a small pudding of a woman dressed in sombre colours, her pale hair in a tight bun under her plain hat, was nowhere to be seen.

"Now remember, Elene. Walk slowly. And don't dump your petals. Like this. See?" My mother motioned, strewing imaginary petals with one arm as if she were an opera star. My sister hung her head.

Elene was slumping again, I noticed, in order to make herself look no taller than the second flower girl. This girl was a cousin to the bride, a plump blonde who looked angelic in the prescribed frills of pink organdie. Elene was almost a year older and the frills did not suit her. The dress was too tight across her chest, and the colour was wrong for her pale, freckled complexion. Below the hem of the full skirt her long legs stuck out like toothpicks.

"Here they come, the bride and groom!" several little girls squealed. A black limousine came slowly down the street. Harry shook off my restraining hand and I let him go. He would go to his father who was ushering in the last guests.

The bridal car, hung about with crepe-paper streamers, chrome glittering in the sun, came to a stop at the bottom of the church steps. A door opened and Adolph, who was Conrad's best man, stepped out.

"Don't call him Adolph," my brother had said to me the evening before at the Verlaffness festivities.

"Why ever not?" I had laughed. "Just because he's a doctor now?" I was surprised. Adolph was still who he had always been to me, Nicholas Wall's youngest brother.

"He's going by his second name now: Andreas. Andrew in English. A name like Adolph is not popular in medical circles in Redwin. Hitler has seen to that. Andrew is more suitable for professional reasons. Doctor Andrew Wall. No one would ever guess he's German," said Conrad proudly.

Ambitious, too? I had smiled. And who would recognize ambition better than Conrad?

Adolph or Andrew, it didn't matter to me, now stood beside the black car, big and handsome as all the Walls were handsome. He could have been a Greek prince. What would account for those eyes and that gleaming cap of black hair?

Perhaps a lovely Mennonite maiden wandering too far from her village and being seduced by a roving Greek peddler?

Another moment and my brother Conrad emerged from the car. He looked young and untried beside his older cousin, his square jaw set. His thick hair would not lie down, not even for his wedding day. Tears gathered in my eyes. Would he always wear that guarded look? I so longed for my brother to be happy.

He turned and held out his arm for his bride who appeared in a froth of white from the back seat of the car.

My mother's complaints had not availed and now Conrad was about to be joined with Nettie forever. Poor Mama. But ever since I had seen Conrad and Nettie down by the creek, I'd known my mother's fretting would change nothing.

I had not meant to spy on them - I had gone to throw tomato prunings over the fence at the bottom of the garden. Beyond the willows which grew along the creek was a partly secluded oak grove with short grass growing under the trees. Conrad and Nettie had lain entangled there on an old picnic blanket I recognized from my mother's hall closet. I saw only a flash of white skin and moving limbs and then I quickly looked away. I felt a stab of envy, remembering the nameless yearning I had felt for Henry and how short-lived it had been. Did I wish for its return? I was not sure. They would marry and they would not be as ignorant as I had been. Their wedding night might be happier than mine had been.

Now Nettie stood beside Conrad, as pretty as a doll. From where I stood I could see her hand reach for his, the sparkle of a smile behind her veil.

Miss Kreuger, the leading dressmaker in Millbach, had made Nettie's dress. Now she straightened the veil that crowned Nettie's blonde head and stood back to admire her work.

My mother had disappeared into the doors of the church. The congregational singing swelled. Conrad with Nettie on his arm walked through the door of the church and proceeded down the aisle. I joined Harry in the back row where his father had likely ordered him. Harry's short legs swung back and forth. Henry stood at the back of the church like a sentinel.

A smiling Elteste Epp rose from behind the pulpit. He looked distinguished in clerical black. His abundant white hair gleamed like the satin ribbons that bound the nuptial chairs together.

The bride and groom reached the chairs and sat down. I looked around to see who had come to Conrad's wedding. Zena was there beside her husband. She wore a dress of coppery green and rust, a wisp of veil and autumn coloured feathers sat on her head like a bird about to fly away. I looked down at my dark blue silk. Why hadn't I been more daring? I could have chosen bright blue, or dark red. Zena's choice of dress always had that effect on me. Part envy, part admiration. She never failed to make everyone else around her look dowdy.

Sophie and Nicholas sat beside Zena and Ben. Nicholas in his old-country black looked like an ambassador from Austria or Hungary. No one would ever guess that twice daily he fed his hens, each of which he had named. Sophie was, as always, elegant in black.

Ruth Unger was there, beside Zena as still as a statue, in a dark red suit with shimmering lights. Had she entertained any romantic notions about Conrad? Had Conrad even tried to win her? I doubted it. Ruth Unger would have swallowed Conrad whole.

After a long preamble to which I had not listened, the bride and groom stood up, the congregation rose and the vows were exchanged. "Do you Conrad, take Aganetha...?" Elteste Epp's voice was mellow. "Do you Aganetha, take Conrad...?" Then it was all over and the congregation stood to sing. The bridal pair escaped down the aisle in almost unseemly haste.

I turned back to take Harry's hand but he was faster and brushed by me to make good his escape.

Elene touched my arm. "I want to go home for a while," she said.

"But don't you want to be with the bridal party?"

Elene shook her head. "I can't stand this silly dress," she said looking down at herself. She was close to tears.

"You look fine, Elene. Someday it will be your turn. It will be you in white," I said. Girls were so touchy at her age.

"Never, never, Anna. Not me. You'll see," my sister blurted.

"I have to go down to the reception to see if everything is ready," I said. "You do what you like."

Elene ran down the long flight of steps. She would not be

far away; nothing was far away in Millbach. She would come back when the supper started.

I turned and went down the inside steps to the basement. It was cool and quiet there - all the guests were still outside seeing the bridal party off. I heard the car go in a squeal of tires, off to the local photographer's studio to have the official bridal portrait taken. Inside the car they would kiss, exchange rings do all those things that bridal couples traditionally did not do inside the churches of Millbach.

In the basement, the long, white-clad tables stretched out into the dimness. Quart jars holding purple asters, tall yellow gladioli and blue phlox with lots of asparagus fern stood centred on each table. Around them crowded bowls of potato salad, platters of ham and baskets of Zweiback. The whole place smelled of fresh baking, cool whitewashed cement and brewing coffee. The ladies in their bright embroidered aprons were busy in the kitchen. Then the first guests began to come down the stairs and soon the basement was full of milling guests.

Both sets of parents sat isolated in embarrassed silence at the head table. Then my father's good manners took over and he engaged in conversation with Nettie's father, who did not look the least like Nettie. He was a thin little man with small blue eyes and white hair, high colouring on his cheeks and a sharp nose. The two men looked uncomfortable here where they could not smoke and my father had no newspaper to hide behind.

I slipped into the kitchen, picked up a knife and began to cut cheese to add to the already overflowing cheese trays. I did not want to be witness to my mother's conversation with Nettie's mother.

I remembered an earlier July morning in the garden, picking the first peas. It was early with dew still on the grass when my mother appeared on the path. "Good morning, Mama. You're up early."

My mother's lips were a grim line, her eyes fixed. She had been arguing with someone. My father? Conrad? Not Peddlar-Braun so early in the morning. Maybe she had guessed about Conrad and Nettie.

"How are you?" I asked and went on pulling pea pods from the vines.

"Everything will be done properly. Conrad and Nettie will take the catechism class and be baptized in the Schonweser church in Redwin," she said abruptly. She sat down beside me and reached into my basket for a pod and split it open with her thumbnail, looked at the bright green beads along the spine. "Too early, Anna, You must not be so impatient." She threw it away and took another.

"Me, impatient?" I could have laughed. The next pod was better. It yielded firm round peas - ripe enough but not too ripe. I would be spared a scolding.

"What about Nettie? Her parents are Plain Brethren. What does her mother say?" I asked.

"Oh, her? She's agreed, of course. What do the Plain Brethren know of theology?" my mother had said as if any objections from the bride's family could be brushed away like annoying flies.

I came out of hiding when I saw Nicholas and Sophie standing hesitantly at the foot of the stairs.

"Come, Sophie, sit here," I said, then saw Ben and Zena behind them. "You too, and Ruth, of course. How nice to see you all." I paused as I heard a commotion at the top of the stairs. "Here's the bridal couple now."

Conrad and Nettie, both flushed and smiling broadly, came down the stairs to sit at their appointed places. The assembled guests bowed their heads over their plates while grace was said. Then my mother signalled to the ladies to begin pouring coffee and the buzz of talk rose into a pleasant hum.

Felix appeared camera in hand, to take photos before the perfection of the bridal table could be sullied with crumbs and spilt coffee. He looked a little nervous. It was his first public appearance as the official photographer for the Millbach News. He was sixteen and would be graduating in the spring. My mother had insisted on a new suit for him, his first real suit. Seeing Conrad and Felix together no one would ever doubt that they were brothers. Felix was a taller, lighter-boned version of Conrad. Soon all the girls would be swarming, Zena had said to me. My mother would have her hands full with his white shirts and girls phoning late at night.

I slipped into my place at the lace-covered table and looked across at the bride and groom. I could not think of Nettie as Conrad's wife, yet.

After the guests had eaten, had talked and laughed, and deposited their beribboned gifts at a side table, they moved over to the bridal couple for congratulations and best wishes. After all the excitement of preparation, I realized with a sudden jolt that it was nearly over. I felt depressed, emotionally flattened. Soon Conrad and Nettie would get up from their places and go to their brand new house just across the creek, built as far away as possible from my mother's house while still on Heppner land. I wondered how Nettie would bear up under my mother's constant barrage of advice.

It had been my mother who insisted on the complete furnishing of Conrad and Nettie's house: stove, bed, table and chairs, even to the curtains, the pictures on the wall. Peddlar-Braun had been busy running back and forth to Redwin, to country auctions. I had said nothing. It was up to Nettie to object.

As the festivities wound down the Walls got up from their place at the table. Nicholas and Sophie came over to my father and Nicholas bent down to whisper into his ear.

"Bitte Enschuldich, Gerthe," I overheard him say, "but the short-wave, the Nachrrichten, the news. Poland.... "

"This morning, already we heard on the short wave, something," Sophie added quietly. "But we wish not to distract from the festivities."

My father looked grave and nodded. He stood up to bow over Sophie's hand and bid her goodbye. Nicholas and Sophie disappeared up the stairs leading to the church foyer and the outside door.

Would the dance at the Giroux Hall be cancelled if the news on the radio was too grim? No matter, Henry and I did not dance. The dance was for the young people and rebels like Zena and Ben and their Schonweser friends from Redwin.

I excused myself and went to the kitchen to help. War or no war, dance or no dance, the cleaning up in the kitchen had to be done. I knew what I was doing in the kitchen. I belonged there.

Chapter Seven

The Sunday morning after Conrad and Nettie's wedding day, I went over to my mother's to return her silver candlesticks that had adorned the bridal table.

"The Germans have invaded Poland," my mother said without a greeting and set a pot of freshly brewed coffee on a trivet on the table.

"It can't be, I can't believe it," my father muttered from where he sat close to the radio. His eyes turned briefly towards the dining table with its cups and breakfast crumbs as if he had never seen them before. "Gott Im Himmel, Albert Siemens was wrong after all. Now there will be war."

"War in Germany? But not here, Papa, surely not?" I sat down on a chair. The desire to spread a roll with jelly left me. The static on the short-wave fading in and out held a nameless dread. News on the radio was almost always bad.

"Poor Katya," my mother sighed as she placed her candlesticks back where they belonged on the buffet. "Poor Katya," she repeated as in a litany. If she had been Catholic, she would have crossed herself. "I told her and told her." My mother turned away from the buffet. "Of all people, Katya should have known better than to follow Albert to Germany."

"Maria, Maria, " my father said. He got up from his chair as if to pour himself a cup of coffee but then sat down again. "You don't understand." He shook his head and turned back to the radio.

He must have been up for hours. The air around his head was blue with tobacco smoke. There was a tiny cut on his cheek where he had nicked himself while shaving. His white shirt tucked into the well-pressed trousers of his good grey suit was still tie-less and unbuttoned.

My mother wore a flowered housecoat beneath which I saw the outlines of her tightly drawn and hooked corset. She had changed into her pumps and silk stockings in preparation for donning a Sunday dress and going off to church with my father.

"I do understand," my mother retorted. "The war is far away. In Poland. The Poles are always fighting amongst themselves. You know that, Gerthe. They have endless feuds, worse than the Irish. A murderous lot. What have we to do with them? Why would Canada go to war for Poland?" My mother stood up from the table, breadbasket in one hand and walked towards the kitchen. "My father always said the Poles didn't..." the end of her sentence was lost as she disappeared from the room and I could not hear what she was saying above the rushing water, the rattle of dishes in the sink. It didn't matter. My father and I had both heard what her father had said at least a hundred times.

"What will happen now, Papa? I asked.

"God only knows, Anna. Both sides armed with tanks and planes. It's insane. They will kill and kill. Nobody can win. Who knows how it will go?" My father stood, then turned and picked up his tie slung on the back of the chair and looped it around his neck. He padded down the hall in stocking feet, looking for his shoes, I supposed.

"Your father remembers the last war," said my mother who had returned to the dining room. "How it was then and the revolution after. There is reason to worry I suppose but this is Canada now, not Russia. There we had no one to protect us, oh, we did have our own Mennonite Forstei - our boys clearing brush, or on leave from the Red Cross, but they were unarmed. Once or twice when the Machnovitz swept through our villages they would try to protect women and children with whatever was at hand, but officially the Mennonites were not to bear arms of any kind. It was not allowed." My mother brushed viciously as if she had one of those Machnovitz bandits by the neck as she swept crumbs from the white tablecloth with a hand reddened by hot dishwater. "I can't bear the thought of Felix and Conrad among the guns, picking up wounded and dying men in their arms." My mother shook her head, grimaced. "Back then, I remember your father would come home on leave from the Red Cross looking like a ghost. He was filthy, lice in his hair, fleas, Mein Gott! It was awful."

"But Mama, wasn't there an agreement with Canadian government or something?"

My mother shook her head slowly. "That was in 1874 and agreements can be broken. It all depends." She began to clear away the rest of the breakfast things.

"On what? Why doesn't Papa trust the agreement?" Butter dish in one hand, milk jug in the other, I walked to the icebox around the corner. It would be a warm day for September.

"I don't know. You know how he is. Always seeing the dark side of things," my mother said, plunging her hands once more into the dishwater.

We did not own a radio that first winter of the war. My mother would tell me what she knew over the telephone. When she suspected that Martha the telephone operator might be listening in - we were on a party line - my mother walked the short distance to my house.

"Your father does nothing but sit beside the radio as if that will change anything. He cannot stop the German Panzer divisions or the Luftwaffe dropping bombs on London all day and all night." She sighed.

The war seemed distant although the headlines screamed out big and black in the daily papers. They spelled victory but if I read further on the inside pages, the news, however carefully worded, spelled withdrawal, defeat.

"Your Papa was right," my mother said one afternoon when she stopped by. She sat down on the stool beside the back door to remove her overshoes.

"About what?" I asked and reluctantly closed my diary. With Harry in school, the early afternoon was my favourite time to write, with the smell of chicken soup still lingering in my tidy kitchen, wintry sun shining through the bare branches of the apple trees.

"The government has refused blanket exemptions for the Mennonites. Now Felix will have to join up. I know him. He's

so young. He'll see the papers - handsome boys waving flags."
My mother undid the buttons of her fur coat. Her cheeks were
pink from the cold. "Gott Sei Dank, for once I'm glad Conrad
is married. The government won't come after him right away."

"You mean no Forstei for our boys, no Sanitaats Dienst?"
Wouldn't the government need extra help in the hospitals?

"Let me take your coat, Mama," I offered but she brushed
past me. I was still trying to absorb what this latest news meant.
She was shaking her head as she walked into the living room.
Harry's cat, Ginger, who had been asleep in the rocking chair
jumped to the floor and stalked off, his tail high with insult.

"Not only my Felix. The others will join up, too. And who
will get the blame?" my mother sat down hard in the rocking
chair. "I can hear the Low Brethren, already. We worldly
Russlenda have spoiled it again. They can't stomach your Papa's
university degrees, his politics. They think us too permissive.
We allow our young folk to dance. They even frown on the
feathers on my hat, the rings on my fingers." She slipped her
arms out of the coat revealing the pale mauve satin lining that
draped in heavy folds around her.

I put another stick of wood into the parlour stove. A puff
of smoke rose and with it the smell of seasoned poplar. "Surely
that's not true, Mama," I said.

"Yes, Anna. I can feel their rebuke when I walk along the
street. Eyes boring into me. You know where the men sit at
Unger's on the bench beside the front door?" She rocked back
and forth. "Russlensch, I feel so Russlensch."

"But Mama, Mama, they mean no harm," I said trying to
soothe her. "It's Millbach after all. You know how it is here." My
mother did flaunt her Russlenda ways - perhaps I had been
lulled into thinking that Millbach had accepted us.

"I would never tell your father this but I blame Mrs.
Peddlar-Braun and her ilk. Running off to those American
revivalists and their Armageddon religion as they do. No
wonder the government doesn't take our petitions seriously.
Besides, what has Mrs. Peddlar-Braun to worry about? She has
only girls." My mother rocked more vigorously. "She has no
Felix to worry about." Her hands clutched and unclutched the
satin lining of her coat.

"Mama, Mama, calm down. Mrs. Peddlar-Braun is

harmless. She means well, I'm sure she does." I picked up my needlepoint, which lay on the table beside my chair and began to stitch.

"Well, maybe so. Then there is your father. He is partly to blame, too. For all these years, he has not taught his sons what it means to be Mennonite."

"How can you say that, Mama? Papa's been a good father." I kept my eyes on the green thread as I pulled it hard through the canvas. I wanted no one, least of all my warrior-like mother to criticize his kind and gentle ways.

"He's been too lax with his children, If he had been sterner..." my mother paused and I took advantage of the break to interrupt her.

"Because Conrad and I laughed ourselves silly when he read us Til Ulenspiegel? Because he didn't read the Bible out loud at the breakfast table? Mama, you can't be serious." I was angry and picked furiously at the knotted thread I had created in my haste.

"My father always read at least one full chapter," my mother said smugly in her pious voice, meanwhile looking out of the window at my leafless garden. She did not guess how angry I was.

"Yes. But you told me he beat you with a leather strap. Hard too, and often, you always said." I only remembered my grandfather vaguely, an old man, crippled and drooling and unable to beat anyone - least of all my mother and her sisters.

"It's out of our hands," my mother said, changing the subject. She did not want to hear my opinion of her autocratic father. "All we can do is pray."

I was sceptical when my mother mentioned prayer, she who always had her own solution for every problem.

She pulled herself from the rocking chair, shrugged her coat back over her shoulders and walked to the kitchen for her overshoes.

After she left I thought of the Book of Martyrs I had grown up with, full of stories of people dying because they refused to become soldiers and kill for their country. Killing was always wrong. But what about letting others do it while one stayed out of the way? Being a Mennonite was more than wearing the plain clothes; Jesus had said love your enemies. That would not be a popular stand in wartime and I knew I was not a hero nor would I make a good martyr.

In November the oldest two of the elder Bauman boys went to Redwin and joined the army. They were the first.

"Oh well, the Baumans," my mother dismissed them. "Hardly Mennonite. Their mother was a Greek Orthodox from Gardenton."

Although Mr. Bauman was from a founding family, he had married out of the fold, and the Baumans lived on the fringes of Millbach society. Mrs. Bauman looked like any other woman in the row of proper black-clad women who sat at the back of the Plain Brethren church, her hair scraped tight under her a black lace cap. But no matter how hard she tried to fit in, no one in Millbach would ever forgot where Mrs. Bauman came from. It was one of the few mixed marriages that I knew of in Millbach. But then, even a Plain Brethren marrying a New Brethren counted as mixed here.

"And the Baumans have such a long row of boys," my mother added as if the Baumans had more boys than they really needed. Now the two oldest of them were apparently grown enough to go off to war. Adya, Padya, Waldmer, Hugo; I remembered four of the six only because in the past I had heard their mother calling them in the long summer evenings when I tucked Harry into bed.

When they came home on leave the first time, I met them on the street. Two almost beardless boys with acne still scarring their cheeks, suddenly transformed into soldiers. I could smell the newness of their stiff uniforms. They nodded politely and passed on, clumping down the street in their heavy new boots. I turned to look back. They had grown tall and burly and seemed to take up the full width of the sidewalk.

Slowly, slowly, even though no bands played, no flags waved, military uniforms appeared on the streets of Millbach. A strange flowering it was. Patches and splotches of alien colour - army, air force, even the navy's bell-bottoms showed up in this place so far from an ocean. The uniforms stood out against the blue denim of the overall-ed farmers passing through the doors of the post-office, against the grey-suited business men in shirts and ties, drinking coffee at the Fruit Store. By spring, when water rushed again in the creek, the trees turned green and apple blossoms lay in drifts beside the printery walls, Millbach had become a different place.

The war caused a flurry of business in Millbach. By the December of 1940, Conrad and Henry were working late nearly every night in the printery. There was the usual noise and bustle of Christmas. My mother spent money as if this might be the last Christmas she could do so. There was talk of rationing and shortages and the New Brethren preached about the coming national registration at their street meetings every Saturday night.

"Pish and twaddle, it's nothing. Such ranting," Sophie scoffed when I met her at Unger's store. She and Nicholas had walked from their house in Hunger Begone for their weekly purchases. "Ridiculous, those New Brethren. They predict we will have the numbers 666 tattooed on our foreheads just because the government wants to register all citizens. They are waiting for the horses to be up to their hocks in blood. These things are taken seriously in Millbach. After all if it says in the Bible…" Sophie rolled her eyes and spoke quietly so as not to be overheard. I did not reply and looked down at Mitzie dancing on the end of her leash beside the counter.

"Come and visit soon, Anna. We'll play Skat." Sophie was never serious for long. She bent down and popped a chocolate drop into Mitzie's open mouth, then picked up her modest purchases smelling of cinnamon and cloves, ready to go home and begin her Christmas baking.

Nicholas came from the back of the store with his empty egg basket and I greeted him. Sophie kissed Zena goodbye and followed Nicholas through the double doors of the store as graceful as a doe on tiny prancing hoofs.

Zena and her helpers had just unpacked the last of the holiday goods which had been ordered the year before the war began. English Meccano sets and toy steam engines, German dolls with exquisite porcelain faces and silky hair, wooden blocks and picture books. Japanese tea sets painted with graceful brush strokes.

"I can't help but think, Anna," said Zena, surveying the display of imported goods arranged on counters draped with Christmas tinsel, "who was it that painted those doll faces and tea sets."

I looked again at the bright display. The people who had fashioned those doll faces, painted the dishes, bound the books; did they really mean to harm us?

"Ben got his exemption," Zena said quietly. "He can stay home and run the store. I don't know how I feel about that." Zena fingered the china rose on the lid of a tiny sugar bowl.

I nodded. Henry had been exempted too. Newspapers were essential industry. I also felt guilty.

We were getting used to the war. The Phoney War, the papers called it. In Millbach, things remained much the same. Then came the shock of Pearl Harbour in December of 1941. Even though it was the United States being attacked, we felt in some way attacked too.

On Christmas Day we were at my parents' house. It smelled of roast goose, peanuts, oranges, as it did every Christmas. The tree stood in the living room with real wax candles and a bucket of sand hidden behind the sofa in case of fire. Conrad and Nettie had left right after dinner to join her parents for the rest of the day. I could hear Elene at the piano working out the chords for White Christmas. Henry had gone into the printery to check on a piece of machinery that had not been working properly.

"Felix will turn eighteen in January," my mother said. We were in the kitchen cleaning up the last of the dinner. I stared out of the window at the drifted snow against the hedge and thought back to the day of Felix's birth and how the cold had pressed in against the thin walls of our first home in Canada.

"He'll join the Air Force. Your father says if he waits until later, until he's drafted... Gott Im Himmel, who knows what will happen." My mother wrung out the dishrag hard and scrubbed, the mottled blue battleship linoleum counter for the hundredth time. It had been the latest thing when Albert Siemens had ordered its installation ten years before. I thought of Albert Siemens. Where was he now? And Ziggie, his son - the same age as Felix. Ziggie could be a soldier in the Wermacht by now. Albert Siemens had held no pacifist convictions. He had inculcated that in his sons no better than my father had.

But that was not why he had never been accepted in

Millbach. The Plain Brethren could never really forgive him for the stories he had written about them. His satire hit too close to home.

"You're smiling, Anna?" my mother's voice broke in. "Don't you care? Felix could be shot down over Germany. His speaking German would not save him, more like the Germans would shoot him as a spy."

"Sorry, sorry. It was just...I was..." I apologized. "Of course I care about Felix, Mama. Maybe he won't be accepted because of his eyesight. And anyway he'll have to train for a while. By then the war could be over." I knew I was clutching at straws.

"Well, anyway, we have to be brave and take it as it comes. Some have it much worse, I guess." My mother went to her bedroom and I moved towards the living room. The presents had been unwrapped, the carcass of the goose stored in my mother's new refrigerator, the wine glasses, the fine dinnerware washed and safely put away. I longed to go home and read the new novel I had received from Felix.

He lay full-length on the carpet among the Christmas wrapping helping Harry with his toy steam engine.

"See, Harry? I told you Uncle Felix would get it to work." I looked down at my brother leaning his head on one elbow. Harry knelt beside him. The toy steam engine puffed bravely like a small teakettle. The smell of spirits and steam hung in the air.

"Thank you for the book, Felix. Agatha Christie is a favourite of mine. *Ten Little Indians*...sounds fascinating." I spoke quietly for my father had dozed off in his chair. I looked at the cover, riffled the pages.

"Shall we shut it down for a while?" Felix asked Harry and pinched the tiny blue flame under the boiler with his long fingers. Harry ran off to find his father and Felix watched him go.

"He's sure to get ink on his good shirt," I said as the door closed behind Harry. Then I turned my attention back to Felix. "Mama says you're joining the Air Force." I kept my voice down, the tone casual. "Will Conrad manage without you?" Felix had graduated the summer before and had been working full-time in the printery.

"Oh, he'll manage. What about you? Wouldn't you like to give it a try?" Felix looked up. The whites of his eyes around the dark pupils were clear, his lashes thick as a girl's. He looked so... splendid came to mind, clean and innocent, his cheeks smooth, his dark hair shining with life. My heart turned over with a lurch. The war. My brother was going off to the war.

I thought of that other war of my childhood, of the silent men, not really soldiers, marauders more like, some said beasts, their filthy clothing torn and bloody, crowding around the steps of our in Russia. I tasted the fear again, metallic on my tongue; heard my mother's voice, sweet, coaxing, the Russian phrases purling from her lips as she handed around her freshly baked bread, all the while keeping us behind her, Conrad and I shielded by her aproned body.

Now Felix broke into my reverie, smiled, his teeth even and white. I could not imagine them shot to pieces, his mouth a bloody cavern.

He rose from his position on the floor. "It's your chance, Anna," he said quietly, unaware of my fearful thoughts. "Conrad will have to hire women for more than just the folding and collating." He stood up and stretched. My father slept on.

I shook my head. "I couldn't do that," I answered as quietly. "You know how Conrad is about women. Not in his shop. Besides there's Harry." I leaned my head against the back of the chair.

"I could show you how to take the photos, leave you the camera. It's not very good. But it will have to do for now. There's really nothing to it, easy as can be." Felix had been a camera buff from the age of six, I thought. What seemed so easy to him might not be so for me.

I shook my head again. Now the ten-year difference in our ages was obvious, like a full generation. Felix did everything so easily and he was too young to know how Conrad felt about the printery - he was possessed by the printery and the newspaper which was a part of it. If we had not been Mennonites and Conrad a peaceful man, I could imagine him driven to violence over its ownership. Felix would not believe me if I told him that. He would laugh. Felix did not fear women or feel threatened by them. I felt like warning him. Don't count on too much, Felix. Don't ever try to come between Conrad and his newspaper. You'll be in deep trouble.

I changed the subject, instead. "What will happen to your band, Felix? Zena says you're getting quite professional. Did you know she stops to do a little dance by her clothesline when she hears you?"

Ben had given Felix and his band permission to practice in the loft of the old Unger barn. The building stood across from the H.W. Unger's big house and behind where Zena's new house now stood. Lately it had rung to the beating of Willie's drums and the wailing of my brother's saxophone. "The boys in the band invite their girls up there to dance, I notice. I see them," Zena had laughed. "Nobody's supposed to know about it. They think we haven't got eyes in our heads."

"Will there still be dances at the Second Floor Club?" I asked now laughing, for that was the club's official name. Felix had even designed official cards and printed them himself. "That Willie is a good drummer," I continued. I could tell Felix was anxious to go but I wanted him to stay and talk to me. "Must you go to the Air Force?" I blurted finally. "Can't you go with Willie to the bush camp?"

"Anna, you don't understand. This is my big chance. Besides Canada didn't start the war. I feel we owe this country. I want to defend it." He sounded solemn, my Felix who scoffed at everything serious.

"Oh, Felix. Nothing is that black and white." I stopped. I would not be the one to persuade him of that. He would have to find it out for himself. "How does Willie feel?" I asked.

Willie's father was an elder in the Plain Brethren Church. Had my mother been right after all? Had my father been too worldly-minded? Or was it as my father said, we lived in different times? Perhaps Mennonites could no longer be *Die Stillen Im Lande*, the quiet ones.

Felix shook his head. He didn't want to say. He shrugged his shoulders, his mouth a firm line and walked into the hall for his coat.

"I have to go." He patted my arm as if I was the child.

I followed him. I longed to reach out and make contact with the energy he gave off, to slow his eagerness to be gone. He had once been my baby brother. I had held him in my arms. I knew that once he was gone from home he would be homesick and I would not be able to spare him that lonely pain.

He ran down the front steps. I watched him slip and slide, with his arms outstretched for balance, on the icy path leading to the street. Instead of proper boots he wore leather shoes. Better for dancing, I thought. This could be his last day with the band at the Second Floor Club.

I wondered what Conrad thought of Felix. How he felt about his brother, caught up in the fever and dangerous excitement of war. Conrad would stay behind, putting out the paper every week with untrained help and antiquated machinery, left alone to deal diplomatically with the Low Brethren in his fractured Platte. Felix was Canadian as Conrad and I would never be. We were Russlenda and would remain so.

When I had first come to Millbach it was an old world village set down intact in the Manitoba bush, its houses and barns exact replicas of what had been left behind along the Dnieper River in Russia. A place where elders still did up their coats with hooks and eyes. A place where the Omas died peacefully in their high feather beds, even as newborn babies babbled in their wooden cradles. Now a war on the other side of the ocean changed all that. As Felix and other young man disappeared from the streets of Millbach, the bush and swamp, the gravel ridges that had isolated Millbach for more than fifty years were no longer enough to keep the rest of the world at bay. The provincial government, which had almost forgotten about Millbach, built a gravel highway right through the village in a sudden fit of wartime nerves. The old settlers, who had so adamantly refused the C.P.R. permission to build a railway through Millbach, remained silent under their weathered tombstones in the churchyard.

With the new road, Millbach was no longer the only place to shop. Now Mrs. Peddlar-Braun could go with her husband to the Woolworth's in Redwin while he attended the auction sales.

"Let her, let her go. Tangee lipstick and Cutex nail polish. Who cares?" Zena grumbled. "Anna, you'll stay loyal, won't you?" Zena cheered up again. She never stayed down for long.

Above the big ledgers by the cash register Ben still wore his satisfied smile. Ben's three older brothers farmed hundreds of acres of Unger land around Millbach. Profits from the store were only one source of the Unger money.

Then, soon after the road was built, Ben's father died. He had been failing for a long time.

"It's a blessing. Poor man, he's better off," Zena said to me, the day before the funeral. She was in the hallway of the big Unger house where she had been helping with the preparations for the funeral reception.

"This old house." Zena looked up at the high ceilings, the long oak staircase. "I hope Ruth will do something once this is over. Looking after the old man for these last months. She needs a change. The whole house, all these rooms have been like this for twenty years. He wouldn't let Ruth change anything. Nothing since Ben's mother died."

I looked at the heavy oak dining room chairs around the table, the huge buffet, the leather upholstery on the oak settle beside the radiator in the corner. The smell of the old man's presence lingered, a mix of urine and Wonder Oil liniment. It lay beneath the smell of wax and furniture polish and the heavy perfume of the funeral wreaths.

The whole village closed its doors to honour the dead, the last original settler and pioneer. Black crepe ribbons hung on the locked front doors of every business and the school closed for the day. H.W. Unger was still a presence in Millbach; everyone went to his funeral.

I left the crowded church early and went home to watch the funeral cortege pass by our gate. The black hearse came slowly down the village street towards the cemetery. The Unger Buick came next with Ben looking stern at the wheel. Zena sat beside him. She looked straight ahead in her black hat, her cheeks pale. Ruth sat in the back seat beside her uncle Machine Unger.

"You'll see, things will change fast now," Zena predicted and she was right. "Ben says the war is good for business. Everybody will have a job. They have to build planes and tanks." She did not mention guns and ammunition. "The soldiers and sailors have money to spend. Ben will modernize the store. We'll go out of groceries and expand into fine furniture, bring in a pharmacist. Millbach is ready for a ladies fashion department. We'll get the dealership for RCA radios."

Perhaps, soon it would not be only my heretical father who owned a radio.

"For your birthday - would you like one?" Henry asked me.

"One what?" I was taken by surprise. "A radio?" Henry usually gave me practical gifts like pots and pans or garden shears. And so a small brown celluloid box joined the canisters, the coffee pot, the breadboard on my kitchen counter. In the afternoons I followed the joys and sorrows of One Man's Family and Ma Perkins. "I'll be seeing you," I crooned along with Bing Crosby. "There'll be bluebirds over the white cliffs of Dover," I sang.

When I met Mrs. Peddlar-Braun in front of the post office, she enthused about KFRB Fargo. "Preaching the true gospel," she trumpeted.

I lied politely, "Yes, indeed, Mrs Peddlar-Braun." I had tuned to that station once. A voice had oozed from the radio promising me a special Bible with the words of Jesus in green ink in exchange for my donation.

Then Hollywood came to Millbach. A Ukrainian from Sarto built a motion picture theatre on the outskirts of Millbach. Just who had sold him that precious acre of land placed so strategically just off our Main Street, Dmitri Savakowski never did say. The town fathers could only fume and fret. They could do nothing. It was out of their jurisdiction.

Mrs. Peddlar-Braun fought hard against it. Her alto voice could be heard as she boomed out sin and damnation at the street meeting in front of the hotel. She was part of a gospel quartet that performed there on Saturday nights. Not many people stopped to listen. This kind of religion was too new and strange for the stalwart Mennonites of Millbach.

On one of those nights when Mrs. Peddlar-Braun was in full spate like a springtime flash flood in the creek, I was threading my way through the crowd gathered in front of the hotel, on my way home from a visit with Zena.

"Hollywood, the whore of Babylon," Mrs. Peddlar-Braun cried. Her voice did not need a microphone. Suddenly her big white hand clamped down on my arm and she held me fast. "Oh, Mrs. Redekop! Beware of the sins of the flesh! We will have no moving pictures here!" Her blue eyes sparked with electricity, her crown of red hair looked as if it might catch fire.

I did not dare shake off her hand. For one blinding instant I even believed her. It was easy to believe her, go along with whatever she said. But then another image flashed - my father horrified and shamed. It would be a betrayal of all he stood for. "So many unsaved souls. The Antichrist himself can not be far off." Mrs. Peddlar-Braun's jowls shook. Tears gathered easily at the corners of her eyes. At last she released me.

I hurried away laughing with embarrassment and relief. I wondered again who owned the land the theatre stood on and who had sold it to the Ukrainian from Sarto. And who in Millbach would dare to be seen going into the theatre?

"We're just poor folk. Can't we have a little enjoyment?" Nicholas had laughed and shrugged his still handsome shoulders, when he heard the news about the theatre being built not far from his small holding. "Can't they leave us with our little sins?" He and Sophie would have no qualms about going to the movies. "You might want to come too, Anna," said Sophie. "You could bring Harry. I see they are showing Little Lord Fauntleroy soon."

But not Henry. He was aghast when I mentioned it. "No, Anna, I'll not go. I have work to do." That was always Henry's excuse. "Besides people already think we Russlenda are quite wicked enough. We don't want them to get even worse ideas about us."

I did go once with Zena when Ben was out at the airfield tinkering on his aeroplane, the Peitpol, as they called it. It had been the talk of the town until it was pre-empted by the theatre.

The building was a long windowless plywood box with a slanted floor. People spilled soft drinks and popcorn beneath the sagging cushions of the second hand seats that the owner had rescued from a defunct theatre in Selkirk. I remembered what Elene had told me - there was bubble gum under every seat. An usher, his flashlight bobbing in the darkness, waved us to our seats. The smell of rubber boots and damp wool clothing made me feel faint and I wondered how I would be able to breathe for a whole evening. But then the movie came on - Gone With the Wind - and I forgot all of that entirely and lived vicariously with Scarlet for the next three hours. When I came out of the theatre into the winter night, I had almost forgotten who I was or where I lived. Large flakes of snow fell silently, sedately.

But it was not often I had need of movies so long as I could read. Whenever I could, I retreated to my library books that I ordered from the Extension Library in Redwin. They came by mail each month wrapped in plain brown paper. No one paid any attention to what I ordered from the catalogue; I could have been reading Moll Flanders or the Kama Sutra for all that anybody in Millbach noticed. I loved books because while I read no one knew what was going on in my head; no one could criticize what I was thinking.

Chapter Eight

Then in the spring of 1942 what Felix had predicted came to pass: Conrad asked me to work in the printery. He did not ask me directly but through Henry, and not because he wanted to but because he had to. There was no other help.

I was given a place at the composing table where Dietrich, the elderly compositor taught me the intricacies of setting cold metal type by hand, letter by letter. He did not speak as his ink-stained fingers unerringly plucked type from the small wooden drawers that held the various sizes he would need to print an auction bill, the scribbled version of which lay beside us. "For Sale by auction" it read, "Allis Chalmers separator, Massey Harris cultivator, Findley kitchen range, oak leather upholstered arm chair and six side chairs." A farmer must be retiring and there would be no room for so many chairs in a smaller house.

I began to line up the type. The metal I worked with was like a lot of men I knew, not malleable, rigid and unforgiving. Yet somehow piecing the letters together reminded me of women's work, of quilting. Of course, quilt squares were softer and more flexible and allowed for small imperfections; you could stretch the cloth a little here and there. Quilt pieces, I mused, were like women who had to fit themselves into the unyielding world of men.

When I was done, Dietrich locked up my letters into a metal chase like a picture frame and showed me how to proof-press a first draft. He smiled for the first time that morning. "You can spell," he said as he positioned the completed chase into the small Gordon press. I pulled the switch on the press as I had watched my brother do many times before and began to feed paper into its steady grasping maw. It was a little like feeding a hungry baby. Later the farmer's son would come for his freshly printed bills and the next day they would appear in every store window in Millbach.

Every weekday morning at half-past eight I left the house I loved so much without a backward glance. On school days Harry waved good-bye and would run ahead of me to meet his school friends gathering at the corner before they crossed the street by the post office. The short walk down the main street was just long enough to fill my lungs with fresh air. In winter the cold reached down to the bottom of my lungs when I took too deep a breath. In the summer during lilac time, the tall bushes blossoming along the street brushed against my face as I hurried by. When I reached the door of the printery and opened it I knew I was where I wanted to be. I did not think of the household chores I had left behind, the washing and ironing, the cleaning and polishing, the knitting and sewing. What was it about the smell of paper and printer's ink that took me by the throat; the rumble of the big press that made my heart beat in time with its rhythm?

When I made mistakes, which I inevitably did, Conrad kindly covered his smile with his hand. He was in the shop less and less, although I still felt his eyes upon me like an extra conscience. In everything, I felt I had to do as well or better than a man. If there was a crisis and the air in the shop became too tense, Elene - who worked in the office after school - would come into the printery and drag Conrad away with some excuse - the telephone, a customer who was asking for him, trouble with her adding machine.

"Ease up, Anna. Conrad's not God," she would hiss before she went back to her invoices. I was reminded of my days at the Strachans and the tears I had shed then. The awful times I'd had with the Yorkshire puddings that the judge so loved and I could never get right. I had learned to do things there that seemed impossible. I refused to cry now. I would show Conrad, show them all. My fingers were as dexterous as any man's, my brain as sharp. Conrad would have to eat his words about women in his all-male shop.

"Give it up, Anna," Henry mumbled before he went to sleep at night. "You'll never satisfy Conrad." I did not give him the satisfaction of a reply.

I had been writing secretly for years. I read a lot. Now I could see that what I really would like to do was just what my father did, edit, so it was a great opportunity for me when I could leave the shop floor and go and help my father with the editing in his office.

"I'll not give up. I'll not," I said to Henry one Saturday as I threw my denim coveralls into the washing machine and followed it with the bandanna I wore all week to keep my hair tied up and out of the way. I let my hands trail in the hot soapy water of the machine to soften the ink and grease so that I could clean under my fingernails for Sunday. The Pumice soap we used at the printery had roughened them. They looked awful. I thought of Conrad's words the day before.

"You're doing well, Anna," he had smiled, not wholeheartedly but not grudgingly either. "Who would have thought it?"

I could almost taste his praise.

That September Harry started school, a solemn little boy in short pants and knee socks.

"Make us proud," Henry said and patted him on the shoulder, man to man, before he left for the printery. My heart lurched. I wanted to shout to Henry, hug him, for pity's sake, please, please. He's scared, at least hug him. He's your flesh and blood. But I kept silent.

Harry did not carry on his usual chatter as, hand in hand, we crossed the wide village street. At the school we climbed the high unfamiliar steps. I placed a kiss on his head. He had that little boy smell of puppy dog and soap. Nervously, I brushed a toast crumb from his mouth. "I'll be here waiting for you after school Liebchen." I swallowed a lump in my throat. I had thought this would be a day of liberation; I would have all that free time that I had so looked forward too, time to write, time to read. And what was I doing? I felt like blubbering like a baby.

Harry eyed me solemnly. "Papa says we have to brave, Mama." He let go of my hand and raised his stern Redekop chin. Other children might cry or cling to their mothers, but Henry had trained his son well. Already he was learning to hide his feelings. I remembered Mrs. Strachan - she would not fall apart at a time like this - and restrained myself, giving his shoulder an extra encouraging squeeze. He was my baby, after all.

On my return from the school, I stopped to avail myself of Zena's comfort. She looked fresh and bright in her tennis whites. "No, no, it's alright Anna, I have time," she said tenderly. "You look all bleary-eyed and in need of something." We went across the street and ordered coffee at the lunch counter in the middle of the store. Business was slow on this weekday morning. "This coffee is undrinkable," Zena said. "We'll end up with ulcers." She took our cups and poured their contents into the sink. "Let's have a coke even though it's not yet noon," she said as she opened two bottles of coke and slid them across the counter. "Now tell me everything. What happened?" She knew it was Harry's first day in school. "Did Harry cry? Did he cling to you? Are you feeling guilty?" Zena rattled on without waiting for my reply. "You know, when I see Harry I think it's really time for me to produce a son and heir for Ben. Then the feeling goes away. But one of these days it won't. It would be just my luck to have a girl, although I'd love that and my mother would be in seventh heaven." She tilted the bottle back and swallowed, quite unconscious of the picture she made. I imagined the coke going down that long graceful throat. My throat would never look like that. My neck was too short and plump.

"Cheer up, Anna, think of the parents' day visits, all the brownies you can bake," Zena laughed. We hugged each other and went on our separate ways - Zena to her tennis game, and I to my house.

When I passed the window of my father's office, he and Nicholas were still huddled around the radio. This morning they each held a thimble-sized glass of colourless Schnapps. Comforting themselves so early in the day? The news must be very bad.

On Saturdays I crowded a week's housekeeping into one day. Harry followed me about with his storybook in his hand. He could read now and excitedly pointed out the words he knew. I helped him with the more difficult ones as I mopped and dusted, baked Kringel, washed clothes. Laboriously, he would spell out the letters on every printed surface that he saw. Magic Baking Powder on a can in my kitchen cupboard. Millbach News on the newspaper spread on the floor to catch drips from our overshoes, Five Roses Flour on the side of the flourmill as we walked to the store.

I tried to be considerate in the shop; it was not a large working space and there was only one washroom. Having me there made Dietrich and Rudy the new pressman uncomfortable. They were not used to a woman in this man's place - I supposed they could not belch and fart as freely when I was there.

As for me, I vowed they would never know of anything female about me. No premenstrual jitters. On those awful days when my period was late and I thought I might be pregnant, no one, man or woman, must guess. Of all the times in my life, I didn't want to be pregnant now. When the welcome blood finally flowed I padded myself until I felt trussed up like a stuffed chicken ready for the oven. No one in the shop would ever learn from me that such a thing as menstruation existed.

"You try too hard," Henry said of my frustration with the keyboard of the linotype. But I refused to listen; he had mastered it so easily and it could well be his pride talking. Henry tried as hard to please as I did, but Henry had his whole life to prove himself. Now, while the men were away at war, I could see only this one chance for me.

It came to feel as if there had always been war. We read of Canadian soldiers landing in Sicily but the thin blue airmail forms from Felix with their military postmarks gave no hint of where he was. "Dear Anna, I am fine." Felix wrote. "Thank you for the pyjamas and the cookies. Good girl. You working in the printery. I knew you could do it. Anna, what I wouldn't give for a cup of your good coffee..." The letters came in clumps of three and four or not at all.

In August of the following summer, Nettie gave birth to a son, the first baby born in the new Millbach hospital. On a Sunday afternoon I went to visit at the hospital and found

Nettie in tears. Conrad had just left the room to walk down to the nursery window with my mother to show off his son.

"Never mind what Mama says, Nettie. If you let her upset you it will just put off your milk. And the bruises from the instruments on the baby's head will disappear in a few days. Just think of how squashed he must have felt right there at the end." I put down the armful of late gladioli I had brought and tried to soothe the crying mother as she shifted gingerly on the high hospital bed. She was trying not to aggravate her stitches. I was not surprised Nettie was in tears. "New mothers are supposed to cry. Difficult births are hard on mothers and babies. What are you going to call him?"

On my way back from the hospital I stopped at Zena's to share the news of the baby's arrival. Zena was wearing yellow shorts and a halter-top, her smooth brown legs and arms shining with lotion in the sunshine, her body completely relaxed in a striped canvas chair. A book, its pages fluttering, lay on the strip of grass beside her. She yawned hugely. "Come and sit. I was almost asleep, bored with the amorous Anthony Adverse. Ben's gone to the airfield with Machine Unger to tinker. I hope that heap of canvas and wires they've glued together will fly." She looked up at the sky as if any minute now she would see Ben and his uncle wave to her from the homemade plane they had been working on for months. "This is the big test. They've installed an engine from an old Ford. Let's hope for the best."

"I just came from the hospital. Nettie's had a boy."

"Yes, I heard. Everything fine? What are they calling him?"

"Richard Gerthe. And guess who delivered him? Dr. Andrew Wall. Apparently he had to use the latest thing in instruments. I was surprised to see him. Did you know that Andrew was here?"

Zena laughed. "Yes, yes. Filling in for Dr. Schilstra. He's not staying in Millbach -wouldn't my parents just love that, though. Just as well." Zena shook her head. She was not much fonder of her young uncle than I was.

"Was Nettie really late or did she count wrong? Being pregnant in August can't be much fun. I saw her ankles the other day. And edema with high blood pressure, too?"

"She'll be fine," I said. Zena still had no idea what labour and birth involved. "He's a lovely baby. Very fair. I held him for a minute and I got such a rush. Newborns do that to me."

"Your mother instinct, Anna. It's all the rage now, having a baby. Didn't you know? All my friends in Redwin. Andrew will be busy when he goes back."

"It must be the war. Replacements for all the killing."

"Ben is after me too, now. He wants a son. A son to take over the store so he can tinker on his aeroplane." Zena laughed again. Her voice softened. "Well okay, I told him. But nothing's happened yet. It's kind of exciting, wondering when, which time."

"Zena, you? Really? I knew it, I knew it! Finally? You haven't told your mother? Does she know?"

She shook her head. Her laugh rippled on like a summer breeze. She slid from the low-slung canvas chair. "Remember Mrs. Peddlar-Braun's prophecies? What she threatened? No baby for that Zena, ever, she said. Remember that?" Zena stretched, tugged at the straps of her yellow halter-top. "I'm not worried. We Walls are a fertile lot. Come, let's walk." She bent to slide her feet back into her canvas sneakers, every movement languid.

I felt suddenly warm in my cotton skirt and sleeveless blouse. I had changed out of my good dress at noon when we came home from church. We walked slowly down the front walk. Behind us Zena's lawn sprinkler sprayed water on the grass under the trees. Her Siamese cat came stalking towards us down the paved driveway. It had eyes the same colour as my new nephew. The green awnings over Zena's kitchen windows flapped lazily. We turned to walk along the path that led to the bridge across the creek and the new hospital.

"Andrew's been for supper twice, now," said Zena. "Ruth too, of course." Zena leaned closer and put her hand with its brightly polished fingernails on my arm. "Don't breathe a word of this to anyone but they are about to be engaged. He showed me the ring. They'll be announcing it soon."

"You mean Andrew and Ruth? Really, Zena? What happened to the Dean's daughter that you told me about? The one at the medical school?"

"Oh, that was nothing much, not serious, anyway. Deep down, Andrew likes tradition. For marriage he's come back to his roots."

"Ruth is Plain Brethren, Zena, hardly close to his roots."

"Close enough. Look at Ben and I. Andrew is more old-fashioned than he lets on." Zena's mouth turned up at the corners. She smiled her lazy smile. Her eyelids drooped. "I wasn't all that surprised about him and Ruth."

"Well, I am. Ruth a doctor's wife in Redwin? I always thought she'd marry another storekeeper or a farmer." I hadn't thought about Ben's sister as sophisticated enough for our doctor cousin who had been squiring the Redwin girls about for what seemed years. Now he had come back to Millbach for a bride?

"Sure. Why not? Andrew will use her money to buy a practice. And Ruth will get a big stone house in River Heights, fill it with antiques, sing in the Easter Cantata at the Schonweser choir. Their daughters will go to the Elmwood Academy. Oh Anna, she'll love it. It's just what she was waiting for. She's already quite taken with my Wall relations and their Russslender Kultur." Zena's voice was edged with irony. She stuck out her little finger as if she was holding a teacup.

"I should think you'd be pleased, Zena. Aren't you glad for her?"

"Of course I am, Anna. I'm making Shputt, for heaven's sake! Our Redwin relations do take themselves so seriously, Anna, you have said so yourself. Ben is always the soul of tact but they think they are better, smarter, more elegant. Ben doesn't have the right accent; he's Plain Brethren and from Millbach, too. Never mind that he has money. They go for the University degrees as if their Seiligkeit depends on it. I'm not talking about your father, Anna," Zena said quickly. "He's a fine, truly educated man. Don't misunderstand me."

"But Zena, we're like that, too. No better, really. My mother cares as much about how we pronounce the Umlaut as yours does." I laughed. "Such a little thing!"

"Is it?"

I did not answer. I remembered that I had corrected Harry that very day. "German or English. Not both together, Harry," I'd said. He sounded a proper Millbacher speaking Platte and it had bothered me, I had to admit.

"No matter, Anna. I'm sure Ruth will be happy. She's like Ben in that. That's what I liked about him right from the first: his Lassigkeit, his nonchalance. I had enough of being a refugee when we landed in Millbach. Sick of having nothing, sick of misery."

"No matter, no matter, you say. No matter what? You're happy by nature, Zena. I always hoped some of that would rub off on me. I'm more of a pessimist."

Zena rubbed her bare arm against mine. "Here, Liebchen."

"Well, it's true, Zena." I touched my arm where she had rubbed. "You're more easy-going than I am. I have to try harder. Maybe it's being married to Henry. Grit and endurance is all that matters with him. Like the Strachans. Stiff upper lip. No compromise."

"Oh Anna, I was very lucky finding Ben. Not the most exciting man in the world, but exciting enough. I'm almost ashamed how easy it was to have him fall in love with me. But he did and I didn't try to stop him." She did not explain. Frank and forthright as Zena was, she and I never talked openly of sex since the day I had asked about the diaphragm. "Andrew is a Wall, too," she said. "The Walls are not romantics in spite of their soulful eyes. He's being pragmatic. It's not the hottest passion in the world, but they're suited well enough. They'll have a good life. Ruth will be good for Andrew." She pushed her sunglasses to the top of her head, squinted. The sun was still too bright so she pulled them down again.

"Has Ruth talked to you?" I asked. "About the wedding? Tell me. I won't say a word to anybody, promise."

"Ruth will want a big wedding - all those Unger relatives! Of course, you know that half of Millbach is related to her. Who knows better than I, Anna?"

"Will they do as Conrad did? Rent the New Brethren church?"

"They'll probably get married in Redwin," Zena said.

"What will Ben say to that?" I asked.

"Ben won't mind, I don't think and at least Ruth can choose a long train on her dress, and can be given away by her brother. The church in Millbach is still in the dark ages."

"But it's changing, Zena. You wouldn't know because you never come to church," I said and bit my tongue. The words were out before I could soften them. I hadn't meant to sound so sharp, but it was true. Zena and Ben did not go to church. In Millbach that was a rare thing. I might not agree with Mrs.

Peddlar-Braun and her hell-fire preaching but I wished Zena would go to church like the rest of us.

"I don't feel...I'm very proud of being part Russian, baptized Orthodox. It means something to me."

Here we were, Zena and I, talking about what could most divide us: baptism. I could not find the words to encompass what I meant by that. Baptism was a sign of the way I understood God. It was a rite of passage. My father, a true Schonweser, talked of growing up, confessing to accountability. It was what my mother had insisted on for Conrad and Nettie. Our forefathers had thought their view of adult baptism was important enough to die for.

"And it meant something to my birth mother. She died with that desire on her lips. It's basic, like my blood type." Zena stopped. She was no better at explaining than I was.

"Early or late, Zena. For me it is a sign, only a sign," I said. I did not want any such thing to come between us.

There was a silence. We stopped on this very ordinary pathway under an ordinary sky and looked at each other.

We could hardly find the words to describe what we felt about baptism, let alone the idea of God. It was what I had felt when my father had taken me to the basilica in Kiev. It was what Mrs. Strachan had knelt down to in the cathedral in Raulston, the presence I had experienced when a wise old hand had rested on my head and water dripped to the floor in the church in Hackett.

"I'm sorry, Zena. Let's not split hairs like our elders," I laughed apologetically.

"No, let's not." Zena laughed too and plucked a tall blade of grass growing close to the path and stripped it of seeds. We walked on, quiet again but peaceful with each other.

"So Ruth and Andrew. Wait until my mother hears."

"Yes, my mother, too. They'll be out shopping the minute they know."

We had reached the bridge. In late August the water in the creek was at its lowest. There was a rank smell and a barely audible trickle. We leaned over the railing but there was not much water to be seen among the moss-clad granite stones left there by the last ice age. Iron in the water had stained the stones with rust. A wave of cool air rose from the creek bed and cooled my face. We turned back towards Zena's.

Back at her house I lingered, resting my hand on the wrought iron railing. It was warm from the sunshine. The glass in her front door reflected the two of us. From this distance we might have been sisters. Dark hair, dark eyes. A pleasant harvest warmth hung in the air. Zena's cat was rubbing against her bare legs.

"Stay a bit longer?" Zena asked.

"Just for a minute." I sat down on the step. The cement felt cool through my skirt. "I've been up till all hours."

"I hardly see you," Zena said. "What's happening at the printery? Any news of Felix? The store's slowed down. Everybody is harvesting."

"Nothing lately from Felix. Conrad's working on an English edition of the Millbach News. The censors might leave us alone if we printed in English. It's the German language gets us in trouble. And Papa's been careful, too. When we started I had no idea..." I looked down at my hands. My nails were faintly rimmed with ink. "Conrad is obsessed with it. I mean it's like his baby. The thing has to be up and running before Felix gets home. As if Conrad's trying to prove something."

"An English paper? About time I'd say, Anna. How about coffee?"

I shook my head. "Thanks, no, I have to go. You're all goose pimples, Zena. Better go in, put on some clothes. I promised Mama we'd come for Faspah. Harry's at home with his dad." I hugged my bare arms. The afternoon was cooling. "And Felix? Mama's dreamt of him dead in a ditch so many times I've lost count. Do you think the war will ever end?"

Later that fall Unger's old barn burned down. Elene came charging into the back room of the printery to tell us. Her parka was open, long hair streaming down her back. "Unger's..." She was out of breath from running. "The old barn's burning."

"Well, that's a relief. I thought for a minute it was the store." I half stood up from my seat at the stapler to look through the window that faced towards Unger's store and Zena's house. I could see nothing but the bare branches of the trees in the neighbouring garden.

"Elene for pity's sake do up your jacket, when you go out. You'll be wheezing and coughing all night." My mother went on collating the printed pages of the book then placed each copy in a neat pile on the stapler. "It was an eyesore, that old barn. It's probably just as well."

I reached for my jacket hanging on a hook behind the door. "It's quite near Zena's house. I'd better go see. And Harry? Where's Harry?"

Elene blocked my way. "No, don't go, Anna. People there, they're saying awful things. Sabotage, Nazis, stuff like that."

"Elene. What are you saying?" my mother asked sharply.

"I heard it. About us, Mama. Saying the Russlenda set the fire. Nazis. Mrs. Peddlar-Braun is saying we're Nazis. It's true, Anna."

"We Russlenda? We? That old barn? Why would we do that?" My mother was now as breathless as Elene. "It's those young boys. Smoking cigarettes, the Plain Brethren - their snotty little boys smoking in that old barn." Her voice rose in indignation.

"No, no. No one believes anything like that," I said firmly. Elene and my mother were close to stuttering.

"They're saying the Russlenda are the Germans and the Peddlar-Brauns are Dutch. We're the bad ones because we speak German. One kid said Papa has a moustache like Hitler's," Elene finished, close to tears.

"Elene, Elene. Wait a minute. Calm down." I put the last stack of books under the paper knife, pulled the lever and shreds of paper littered the floor. "I better go find Harry." I didn't want him hearing gossip about his grandfather. I stepped into my boots standing beside the door. "Calm down, now. You too, Mama. I'll go and see about this and I'll stop by the post office and see if there isn't a letter from Felix."

"I hope Mrs Peddlar-Braun's house burns down. I don't care if the whole town burns down, Anna. I hate this place. I wish we'd never come here." Elene squeezed her eyes shut. "That woman, Mrs. Peddlar-Braun. She always looks at me as if...as if I might be wearing dirty underwear."

"Now, now, Elene." I did not want to think of anyone

saying such things about us, especially Mrs. Peddlar-Braun. Did we still seem like outsiders even after these years? When would we finally belong? Did we first have to bury a full set of ancestors in the churchyard? I had thought we were already accepted here.

I looked through the window again and this time I saw smoke and low flames. I looked back to see Henry above the tables and cabinets. He was standing up, bent over the linotype like a priest at the altar. I slammed through the front door.

It was still light. Further down the street I could see more smoke but no flames now. It was quiet except for distant shouts. The whistle on top of the flourmill sounded. It must be a big fire.

Suddenly, Nettie pushing her pram appeared through the smoke billowing out halfway across the wide street. She wore her good black coat with the mink trim. A silk kerchief covered her head and was tied under her round chin. I ran up to her.

"Have you seen Harry? I have to find him."

"Oh, don't worry about him. He was in the office with his grandpa when I went by there, half an hour ago." I hadn't thought to check although Harry often visited his grandpa there. Nettie leaned on the pram. "I could see the fire from my kitchen window. I had to come and see. It's almost out now, nothing like it was. You missed it, Anna." She sounded almost gleeful as she pointed to the smoke, darker now and climbing high into the sky behind the trees.

"From our place it looked like the Unger store was burning. Serve them right, too," she muttered under her breath.

"Thank God it's only the barn, Nettie. If it was the store that would be terrible."

"Oh, I don't know, those Ungers. They've lorded it over us for too long." Nettie shot out the words as she rocked the pram back and forth, the rubber tires swishing a little on the patches of wet pavement. It was trying to snow, but every flake that came down melted on contact with the warm earth. "You admire them so much. Really, I don't know why. There are things you don't know about the Ungers, Anna," Nettie continued.

"Well, you've lived here all your life. You've known them

longer, of course, Nettie but - I mean Zena is my best friend. Don't you care about their family?"

"I'm not talking about Zena. It's the Ungers. Really I know what I know." Nettie sniffed, pulled a handkerchief from her coat pocket and wiped her nose. No sound came from the depths of the pram. Richard must have gone to sleep.

"What is so bad about the Ungers, Nettie? Tell me." I turned so I could watch the fire and talk to Nettie. I could see knots of people still standing about.

"They...I don't know. Something wrong about them, that old place," Nettie said. Above the trees the last sparks rose. A sigh rose from the little crowd as the building collapsed upon itself. "It was a house and barn once you know," Nettie said so quietly I had to lean over to hear.

I had heard the old story that Nettie alluded to from Zena when she showed me over the place soon after I arrived in Millbach. I remembered that Ben's great grandfather, who had lived in the house and barn, had married a young girl in his later years. It was his third wife. There wasn't quite a scandal because of his standing in the church but rumours abounded about his young red-haired bride.

"Old Unger's young wife, her babies all died. My mother told me," Nettie said self-righteously. "There's a row of little graves in the churchyard: Dietrich and Heinrich and Klaus and a girl too, called Aganetha."

"But that has nothing to do with Ben, Nettie."

"Maybe not." Nettie's cheeks reddened. She bent to straighten the blanket that covered her baby. "But if they hadn't all died Ben wouldn't be who he is today - living in the nicest house in Millbach, driving to Redwin in his new car, parading Zena about. Someone said - isn't she a kind of gypsy?"

"You don't like Zena much, do you, Nettie?" I said defensively.

"Of course I do, Anna. It's just that, well..." Nettie's mouth turned down. "The Ungers cheated my father. My father had a store, just as good as Unger's and they drove him out of business. My father went bankrupt. A shameful thing. They still look down on us." Now I understood the real reason for Nettie's animosity.

"But Nettie, that's a long time ago, now. How long—"

Nettie interrupted me. "And your mother's as bad. She copies them, the Ungers. Looks down on me but just wait. I've got Conrad now and in the end, well, we'll see." Nettie's voice stopped. She rocked the pram.

We turned and walked back to the printery in silence. I could see Conrad look up from his desk as Nettie pushed the pram through the front door. I followed her and went straight to my father's office in search of Harry. He was writing happily on scraps of paper my father had given him. I leaned against the doorframe watching him, thinking about all I had just learned.

It was just a fire, an old barn burning down. What was it about a fire that could rekindle such ancient animosities? First, Mrs. Peddlar-Braun's name-calling - I believed it, Elene would not make up something like that. Sabotage, Nazis, Hitler's moustache. I shook my head. It sounded just like Mrs. Peddlar-Braun. And if that wasn't bad enough, now Nettie with a long buried grievance against the Ungers. She must have harboured her animosity through her childhood and into adulthood. I had been stunned by the words flowing from her lips, words as hot as the fire itself. I had always known there was more to Nettie than blonde hair, a pretty face and breasts.

Through the front windows of the printery I could see Henry still at his keyboard. I wanted to go and touch him on the shoulder as if to reassure myself, of what I wasn't sure. But Henry did not look up. I went around to the side door of my father's office.

That night I dreamt of the old Unger house and barn. In the dream Zena and I climbed the steep flight of narrow steps. Down below us light filtered through dusty panes of glass. In the shadows nearby odd shapes draped in cobwebs loomed. "Machine Unger's inventions," said a red-haired girl who stood on the upper landing. "Stillborn." Her voice echoed tinnily as if she were in a hollow drum. Did stillborn refer to her dead babies or Machine Unger's inventions? She looked quite normal in my dream, not crazy as some claimed, not the least bit like she had buried four babies in a row. We three stood in the centre of the floor with the ceiling sloping down on all sides. The doorframes and windowsills were all painted delft blue.

"To ward off evil," the red-haired girl said, with her voice still a kind of echo only this time from farther away. Suddenly Harry was there. "You won't die," I said to him and took his hand. He led me to a low door that led to the loft of the barn. I smelled hay and down below cows moved and horse stamped their feet in the dark. I could smell cigarette smoke and saw a row of four tiny lights glowing in the dark. "You'll never smoke," I said to Harry. Then suddenly it was Henry taking my arm and leading me in a slow waltz on the wooden floor polished by years of hay sliding across it. "You can dance," I said in surprise to Henry. He nodded gravely and I woke up.

Chapter Nine

The following September, Elene went away to the Elmwood Academy for her first year of high school. All summer my mother and the seamstress, Miss Kreuger, basted and stitched Elene's uniforms - dark blue tunics and grey shirts, white blouses for choir and other special occasions. Elene was persuaded to hold still long enough to be measured for the correct skirt length one inch above her black-clad knees.

But when it was time to take Elene to Redwin, Mama declined to come along with us. "You and Zena take her," she said to me as she tightened the strap for the third time on Elene's suitcase.

"But Mama, don't you want to see Elene settled in her dormitory?"

"No, I'll take care of things for you here, mind the front office, cook supper for our men folk. You take the day off, enjoy yourself."

"Are you sure? Zena thought she might go shopping afterwards and then to her aunt's. You'd like that."

"No, please Anna. Those high and mighty Russlenda in Redwin put on such airs. I can't take it right now. They'll ask about Felix. I don't know. They go on and on. If a son is not in medical school then he's in seminary in Bethel. The daughters are all engaged to dentists at the very least." She checked the address labels on Elene's bags as if Elene was going overseas. Elmwood Academy was only a few miles north of Redwin on the banks of the Red River.

"Probably that nasty Hedwig Wall has spread her lies all

around the Schonweser Church, although Sophie says it's not so. Hedwig is still angry, claims I fired her wrongly, although it's been how many years now."

"But you said...you said..." I gaped in surprise.

"Well how else could I get her out of the printery? Henry needed that linotype job. I had to, Anna."

"So all this time...that's why? Hedwig still holds that against you? Mama, I didn't know. I...it's hard to believe." I was flabbergasted. My mother always surprised me. I had misunderstood. Apparently there had been more to Hedwig's sudden leave-taking before Henry and I arrived in Millbach than I had been aware of at the time. In her letters, my mother had been vague about the exact circumstances and we had been desperate. Henry had really needed that job. She must have done it for me, certainly not for Henry's sake. She barely tolerated him.

Now I looked at her with new eyes and I thought of Harry. I would do the same for my son. Mothers could be ruthless.

"You know what the Walls are like. Never give an inch. Now Hedwig teaches music at the academy. What if she takes her grudges out on Elene? I want Elene to do well in music. Best that Hedwig is not reminded that Elene is a Heppner."

"Well, if you say so, Mama. Of course I'll go if you really think it will make a difference."

"I'm sure it will, Anna," my mother said.

The next morning Zena pulled into the drive at the appointed time. Sophie climbed out of the car holding a tapestry bag bulging with white crochet yarn. Mitzi pranced about at Sophie's heels.

"Lovely morning, Anna," she trilled.

"It is indeed, Sophie." I had noticed the lovely morning earlier as Harry and I walked the short distance from our house to the printery.

"Mommy, I want to come, too," he had begged as he dragged along behind me.

"Next time, Harry. Now I have to go with Zena to take Elene to her new school."

"You're all done up, like for church, Mama." Harry had squinted up at me, his blue eyes as clean and pure as a rain-washed sky. He sniffed at my wrist like a puppy. "You smell like flowers," he said.

I had dressed for the trip to Redwin and the Academy in my best. I had thought of Mrs. Strachan as I pulled on the blue tweed skirt - I finally had a suit whose tailoring satisfied me - an off-white pullover, my pearls and then the jacket. The day would be sunny and cool according to the forecast on the radio. I wore my one and only pair of pre-war silk stockings. They were fragile. When these wore out I would have to resort to painting my legs as the younger girls did, drawing a black line down the back of both my legs with my eyebrow pencil.

Elene came from the side door of the office. She had bid her father goodbye unobserved by anyone else. I thought of what my father would have said - words reminding me of my own leave-taking. It seemed so long ago, now.

Elene was now nearly as tall as my father - a long-legged swan among the stockier Heppners, her bronze eyes an anomaly, her pale hair a halo around her head. Harry gave Elene one of those nonchalant hugs that young boys take such pride in and then left reluctantly for school.

Sophie hugged Elene, as well. "Dear girl. Bless you," she said and stepped well back from the car. My mother kissed Elene briefly on the lips then emotion overcame her. She held to her daughter's arm and Elene had to remove my mother's hand to climb into the back seat of Zena's car. She sank back into its padded softness and I climbed into the passenger seat beside Zena. The inside of the car smelled Detroit-factory new. From the back seat, Elene rolled down the window to wave goodbye as the car backed off the drive. She was solemn - it would be her first time away from home.

When I looked back, my mother and Sophie had already disappeared. We would not see her tears, nor Sophie, her dearest friend, comforting her.

"Your mother is so tough, but underneath? She is good at pretending," Zena said sympathetically as she turned the car onto Millbach's main street. We passed the Unger's store and Zena gave it a cursory glance. There were a few trucks and a car parked by the long railing in front of the store. Business was going on without her.

"Your mother is good, too, Zena," I said. "Mama's lucky to have Sophie."

Zena nodded. "She is. A healer if there ever was one. They'll be friends forever, eh? They'll drink coffee, sit in the sun. Hash over Andrew and Ruth's wedding again, who said what to who," Zena laughed as she changed into second gear and turned on to the highway, gravel spurting under the wheels.

Ruth and Andrew had married in June in the Schonweser church in Redwin. For weeks before my mother and Sophie had discussed the pros and cons of satin versus taffeta, a swooping brim on a hat or a froth of veil and feathers, short or long gloves. My own flowered silk finery had hung ready and waiting in my closet. But then the day before the wedding Harry had showed the very obvious spots of measles. Of course we couldn't go. Henry had not been too disappointed, he was never one for social occasions - he went off quite happily to his work, but I was sorry. I would have liked to go. Instead, I had gotten all the details second-hand from my mother.

"I've heard enough, Zena. The famous people that were there, the fine food..." I stared through the windshield as the road divided before us. "Too bad, but Harry was so sick. I couldn't leave him."

"Ah well, Anna, you can be in at the child dedication," said Zena, mischievously. "That'll be next and not too long either. Andrew and Ruth won't dawdle around. Andrew has been in school forever and Ruth is almost thirty," Zena said keeping her eyes on the road. "Mama would dearly love a grandchild. She's given up on me. Andrew's children will delight her." Zena's voice softened. "I'm going all mushy. It's time Ben and I got to it, had a baby, eh?" She directed the last comment over her shoulder at Elene who looked up from her magazine.

"Babies? Not me, Zena. Never." Elene blushed and returned to the pages of Chatelaine with a frown.

"Smart girl. Just stick with that." Zena was watching Elene in the rear-view mirror. "I hear you had the highest marks in your class," she said over the sound of the humming motor.

I looked over at my sister. Now that her blush had faded her freckles stood out. "Are you getting nervous, yet?" I asked jokingly.

She shook her head.

"Don't ever let it bother you, Elene," Zena said. "Those girls from Redwin. They're nothing to worry about. Just do as if you own the world. They'll be overwhelmed; they'll introduce you to their older brothers. I can see it all happening already." Zena smacked her lips as if she was tasting something delicious.

"Don't tell her about boys, Zena," I protested. "My father would have your head. The boys will only get in her way, take her mind off her studies. She has years and years to find out about the boys." I was not really worried. I knew Elene would decide for herself, she was that kind of girl.

I looked out the car window at the fields surrounding Millbach. Only a few months earlier Japanese internees had dotted the fields. They did not look up as they knelt on the moist black earth and thinned out the long green rows of beets that stretched into the distance. From the road you could not tell whether they were men or women - their straw hats hiding their faces. After a few weeks, the beets were thinned and the figures with their thin child-like bodies clad in faded cotton had disappeared. The flashing hooked knives of the beet toppers had come and gone, but where did they go? The newspapers said the beet-thinners were enemy aliens. The beet farmers had been strangely silent.

After Elene went away to school my mother came to help me in the printery nearly every day. In the rhythm of our work, collating books, folding newspapers, we found a rare harmony of purpose. And so the fall and winter passed. The war seemed far away.

"Letters, Mama," I greeted her one spring morning. The daylight had been so bright on my walk back from the post office it made my eyes water. Returning crows cawed rustily in the branches of the trees.

"Letters, Mama. One from Felix." I opened the leather briefcase we used to transport the office mail and dumped it on the front desk. I recognized my brother's large good-natured scrawl on the thin blue airmail form. "Shall I open it?"

"Gott Im Himmel and about time too, Anna." My mother had just come from her kitchen in the living quarters. She still wore her house apron over her workaday dress. There were no customers in the office so early in the morning.

She picked up the envelope and held it up close to her eyes, then handed it to me. With one thumb and forefinger she rubbed the dirty lenses of her glasses hanging on a cord around her neck.

I sighed. At home in the evening my mother crocheted by feel, her fingers flying relentlessly. But here in the printery she could no longer pretend that her eyesight was perfect and she hated to admit it.

"So read, Anna. What does he say?" she said and began to remove her apron.

I slit open the airmail form and spread it out on the desk. "Does he say where he is?" she asked.

"You can't tell where he is by the military post mark," I said, my eyes running down the page.

"Oh dear," I said and looked up.

"What? What? Will he be home for Easter?"

"Here Mama, it's not bad news. Felix has... better sit down," I said and led her to a chair that stood before the still-shrouded typewriter. "Here, Mama. Felix is fine. Maybe you should read it yourself. It's not bad news, Mama. Don't be worried. Felix has... is married."

"But he promised me." My mother rose from the chair. "There was that one French girl in, where was it, Dorval or St. Thomas that he mentioned when he cancelled his leave. Not that one?"

"Here read it for yourself. Her name is Alice. That's not a French name."

My mother looked down at the flimsy paper as if it would bite her. "What possessed the boy?" she moaned. "It's wartime. He's so young."

"Well, here. I'll read it to you." I began to read aloud.

"Her name is Alice Bradford. I know you will be surprised; I'm surprised, too, but I had a ten-day leave and we decided not to wait until after the war. You'll love Alice once you know her," my brother wrote. "Her mother came for the wedding. Her father died long ago in India when she was a small child. When you meet her, you'll know everything, Mama. We're happy.

Alice will write to you, too, send pictures of the wedding. I know it's sudden. But it will work out, Mama. Love Felix."

Tears rolled down my mother's cheeks. "Well, Felix," she said. "Well, I could have known. Always so reckless. Well," she said again for want of a better word.

I read the P.S. at the bottom of the page. "Married at the Cathedral of St Thomas, Hamilton on the Mountain, Ontario." I shook my head and thought of Mrs. Strachan and the cathedral in Raulston. "She'll be English, Mama. Her family Empire-Loyalist probably."

My mother gulped back a sob and taking the letter from me, hurried through the door to my father's office. I thought of all the British novels I had read about Empire Loyalists, books by Mazo de La Roche and others. Felix's new wife might be a character in one of those novels. She probably lived in three-storey red brick house surrounded by orchards. Her family would have been settled there for many generations. Alice could not possibly fit in with our Mennonite ways here in Millbach. I followed my mother to my father's office where he sat reading the letter. He looked surprised but not unduly so. He looked up with a little smile. "He's a man, Maria. Felix is old enough to make up his own mind."

"But Gerthe, so young and a strange girl. What will I tell Sophie and the others? And Conrad?"

By the time the pictures arrived it was truly spring, the trees sticky with buds and my mother had grown accustomed to the news of her youngest son. In fact, to neighbours and friends she gushed.

"Felix, my darling boy, it's really true. Married." My mother came into the office to hand a photograph to me.

I took it and looked down Felix and his bride stood on the outside steps of a chapel, the stone arch of the doorway high above them. No long wedding dress. No veil. A real wartime wedding. Felix smiled straight into the camera. Light snow fell on his shoulders of his uniform as it did on Alice's dark skirt and the fur jacket she had draped over her shoulders. The rector in white vestments stood beside them. I laid the picture down on the table.

The girl had written a short note. "I'm looking forward to meeting you all. Felix just had his embarkation leave." That was all. I looked through the window. The previous fall's leaves lay in sodden heaps under the trees. New leaves were about to unfurl.

"Will Felix bring that girl to live here?" I wondered aloud to Conrad that evening. We were alone in the printery, the room partially lit. The only light was the one above Conrad's desk. My pencil moved through the columns of type, slashing here and as I edited the district news. The words would become lines of type on a page in the new English edition of the Millbach News.

"I have been thinking of a name," Conrad said ignoring my question. "We can't keep calling it the new English edition of the Millbach News. It's far more than that, really a separate thing. We never had hockey scores from Woodridge, the obituary of a Gardenton pioneer, news of a whist drive in Piney."

I put thoughts of Felix and Alice and whether they would fit in aside and went on with my work. I loved it and I was proud of our name painted in bold letters across the front of our building, Heppner Printers and Publishers.

War's end when it finally came caught me by surprise. For those last weeks of March and April of 1945, my father and Nicholas Wall closeted themselves in the office much as they had at the beginning of the war, six years before.

"Murderous Bolsheviks. Why do the Allies not take Berlin? Why don't they realize?" I heard my father ask Nicholas over the hysterical voice on the radio reciting the latest news. But even Nicholas could not explain why the advance and retreat of armies was not as my father had hoped.

"The Allies don't realize, Gerthe." Nicholas sounded sad and weary, disappointed, old. I moved closer to the partly opened door. Realize what? I had stopped paying attention to the daily newspaper from Redwin, one black ominous headline after the other in ink so thick it smeared across the page. I gently pushed the door open. A cloud of tobacco smoke hung in the room, the two men hunched over the desk. "Stalin, Stalin. They don't know Stalin. Roosevelt, Eisenhower. What is the matter with that man? He's letting the Russians take Berlin!" I went back to my proofreading.

Allied war correspondents waxed poetic in their newspaper columns but the liberation of Paris meant little to me. It was a place for a Madame Bovary, a Marie Antoinette, both women I disliked. But the Millbach News must go to press on time and I cleared my head of all other thoughts as I ran my pencil down the last page of the Familien Freund, checking for spelling errors.

On VE Day, Millbach was unusually quiet. There was no victory parade, no marching bands, no speeches, although special Thanksgiving services were held in all the churches. Millbach would welcome its veterans, maybe build a small cairn but there would be no memorial for the conscientious objectors who returned from bush camps and national parks at the same time.

We had our own Schonweser church now. It was a small renovated schoolhouse with windows in the gothic style and the final touch, an imposing steeple. That Sunday I prayed that peace might reign. I saw my father, the crease between his brows deepening as he bowed his head. He still worried about the Russians. I prayed for Felix. He was somewhere in Germany.

At the end of that eventful May, a letter arrived from Felix addressed to my father. I was surprised - his letters were usually addressed to my mother. I fingered its thickness - several pages - before I laid it on my father's desk. It was much fatter than the ones my mother received.

"Papa will not say more except that Felix will not be home for a while yet," my mother told me later on her way for an afternoon visit with Sophie. She was taking the afternoon off from the printery as she had begun to do every day. Our pressman and linotype operator had returned, one from the mines in Flin Flon, one discharged from the Air Force. Slowly we women were being displaced. I worked half-days now, training a new clerk in an office suddenly crowded with extra help.

"Nuremberg, Nuremberg," my mother repeated while she tucked her crochet work further into her bag. "Felix writes from Nuremburg, that is the city of the engraver Albert Durer. Papa has somehow misplaced the letter or else I could tell you more, but I haven't read it yet. So careless, Gerthe, all those papers on his desk. No wonder he loses things. And the pictures Felix enclosed, too." She shook her head, the amber combs set just so in her hair shone. She draped a bright scarf over her shoulders and hurried out the door.

"Lost on purpose?" Elene asked idly and looked up from her typewriter. She was home for the summer holidays, grown thin on cafeteria food and too much studying, her round cheeks lost forever.

"Why would he do that?" I asked. "They'll show up."

"Have you read the papers? Maybe Felix has found out some things about the Germans," she said cryptically. "Poor Papa - he always loved all things German, the philosophy, the music. And Felix, too. But now..." her voice trailed off.

"All that about the camps, Elene, could it be true?"

"I really don't know," she answered thoughtfully. "If it is true, it's terrible. Remember the fire and Mrs. Peddlar-Braun? How could we ever call ourselves German again?"

"We aren't German," I said quickly, "we're Mennonite. We haven't been German for hundreds of years."

"Don't say that, Anna. You sound like Mrs. Peddlar-Braun. I wonder what she'd be saying if the Germans had won."

"But Elene it's true, besides we're Canadian Mennonites now, aren't we?"

"I suppose," she said thoughtfully and turned back to her typing.

I needed to talk to my father to find out more. He would know. I left her to go and look for him in his office. He was sitting at his desk gazing absently out of the window.

"Have you found the letter, yet, Papa?" I asked.

He rooted through his papers and handed me the photographs Felix had enclosed. "I've put the letter somewhere. It's here. I'll find it. It was mostly for me, anyway."

My father was not a devious man. There must be something in the letter he was shielding us from. I took the photos to the window to see them better.

In the first, Felix smiled back at me from behind a large stein of beer. He was bare headed, his dark hair gleamed, the collar of his battle dress open to a casual white t-shirt. His cap lay on the table beside him. It must have been taken in an outdoor cafe. A striped sun umbrella had somehow survived the bombing. Even the shrubbery which grew along a stonewall looked intact. He had written about the camera that must have been used to take this photo, how he had traded a pound of coffee and some cigarettes for it. I fingered the studio quality of the photo. I was astonished at its excellence. This and the jauntily striped umbrella seemed out of place with what I had read in the papers about a Germany bombed into rubble. .

I looked closer. The fine lens had caught Felix in a pensive mood. Even behind his glasses, I could see that his eyes had a sad wistful quality about them and I wondered if it had something to do with the contents of the letter.

Felix spent a year in Germany after the war's end. It took me that long to believe the war was really over and we had survived almost intact, although my father heard the rumblings of the cold war to come. We younger Heppners did not want to hear about another war, hot or cold. We were secretly embarrassed by our newfound prosperity and worried about another Depression waiting in the wings to flatten us again.

On the surface, Henry carried on as usual and did not allow himself to be swept away by the euphoria. I was like a befuddled child who has stood too long on the outside of the toy shop window and when finally let in cannot decide which toy to choose. The talk was all of new houses, new cars, miracle fabrics, miracle drugs. It was impossible for me to change my thrifty ways overnight. I still counted pennies, mended socks and turned shirt collars. Conrad could not quite conceal his delight in the ever-expanding Millbach Post. That was the name he had given to his upstart English edition of the old Millbach News. Soon the newly installed presses straight from the resurrected factories in Heidelberg, Germany, gleaming with paint, hummed efficiently day and night. Conrad was revealed as a person with power, a man to be reckoned with. Nettie, like I, held back. She had been taught to be modest in her desires.

On a warm morning in June, I set out for my mother's house. Outside the air was fresh. Birds hooted their early morning calls to each other. The sun shone through the hedge in strips of light across the back lawn. Everywhere was the lush green of leaves and flowers. A visitor would have denied that only three months ago this place had been locked in ice and snow. Now my mother's peonies nodded heavy heads and strewed their petals in a thick rose carpet over the moist soil of her perennial border.

I had dug out a sleeveless summer dress from the storage closet. It had a flared skirt cut on the bias and was gathered at the waist. I had draped a white cardigan over my shoulders for the morning. Gone were the dark blue coveralls I had worn every working day for almost six years. Now that the men were back in the printery and I worked only in the office one or two days a week, I could afford to look like a woman, wear a dress, perfume, jewellery. Cool air flowed around my winter white legs. My feet felt strange in sandals.

"Who can believe this?" my mother said even before I was quite through door of her kitchen. "Who can believe this?" she repeated in case I had not heard the first time. She came towards me through the brightness of her kitchen, her half-eaten breakfast still on the table beside her.

"Believe what?" I asked and sat down. My father had already gone to his work and by now would be having his after breakfast cigarette in the quiet of his office. I took the letter my mother held out. "What's this?" The letter displayed a bright red cross at the top.

"Sarah, it's Sarah my sister, Sarah. It came in last night's mail." My mother laughed out loud. "Your Papa applied to these people a month ago but said nothing to me. Imagine keeping it from me." A slight frown appeared on her face then just as quickly disappeared. "He didn't want to get my hopes up." She laughed again, this time fondly. "Dear man. He has located Sarah, Anna. All night I have been lying awake."

"Not Aunt Sarah? You mean she's still alive? I can't believe it."

My mother nodded happily. "It's like a dream," she said. "Pinch me." She held out her arm clothed in a quilted pink dressing gown. I picked up the letter instead.

"In answer to your enquiry of the seventeenth instant," I read aloud. "Our refugee files are incomplete..." Then came a long stream of names and birth dates, locations, refugees in *lagers* and camps along the Dutch border, refugees displaced from Poland, the Ukraine, Bulgaria, Roumania, Jugoslavia.

Meanwhile my mother rushed on. "Sarah. Sarah is alive, like someone rising from the dead. And her two children, surviving!"

"What about your other sisters - and brothers?" I put down the letter.

"No one really knows. They must be dead, killed. Just as Gerthe feared, Stalin's purges..." her voiced trailed weakly away. "The Red Cross can't say. I can't bear to think about it, Anna." My mother's shoulders slumped. "Let me be glad about Sarah, now."

"You're right, " I said quickly. "Let's be glad for that. "

"Poor Sarah. I'm afraid, Anna. I almost dread to see her. Like from the dead after twenty years. She was just a child when we left." Tears gathered in my mother's eyes. We both sat down; my mother leaned her elbows on the table and looked down at her plate. Silently, I patted a pink clad shoulder.

"Oh, Anna, I don't know," my mother said after a long silence. "My brother David - before I could always believe he was alive. He was so resourceful, we would say, setting up a factory for manufacturing farm implements. Ingenious, they called him. A man like that would surely have the good sense to escape with his family, head for the east, cross over the mountains through China. I always wanted to believe he was in Vladivostok, building cranes for the shipyards there."

"And do you still believe that?" I asked gently. I had heard that story since I was a child but no word had ever come from Vladivostock for my mother.

"No, no," my mother said heavily, "but it was easier than believing the truth, that my brother David never escaped the Soviet Inferno." She shook her head. "Such a dreamer we always said, his nose constantly in a book."

"Maybe it's better to know the truth, Mama."

"Is it?" My mother stared out at the birds wheeling from the maple tree, but she did not see them.

She stood up from the table. "I must send a parcel. Coffee and chocolate, warm socks, soap." She was all briskness. "Sarah and her children must come to us. Gerthe will arrange for their passage."

I wrote down the whereabouts of my aunt with a pen my father had left behind. I would send a parcel too. I remembered

Sarah, she had brought me oranges when I had the chicken pox, taught me my letters from the German Fibel. It would be good to have an aunt, like having another Sophie.

I wondered where our family would be right now if it wasn't for my father being ousted from his position at the Zentralschule by the Soviets. What if we hadn't come to Canada? Would we be refugees waiting for someone to claim us?

When Sarah's first letter arrived a month later my mother dissolved in tears. She had been waiting impatiently, asking us every day, sure that Elene had not looked carefully enough among the raft of business correspondence, had maybe even dropped letters when she transferred mail from the drawer in the post office into the leather bag we used to transport it back and forth. When Elene handed her the flimsy envelope with the foreign postmarks, my mother's hands trembled. Elene disappeared through the door leading to the shop. Without a word I took it and slit it open with letter opener that lay on the desk in the front office.

"I can't see," my mother fumbled for her glasses that hung on a chain around her neck, "you read."

My father had come from his office and stood in the doorway. I began to read aloud. "We received your parcel," my aunt wrote. "How can we thank you enough? And what do we see one day but a young man in the uniform seeking us out. Gott Im Himmel, for a minute I thought it was your Gerthe from so long ago. But no, no, it is his son come to bring us the good news."

"Felix, our Felix? " my mother half-shouted.

"Good! Good! He has found them," my father said more quietly. By now Henry also stood in the doorway beside my father.

"What's all the excitement?" he asked.

I continued to read. "We will not be sent back to Russia. No more refugees will be sent back." I looked up. Had there ever been any doubt?

"Felix wrote and said the British Occupation has changed their policy," my father explained. He looked relieved. "They have finally caught on to the Russians. Thank God for that."

"Vielen Dank for the parcel," my aunt wrote, "for the milk powder, the coffee, the jelly - we are so grateful. Vasily is too thin. The doctors test him for the Lungen Ensindung, the consumption. Vasily has suffered the most. The doctors shake their heads."

"Not like Conrad with the Trachoma. Not that," my mother wailed. "Not being in the quarantine. Surely the immigration doesn't still do that."

My father frowned slightly, reached out his hand to quiet my mother. "Go on, Anna. Read on to the end."

My aunt's letter continued, "If all goes well, we will not be a burden on you. Ursula is a big girl, now. We will both work hard, I promise you. Gott Sei Dank we are safe for now in a Lager in the British zone.

"She got my letter, too." I looked up at my parents and read on. "We hear from Anna. To think - you're little Anna, grown and married with a child of her own. So many years, so much to tell you, Maria. If the Lord permits, if Vasily improves, we will greet each other in the flesh once more. With love and thanks, Sarah."

My mother stopped crying and her face took on that purposeful look when she has decided how things are going to go. Henry had gone back to his linotype. I heard it clicking and zinging in the background.

"Gerthe, we must see to it," she said, her lips a firm line. "We must send money for the passage. If there is not enough Conrad will go to the bank. I insist on it. These are our people, our own flesh and blood."

My father smilingly nodded in agreement and patted my mother on the shoulder with one hand and me with the other, encircling us. Elene had come up behind my father. "So it's good news?" She smiled and moved around my father to peer at the letter I held.

Conrad, his hair blown by the wind, came through the front door, a large advertising folio under his arm.

"What's up?" he said when he saw us. "I just got a full page from Penner's Ford. Those car dealers have money to burn."

Chapter Ten

My father did what he promised. He spent the better part of that year pulling both financial and political strings to bring Sarah and her two children to Canada. But a month before they were to arrive our anticipation of their coming was eclipsed by the greater joy of Felix's return to Millbach with Alice.

On a Saturday evening in early summer Henry and I and Harry went over to my mother's to greet them. The whole family had gathered and milled about in my mother's dining room, Harry chasing his cousin Richard around and around practically under our feet. Mama tried to marshal us to the table for an evening snack.

"Welcome home, Felix. How are you?" I hugged him. He had filled out and seemed bigger than when he went away. In his uniform I recognized the young man in the photograph with the same smile but now there was a twinkle in his eye.

"Hello, Anna. Good to see," he said and reached back to put his arm around the shoulders of the girl on whom everyone's eyes rested. "Here's my sister Anna, Alice."

Alice and I were face to face. She had hazel eyes. She wore her dark blonde hair short, held back by a blue hair band. Her blue slacks were belted with narrow red leather at the waist; the striped red and blue jersey fit her just so, not too loose, not too tight. A perfect size eight. She probably wore an up-lift brassiere, Gothic or Maiden-form. She reached just to my brother's shoulder.

"Welcome to Millbach," I murmured and took her outstretched hand. Should I kiss her, hug her? I wasn't sure but threw caution aside, after all, she was my brother's wife. I was aware of her fine bones and a faint scent - Lotus or Chanel.

"I hope we'll be good friends," she said and stepped back to stand closer to Felix. "You have those lovely Heppner eyes. I hope our children will inherit them." She smiled. She had perfect teeth. Her English was not Millbach English, which had a flat sound interspersed with many Platte words. But it was not quite B.B.C. English, either. More like Mrs. Strachan's English.

The following morning I sat in church where I always sat, surrounded on all sides by other women and their children. Harry was in Sunday school. There was a stir and heads turned as Felix came down the aisle with Alice at his side. They chose a pew near the front of the church on the men's side and sat down. I felt rather than heard a kind of communal gasp. Elene who was the accompanist for the summer choir, turned from the piano, then turned back to her music and continued to play the prelude. She had heard it too. My mother who sat beside me tugged her hat more firmly in place.

Zena had said the times would be changing. Too bad she was not here to see this for Alice and Felix had just upset a hoary old tradition. Felix had not told her and she could not know it, but women did not sit with their menfolk in our church except for funerals and sometimes weddings. Oh, sometimes a small girl ran over to her father to be comforted, pushed past the row of seated men until she found the right pair of knees. Felix's boldness was a small thing but a signal of more to come.

We stood for the invocation. I looked up at the motto high above the choir loft "Nun Danket Alle Gott," Now thank we all our God. I smiled. Would we be thankful for Alice? When we sat down I stole a glance at them. They sat close together. Felix had his arm along the back of the bench, not quite touching Alice. He wore a navy flannel blazer, one from before the war. It seemed a little tight across the shoulders. His hair was trimmed short and the back of his neck looked vulnerable. Atop Alice's head was a cluster of blue petals and a wisp of veil perched like a bird about to take flight.

Everyone came to my parents' house for Sunday dinner. As we sat around the table and bowed our heads for grace, I looked covertly around. My father, his shoulders broad in his church-going suit and buttoned vest sat at the head of the table, his big hands folded on its linen-clad edge. Soon he would raise his massive greying head and with a brief nod give a quick 'Amen.' My mother sat opposite my father at the other end of the table. With head bowed, her favourite amber combs glowed in her thinning hair. Her cheeks were flushed after all the preparation and I knew how strained she was, how she wanted everything to be perfect.

Felix and Conrad were seated across the table from each other on either side of my father. Conrad wore his usual enigmatic smile. Through all the days of observing him across an editorial desk I had not yet learned to read that smile. He was beginning to wear the trappings of a successful business man - the silk tie, the gold watch band, the Rotary badge in his lapel and they suited him. In comparison Felix looked young, so young. His long, piano playing fingers played with the clasp on Alice's pearls. Alice smiled faintly, her head remained bowed.

Sunshine poured through the dining room windows over my mother's bank of houseplants. It lit up the red highlights on Elene's bowed head, the pale skin at the nape of her neck. She looked up at me, caught my eye on her and smiled secretively. I smiled back. It was good to have her home from school for the summer.

Nettie, looking plump and satisfied, sat up straight; I could imagine her tight girdle and her short skirt revealing nylon-clad knees under the table. Three-year-old Richard sat beside her, banging his spoon on his plate. Nettie reached over and moved the plate so that his spoon fell on the tablecloth where its clanging was muffled. Richard had not inherited the Heppner bones and colouring but was an image of his pretty mother.

I put out my hand and laid it on my own son's shoulder to stop him kicking back and forth with his legs. Harry did not look like a Heppner either. He was a true Redekop, thin like his father, with a narrow freckled face and a question always in his grey-blue eyes. At least he was past the stage of playing with the cutlery but I could feel him swinging his legs beneath the table while he watched Alice and Felix, the newcomers. He leaned over to his father and whispered something.

Henry smiled faintly, reached down beneath the table to

still Harry's legs. Henry's gentleness with his son often caught me by the throat with a rush of emotion.

"Amen," my father said. The Heppners did not dwell on the Almighty overlong.

My mother had set the table with her best: white china with a dark blue and gold band around a floral centre, a white linen cloth. She must have set it earlier that morning before church because the lilacs in the crystal bowl were drooping a little. We began to pass platters of ham and browned potatoes from hand to hand.

Felix, though repeatedly asked, avoided talk of the war. "It was alright, I guess. Terrible food. It's great to be back," I heard him say when someone asked.

"Did you have a real gun?" Harry asked now leaning forward to see past Alice to his uncle.

"Yeah, sorry Harry. I left my gun in Germany." Felix smiled at Harry, then popped a piece of ham into his mouth.

I stood to cut more slices of ham. Felix was beginning to relax. I sensed that he wanted things to go well, too, wanted his wife to think well of his family. He was beginning to sound more and more like the Felix I knew before he went away. I heaved a sigh of relief. That sad look I had seen in his eyes in the photos from Germany - maybe it was only a trick of the light, or I had imagined it.

"But, here's something for you," I heard him say to Harry who let out a loud squeal of pleasure and came rushing towards me carrying a small box. "A medal! Uncle Felix says I can have it." Inside the box a medal hung on a striped ribbon. "Voluntary Service 1939-1945" was stamped around the edge. The head of King George the Sixth was embossed on one side, the British lion on the other.

"You're not serious, Felix?" I asked incredulously. "You want to keep that for your own son, don't you?"

"It's nothing special. Everybody who volunteered got those, Anna. You must know that. They're nothing like Alice's father had." Felix put an arm around her shoulders. "Let Harry strut about with it for a while."

Conrad and Henry were talking about the columns of district news, and the advertising for next week's paper. Nettie reached over for another roll and spread it thickly with butter.

My mother watched disapprovingly. I looked over to see my father smiling through his after dinner smoke at the head of the table.

"What about the concentration camps?" Elene asked abruptly. We all fell silent. "Why is everybody so secretive? And the Nurumberg Trials - is it like the papers say?" This was unusual from our shy, retiring Elene. What was she learning besides mathematics and music at her academy?

Throughout the meal my father had mostly listened, now he spoke, his voice low. "Not now, Elene. Please, not here," he said.

My mother looked over to him as if responding to a signal. "Mahlzeit," she said, indicating that dinner was over and we were excused. She rose from the table.

But Felix smiled with a shake of the head and bent down to light a cigarette. "Elene, Papa's right. It's not a fit subject for the table, those camps. That shakes anybody up. And now all the different occupation zones. Nobody knows what they're doing half the time." He patted Alice's thigh, and stood up to follow the other men, who were already away from the table and heading towards the door that led to the printery.

"But Felix, darling?" Alice struggled out of her chair to follow him.

"I'll be back. We have to talk business," he said gently.

Alice looked surprised.

My mother heaved a relieved sigh. Men sitting around made her nervous. I began to collect the plates. I would have liked to hear what the men talked about as much as Alice.

"Will Felix be going to the University?" Elene asked Alice suddenly from across the table. "My friend's brother, well, she has two brothers actually, they're both going - one to medical school," Elene said. "I'm sure going to go - just as soon as I finish high school."

Alice shook her head. "We'll have to see, Felix has a lot of things to think about. And I've moved so much in my life from one army base to another. I don't know how my mother stood it. But what with all the things going on in the world, Millbach looks like such a peaceful, contented place. I'd like to live in a house like normal people, settle down, have a baby. "

Elene looked away. She was not much interested in a brother whose wife wanted to settle down. I wondered if Felix had told Alice anything about Millbach. I didn't want to be the one but somebody ought to tell her what Millbach could be like. How would Alice get along with people like Mrs. Peddlar-Braun?

"I wonder if you would like it here, Alice. People are quite set in their ways although that is changing, too. I mean, wouldn't you miss your mother? Or your old friends?" I asked to make up for Elene's lack of interest. I had to; I wanted her to feel welcome.

Alice turned to me. "Felix would like to work on the newspaper. He wants something of his own, something he can belong to." Then she looked at me. Calculating how much she should tell me? She frowned and carried on. She had decided I was to be trusted. "I don't know. Felix will have to make the final decision whether we stay her. Poor Felix, he has gone through some traumatic times. He has bad dreams at night about the refugees that got sent back to Russia. He blames himself. But there is no way he could have changed that. He did the best he could."

"They sent back refugees to Stalin?" I asked in bewilderment. "Who? Not the British. Maybe the Americans?"

"It was in the papers, Felix said. I didn't read it myself. Apparently it was part of the Potsdam agreement, signed by Churchill and Truman," Alice added. "And Churchill is Felix's hero."

"That's hard to believe. After all they have been through. Why would they do that?" I really did not want to believe it, yet that could explain what I had seen in the photo of Felix. Alice moved over to look out of the dining room window and I retreated to the kitchen, still unconvinced, still not understanding. My mother was rinsing the roasting pan in the sink. Stacks of clean plates and cutlery stood on the table ready to be put back into the buffet.

I was sorry that the men had gone. My father would be full of details about things I had read about like the Marshall Plan and the Potsdam Agreement. But it was a foregone conclusion -Conrad and Felix would always go back to business and the newspaper - discussing the pros and cons of the Heidelberg press. I wondered to myself how soon Felix would clue into the fact that it was Conrad's paper. The Millbach News belonged to Conrad. He would lay down his life for it. If Felix really wanted something of his own he might be better off going to the University and getting a degree to become a doctor or a lawyer. The veterans' benefits were very generous, according to the papers.

Suddenly I was tired of other peoples' problems and how they would be decided. I wanted to get out and breathe fresh air. My mother's house with all the people in it seemed stifling. I would go and pull up weeds in my garden - no, I was too restless. I would go and visit Zena and we would go for a long walk. I would tell Zena all about Felix and Alice, how Alice who had all the choices in the world before her, wanted to settle down and have a baby.

But then again Zena might agree with Alice. Zena, who was finally having a baby. Why not leave the Millbach News to the men? They were coming back from the war and needed jobs. What could a woman do? I could have another baby, too. I knew Henry would love another child.

Suddenly, it seemed the right thing to do. And this time it would be different. I would be pampered, go to the hairdresser and have my hair done. Buy flowered sheets for the bed instead of white and towels to match. I carried the last stack of dishes to the buffet in the dining room. Alice had disappeared. She had been drawn like a magnet to where the men sat in my father's office. Alice would not be so easily shaken off. They would have to get used to her. I shook my head as I let myself out the front door of my mother's house. Conrad might not like it but she was not like Nettie. She would not hesitate to have her say.

Felix took to post-war life with his usual nervous energy. He thrived on newness and innovation. The new processes for photo-engraving made it easier to publish photos in the newspaper. Felix's photos of graduations, hockey teams, prize cows and parades now enlivened every page of the Heppner newspapers. It seemed he and Alice were perfectly fitted for the fifties' affluence and they set the pace in Millbach. It was something to watch.

Felix and Alice didn't invite you to supper, they

"entertained." Alice was not uncomfortable with money and knew how to spend it. She bought soup in cans, fresh fish, lettuce out of season, was not ashamed to use cake mix. Alice served white wine in fine glasses etched with flying birds, mushroom canapés on a silver tray while music from the Sleeping Beauty played on their stereo.

Inevitably, Alice changed Felix. Almost casually he abandoned his Mennonite heritage and was baptized and taken into the fold of Alice's Anglican faith. When Alice and Felix went to church now, it was to the shabby little Anglican chapel just down the old highway in Clear Springs where a young priest came out once a month for services. A tiny settlement of English immigrants from Ontario had survived there since the beginning of the century, completely surrounded by the more prolific Mennonites.

"God bless you, Felix," I said as warmly as I could on the day of his baptism. The priest had not talked about being saved or born again. Thank God for that, I thought. That was all one heard from the pulpits of the churches in Millbach. Our Schonweser church still preached in German. The Gospel seemed to mellow and take on a richness the words did not have in English. If God spoke any language at all, I thought I would like it to be German.

We had gathered as a family around the font at the front of the sanctuary. No one quite knew what to say. The Heppners were always shy about using religious words. My mother stood beside a smiling Alice, unable to speak. My father looked thoughtful. Conrad and Nettie stood as far away as was possible in such a small space. Felix grinned, suddenly shy. The chapel was half empty. There were not many Anglicans around Millbach. I thought of all the people that would have assembled if this had taken place in the Mennonite church a few miles down the road.

A year later Alice and Felix had a son who was christened from the same font where his father had been baptized. They called him Bradford after his mother's family name. I had to laugh. Alice and Felix behaved as though they had invented babies. My mother was kept busy cooking meals for Felix while Alice was in hospital. I wondered if Alice knew what my mother was like. Her gifts often came with strings attached.

We had a baby too, another son, Philip. It was almost an anti-climax after Bradford, although everything had gone the way I wanted and Henry was truly delighted. Harry doted on his brother. I was content. It was fine.

Soon after, Alice and Felix moved into their fine new home financed by the generosity of Veterans' Land Act and Alice's inheritance. We were all a little envious, especially Nettie.

"All that money is burning a hole in Alice's purse," she had said angrily. Only occasionally did Nettie let down her guard and let me know how she felt about Alice. She would say something like - who does she think she is? Where does she think the money comes from? I did not have to ask her whom she meant.

Nettie did not take into account that Alice had money of her own - in a trust fund she had inherited from her father. I wondered if Alice would have been so free without it. Money or the lack of it had an effect on people. I knew Zena was free and easy with Ben's money. But Nettie had never learned that, even when Conrad had lots of it.

It was about this time also that Alice began insisting on a cottage at the lake.

"We need a place to go for weekends, we need to think of summer holidays. Children have to have a place to play," she said.

"Maybe they do where you came from, Alice," I said as I placed the dish of beet relish on my mother's white linen cloth before we all sat down to Faspa, "but people in Millbach don't go for holidays or have weekends. They work six days a week and go to church on Sunday."

"But...but," Alice stuttered, at a loss for words at this very Mennonite attitude. I had taken her by surprise. She reached out to catch Bradford before he fell down in the path of Richard's tricycle. He looked up to give his mother a beaming smile.

"Who would weed our garden if we sat at the beach all summer?" My mother's voice came from the kitchen. She had heard Alice. "And by that time the string beans are ready. Besides it's too far away, seventy miles, even further than to Redwin." She came into the room and surveyed the table to make sure everything was in order.

"Bitte, Bitte," my mother called. Alice, followed by the men, came to the table.

"Sparrow Lake is not far, really," Alice said as she picked up her squirming toddler son and placed him in his high chair. She sat down beside him. "Don't you like to fish, Dad? You'd love it." She fiddled with the gold bangles on her arm and looked at my father, sitting at the head of the table. She was the only one of us who called him Dad. He smiled warmly at her, nodding as he did when an important politician engaged him in talk and reached for one of my mother's rolls.

My father fishing? I thought of Judge Strachan in his leaky boat on Lost Mountain Lake. But on the other hand, it might be good for our family. Maybe we could stop working all the time. I got up to go to the kitchen. Maybe it would be good for us to have a cottage. Maybe I would like it better than I thought.

"Felix has applied for a ninety-nine year lease on a lot with a sandy beach and a little creek to one side." From the kitchen where I was cutting up the fruitcake, I could feel the silence at this news.

"Shall I make the tea, Anna?" Alice had come into the kitchen. "Felix doesn't like it drowned."

Stubbornly I poured hot coffee for the rest of us. We had been taught that tea was for weaklings and sick people.

"Brad and Mupps will love it at the beach," Alice said as the water came to a boil and she poured it over the tea leaves. Mupps was Brad's puppy, a cocker spaniel.

"How is Mupps on your new carpets?" I asked and thought of the Strachan's Fletcher so long ago. I had never had a dog. Henry thought dogs belonged in a barn.

"Not bad, he slobbers," Alice said cheerfully and plucked half a devilled egg from the tray on the counter and took a bite. "Mmm...good, and your rolls, Anna." Her even white teeth bit into the one she held in her other hand. "Everything tastes so good. I must learn from you. I'm even afraid to stuff a turkey." She led the way back to the dining room where we rejoined the others at the table.

Nettie was eating as though her life depended on it. She was always quiet around Alice, not afraid of her but cautious. Across the table from her, I watched as Alice cut up her meat in the English way, holding the fork in her left hand and knife in her right just as the judge and Mrs. Strachan had done.

By the time the family cottage rose among the spruce and birch on the shores of Sparrow Lake, Alice announced she was pregnant again. We had come out by car to see how the construction was going and were standing just below the new deck facing the lake which could be seen blue and tranquil through the trees.

"Two babies! My goodness!" I was astounded. "You'll have your hands full." I hardly knew what to say. Should I be glad for her? Should I be sad? Alice? I thought she would have one baby to prove she could do it, and that would be it. It felt like I was from another generation. Mine had tried to avoid just such situations and now here was Alice.

"I'm thrilled. Bradford will not grow up as an only child," Alice said. "I had enough of that when I was growing up."

So it wasn't an accident. I looked again at Alice. Her hair was short and bleached in streaks from hours of sun. She looked not much older than Harry. She wore an old white shirt of Felix's over her halter-top and tight-fitting blue jeans, the first I had seen. I had always thought that denim was for farmers but now apparently it was the latest thing. At least so Alice said. She and Felix had just returned from a trip to the States. They had left their baby at home with a nanny. I could not have done that. But Alice just did things differently.

"Well, anyway, congratulations," I said and slapped at a mosquito.

"Thanks," she smiled with her perfect teeth, tucked the tips of her fingers into the tight waistband of her jeans. She looked about eight years old, thin as a rail.

"We must go, " I said, "Mama is in the car with Philip. He's going to want his bottle before we get home." I turned and began to walk back towards our car parked just behind Alice's. The cars were like two bright toys among between the tree stumps; nearby smooth Precambrian rock heaved up like the back of a whale through the grass and the mulch of fallen leaves. Alice called it the driveway. I looked around me. There was still a lot of work to be done before this would be the paradise that Alice and Felix dreamt of.

I reached the car where my mother sat in the back seat with the window rolled down, Philip in a car seat beside her. They were both having a little nap although my mother would never admit to it. I leaned against the sun-warmed side of the car. It still smelled of the factory- paint and fresh rubber. It was our first car. Henry had talked of teaching me to drive but so far it had only been talk. To tell the truth, I was a little nervous.

Alice stopped to watch two workmen as they built up the cottage chimney brick by brick. Amongst the green of growing things the smell of cedar shavings and varnish hung in the air. The waters of the lake shone with brief flickers of blue through the trees and I saw my father, Henry and Harry coming up from the lake where the aluminum boat bumped against the dock. My mother had opened her eyes, but Philip slept on. As the men drew near I smelled engine oil, mosquito lotion and fish. They looked delighted at the world, their faces tanned from the sun and air.

I climbed into the back seat beside my mother. "Not my idea of a holiday," I said to no one in particular. "Reminds me of Regina Beach and the Strachans."

"The fish are jumping," my father said as he climbed into the passenger seat with Harry wedged in between himself and Henry in the driver's seat. Felix waved his shirt from the porch where he was doing something we could not properly see from this distance.

"Maybe once there is a stove in the kitchen and we can fry the fish and set the table properly," my mother said doubtfully. "But this barbecuing and sitting about on the beach, sun-bathing? What a waste of time." I had managed to coax her away from her garden for this one day, but would not do that many more times.

Nettie and Conrad had not come; they seldom did. Conrad said he had to see to his horses. He had bought a small acreage just outside of Millbach where he kept them and he spent all his spare time there. He seldom talked about the years on the farm but he had never lost his love for horses.

After the cottage was complete we made countless weekend pilgrimages to the lake. I tried to enjoy that kind of life, but it was Felix and Alice and Elene who loved it most at Sparrow Lake. It was as if all three of them had not had enough of hard living. They cheerfully chopped wood, cleaned lamp chimneys, carried water. In the evenings they drank beer in the lamplight, smoked cigarettes, argued politics over endless games of Canasta.

I did not have to go to the family cottage at Sparrow Lake to enjoy myself. We had our two boys and the time passed pleasantly enough, through music lessons and hockey games, report cards and Christmas programs. But no matter how well Harry and Phillip did, Richard was still my mother's favourite.

"That Richard is Conrad all over again," my mother would say, though never when Alice was present. "He'll make a fine head of the family when the time comes."

Nettie would try not to smile.

I would bend further over my needle point, "What about Bradford? Felix might have something to say about that," I would say quietly not daring to look up from my stitching.

"Our sons will not be beholden to the Heppners," Henry said in a low voice so that the boys would not hear him. It was night and we were already in bed. He was tired from a long day at the linotype. Conrad had just ordered another automatic press; and Henry was nervous - all the printing processes were changing. "Now Felix is talking of an off-set press. That means there will be no use for a linotype...and your mother..." he began on another note, but then shrugged his shoulders angrily. I could always tell when she had been ranting at him. If she did not have my father to nag she picked on Henry. Conrad could always shrug her off, but Henry was from the old school of Hoflichkeit - far too polite for that.

"But there is always the German paper, Henry. Relax a little." However I understood Henry's unease. He was a natural worrier. Once you had been poor and almost destitute, you never forgot that feeling. Neither did I of course, or Conrad, although he would deny it with his last breath.

"Depression fever," Felix would josh at Henry. Felix had no trouble with the good times.

"They will go to the university," I said that night to reassure him, but he had turned over and gone to sleep.

Our boys would be like their aunt Elene, I thought. She has a good life, interesting, meeting new people, learning new things. Philip and Harry were quiet and reserved like their father but did well in school. Much better than Richard, something my mother ignored. She did not think a life of learning, like Elene had chosen and my father admired, amounted to much.

But everything was easier when you had money. I thought back to when Philip was born. I had had all the extras just as I had promised myself - the semi-private room in the hospital, the flowers by my bed, the satin bed jacket, my baby brought to me by a smiling nurse.

As my boys grew older I had time on my hands. No one suggested that I go back to work in the printery although I sometimes helped out when there was a big job which had to be finished on time. When I wrote, I wrote for myself and about my family, my garden, what I thought about the world. I read library books and even became the secretary of the Women's Institute. It was the only organization in Millbach that was not connected to a church. We tried to make the meetings educational and invited speakers - often boring men in suits from the government or the university. It was an excuse to go out, wearing our best hats and high-heeled shoes. Neither Nettie nor Alice ever joined, Nettie because she thought that the women there would look down on her. Zena and I went to all the Womens' Institute conventions in Redwin where we mingled with white-gloved ladies in their extravagant hats and on the long ride home we laughed and sang through the summer dark.

Zena never did have the son that Ben wished for but he was quietly thrilled with his two girls. And he could always console himself by flying his aeroplane with his uncle, Machine Unger, a handy mechanical wizard in the seat beside him. And if not there, then he was down on the ground with both arms up, guiding Ben towards the front of a ramshackle excuse for a hangar in one corner of what had once been the community pasture. The cowherd had passed into history, his bugle an artifact behind the glass at the newly dedicated museum. The old pasture alongside Ben's hangar had been grandly named a sports field, where every July first the baseball teams of the surrounding districts battled for supremacy. The ragged cheers of their various supporters, with their chewing gum and their pop bottles, rang out from behind the backstop while the black clad umpire kept track of the balls and the strikes with his fingers outstretched.

Chapter Eleven

Those were the golden years, the years right after the war. The Heppners flourished, the Millbach News grew. Conrad and Felix kept avid eyes on the subscription list as it got longer and longer. And with it, Millbach transformed itself from a village into a town with all its virtues and faults intact. There was still no railroad, but the big trucks and eighteen-wheelers pounded down the highway to Redwin and back daily taking goods and bringing goods back. The flour mill with its quiet droning machinery had been the tallest building; now the New Brethren built a church that loomed over us like an embattled fortress. Its towering neon sign advertised the revival meetings held there regularly with thousands in attendance or so it seemed to me. I never went and did not encourage my children to go.

On Main Street the old settler houses, with their small glass panes set in the white washed cedar shingle walls were being torn down one by one. Around the gaping cellar holes the Spiraea and lilac bushes planted by the long-dead Omas looked orphaned, derelict and forlorn. Here and there, a few whitewashed stones still marked the pebbled walkways now leading nowhere. I realized that our old settler house was the last one in Millbach now. I cherished it now even more as if my own ancestors had built it and endowed me with it.

The rows of cottonwoods and poplar still lined the street, now giving shade to imitation brick and plate glass storefronts. Another hardware store, then a drug store, and soon several clothing stores and a stationery store. A new jewellery store sold rings, brooches and bracelets beside the usual watches and clocks. The Old Brethren did not like it but there was nothing they could do. The Unger store had stayed the same. Above its long aisles the embossed ceiling grew dimmer year by year, its fine oak cabinetwork and plate glass counters still showed signs of its former splendour, but Ben had lost interest in the store; it had become a sideline. He had other interests, Zena told me.

Occasionally I would turn the pages of my diary to the past. Over the years it had become more like a journal. I would pause over the happy times - our arrival in Millbach, Conrad's approval in the printery, Phillip's birth - how different from Harry's! At times I could almost feel my anger rising from the page and I would turn away from the unhappy times. Best not to dwell on them. But always when I turned back the pages it felt as though our family and the town itself was part of a play. When I would describe this feeling to Zena, she would just laugh and say I should stop mooning about. Life was too short to be thinking about its meaning all the time. Elene, when she held still long enough to listen, said I should come to Redwin, go to university, there was an excellent program for mature students.

"You have a scholar's mind," she said.

"With Harry practically in high school?" I said. "Come on, Elene." I laughed. But I continued to order more books from the extension library. I wrote some poetry. The poetry had to come like a flash of light, be there, whole. The diary was a like washing your face or weeding your garden. It was what had to be done. It was routine. How could I live my life without it?

Every January first I stacked another journal high up on my closet shelf.

In April, a few years after we had completed the cottage at Sparrow Lake, my father died suddenly. We should not have been shocked; all the Heppners died suddenly, my mother always claimed in that wry voice she had. They did not suffer lingering illnesses, bid tearful farewells, nor confess to long held secrets on their deathbeds. They just dropped dead. For years we had treated it as a joke in our family.

I was still numb with shock on the day of his funeral. Nothing seemed to get through to my muddled mind, my grieving heart. I dimly heard the respectful shuffling of many feet as the congregation behind us rose to sing. I looked at Henry and our two boys between us. They looked solemn with their new haircuts and well-pressed white shirts. Somehow I could not remember when I had ironed them.

No sound came from my throat as the congregations sang, Was Gott tut das ist whohlgetan, What God does is well and good. I could not get my tongue around the words. How could it be? One minute my father was here, then he was gone forever. My father gone with all his thoughts and wishes, his little habits, his warm hands. I blinked. The brass handles on the casket that stood below the pulpit caught the light.

Conrad, the eldest son, sat with my mother, according to custom. His hair had been recently cut. I wanted to reach out and touch it as I had when we were children comforting each other. Nettie sat beside him with Richard.

I thought of Conrad's ambitions for that blonde, blue-eyed son who carried the Heppner name. Conrad never spelled it out exactly, but I knew how determined he was. It seemed inevitable that his son would inherit the Millbach News. For years I had known deep down that my two boys would have to go elsewhere to make something of their lives. Like rival princes in the bible stories we had heard as children, my sons were a threat to Conrad's plans.

I caught a faint whiff of Alice's perfume and I thought of Felix and Alice and Bradford sitting behind us. Was Felix as ambitious for his own son? I folded my hands in my lap as the congregation sang the last notes.

"Seit Stille. Be still and know," said the Elteste beginning his funeral oration.

Elene, her pale red hair held back with a broad amber clip, her eyes downcast, sat at the far end of the front pew. She looked orphaned, more so because of the traditional black she wore. Black did not suit my sister. Elene, I felt like saying, sit closer to Mama where you belong. But then, Elene had been distancing herself from us ever since she went off to the University.

"Seit Stille. Be still and know that I am God," I heard the Elteste say again. I wondered why he had chosen that text. Still as the incense in a cathedral? Still as the murals of Byzantium priests and prophets, rich with colour on the soaring walls of the half-remembered basilica I had visited so long ago with my father?

I looked around at the walls of the church that my father had helped to establish. The planes and angles of light on the white walls, the clear glass in the windows and the high white ceiling looked as stark as a Benedictine chapter house and as austere - like a theorem in geometry. After the blood and fire of the Reformation, our ancestors had stripped away every outward excess of the Roman church. But over the years the world had begun to creep back in, at least so a few of our elders hinted - the watchful ones, those who saw a threat in every change. In spite of them, crimson velvet now hung from the brass choir rail, flowers stood on the communion table. There was even a cross above the pulpit but without its suffering Christ. Lately there had been a great fuss about candles "reeking of Catholicism" on the communion table. It was not only our Anglican Alice who had deep religious traditions.

"Seit Still. Be still and know." The Elteste must be reaching the end of his sermon. "Gott Segne Euch, Gott Beheute Euch." The Elteste pronounced the ancient blessing. God bless you, God keep you in His care. My mother looked up and nodded as if there was comfort in the words almost visible in the air above her and the long line of mourners began to file by the open casket to pay their last respects to my father. I reached for my handbag. I did not want to meet the sympathetic eyes of anyone - especially not Zena. I knew we would both dissolve in tears if that happened.

Finally the shuffling of feet stopped. Instead of the press and heat of bodies I felt waves of fresh air against my neck. The organ rumbled on. The funeral director came forward and gently folded the white satin over my father's face. I turned away as his hands lowered the mahogany lid with a barely audible click. I thought suddenly of Albert Seimens, my father's oldest friend who had died only the year before. At that time, I had not given his death much thought. I remembered his small black moustache and shiny black shoes, with his black homburg firmly set on his head, the fur collar of his coat turned up like a diplomat or, some said, like a spy. They would closet themselves in my father's office for hours, then go quietly out the side door, leaving an office wreathed with smoke, their empty Schnapps glasses sticking to the scarred wood of my father's desk. Through the window I would see them arm in arm, still talking quietly as they walked through the snowy twilight until they passed from my sight. Such good friends; it brought tears. I wanted to see them like that again. Might they be two friendly ghosts now, drifting down the path beside the creek, carrying on their endless philosophical discussions with no wives or children to interrupt them? My mother would have been incensed at my thoughts. Albert Siemens that agnostic, in Heaven with my father? After what he had done? Adulterer. Betrayer. My mother had somehow forgotten that it was Albert Siemens who brought us to Millbach and our promised land.

The last of the mourners passed and we rose as a family to follow the casket up the aisle. Knots of people stood about watching and waiting respectfully for us to be gone so that they could go on with their chatting.

Later at the funeral reception I tried to forget the hump of frozen earth, massed with the flowers we had left behind in the cemetery. Frost would glaze each leaf and petal, then the brightness would fade into the dreary landscape of a Manitoba spring. The dark would come down. A sugar lump held between my teeth as I drank bitter coffee did not sweeten the metallic taste of my grief. I wanted this day to be over. I wished for it to be a month or a year from now.

On the Sunday after the funeral, Ernest Derksen, our family lawyer came to read my father's will. My mother refused to join us in my father's office.

"Don't you want to hear?" I asked.

She shook her head. "Come and tell me later, Anna." She stroked her forehead as if she had a headache and hobbled down the back-hall in her painfully fitted dress shoes into the bedroom she had shared with my father.

Nettie and Alice had also excused themselves so I followed my sister and brothers and my husband into the office where Ernest waited behind the broad desk so lately vacated by my father. Someone had bared it of its usual clutter and drift of papers and the scars of endless smouldering cigarettes lay revealed.

Through the window I could see Alice's blue and silver Dodge pull away, its chrome tail fins flashing, her two small children beside her in the passenger seat. In the far distance, Nettie's figure grew smaller as she crossed the footbridge spanning the rush of snow melt in the creek and then disappeared from view.

I turned my eyes back to the others. My sister Elene sat on stool beside the bookshelves, her longs legs in black tights folded awkwardly. She had her own life elsewhere. She would go back to her the university in Redwin and her obscure studies there. Henry, his eyes cast down, sat beside Elene. He was always a shade withdrawn in a gathering of Heppners.

Felix was pacing back and forth, restless as usual. Felix is not afraid, Felix is fine, I thought to myself. Whatever Papa has decided will be fine with him. He is our first Canadian; born belonging, clear of all our immigrant baggage, confident that no matter what, he would be alright. He had no memory of misfortune. I wondered how his conflicting desires to please both Conrad and himself would be resolved.

Conrad stood in the light of the window, tugging on the tassel of the dark green window blind until it flipped up with a dusty snap. Conrad, my mother's favourite. I thought of my mother hiding away in her bedroom. "I'm sorry. I'm sorry," she had said to Conrad on a hundred different occasions, it seemed to me. Sorry, sorry. Always sorry to Conrad. My mother had always blamed herself. Conrad, his mother's darling. Conrad with a loathsome eye disease caught on board the filthy immigrant ship. Conrad in the hands of French Canadian doctors who spoke not a word my mother could understand. Then the worst - Conrad left behind. Conrad, in quarantine in Quebec, brave little Conrad, crossing a wide continent by himself to be returned to her at last. What if it had not been Conrad, what if it had been me left behind in that terrible hospital? Would my mother have cared as much? "I owe him, I owe him," I would hear her say to my father and I knew she meant Conrad. The separation had done something to Conrad, too, I thought as I looked at my brother jingling the coins in his pockets as we waited for the lawyer to begin. He did not trust easily. It's alright Conrad, I wanted to say. You have your place. No one will take anything away from you.

Ernest slit open the seal of the heavy envelope. He cleared his throat and began to read.

"This is the last will and Testament of Gerthe Sebastian Heppner, in the village of Millbach, the Province of Manitoba, revoking all earlier wills and testamentary dispositions, " Ernest paused to make sure we were following his words. "If my wife Maria Unruh Heppner survives me..." He read quickly through the provisions made for my mother, then slowed.

"Whereas in accordance with previous promises and agreements..." Ernest's voice faded in and out like a short-wave radio.

Promises? Agreements? My father's promise to me?

"I bequeath to my children Anna, Conrad, Felix and Elene equally, equally," Ernest repeated himself, "all my worldly goods."

Conrad gasped as if he had been struck. Other than that the room was silent. I stole a quick glance at Elene. She looked as shocked as I felt. Although Ernest continued to read I knew none of us were listening any more. The word "equally" echoed in the room and I could feel the tension growing with each second until I didn't know what to do. I had to leave. Without looking at anyone I left the office to stand in the hallway of the printery, the sound of Conrad's withdrawn breath still with me. It was quiet here except for an electrical buzz from the linotype. The lights were off, and in the muted light from the windows, the folder, the type cabinets and the paper knife cast strange shadows. I could smell paper, ink and the warm lead from the linotypes.

My father had kept his promise to me. He had not forgotten the years I spent at the Strachans. He knew that it was not only Conrad who had sacrificed his days and nights with the Millbach News. In my father's eyes, I was Conrad's equal.

I imagined my father sitting with Ernest weighing the pros and cons of what he was about to do. My father always trying to do what was right and good, yet what he had done could tear our family apart. I stood still. Be still and know, the Elteste had said. What was my father telling me? He had just given me the choice. Would he tell me that sometimes to give up was to gain?

175

Or was he saying now is your time, when you come into your own?

Be still and know. Suddenly I was terribly tired and could not face my brothers and Elene. I wanted nothing more than to lay my head on a pillow.

Later that afternoon I woke up on the bed in the dimness of my mother's guest room, pushed away the afghan I had covered myself with and stared up at the blank whiteness of the ceiling and thought about what was the best thing to do. I did not hear the door open. Suddenly Henry stood beside the bed.

"There will be trouble, Anna. Conrad left. I heard his car." Henry cracked his knuckles. He looked like Harry, when he was about to tell me something he knew I would not like.

"Did he say anything at all?" I got up from the bed and sat down at the dressing table to fix my hair. I could see him behind me reflected in the mirror.

He shook his head. "He's stormed off somewhere," he said and sat down on the bed. "Conrad knows what this means, Anna. Think of it. You have equal shares with him in the printery."

"Conrad is my brother, Henry. I still can't quite believe that my father did this." I put down the hairbrush.

"You're going to be rich - you can buy your own car, travel." Henry laughed outright. Although he would never say it, he relished the thought that for once Conrad had been confounded. Henry was a proud man. He did not let go of his grievances easily.

I turned to look at him.

His eyes held something as close to a satisfied twinkle as I had ever seen. "But you must decide, Anna. I will have nothing to do with it. It's your decision."

"You mean that?" I couldn't believe what I was hearing. Henry had always been the head of our household. I turned back to the mirror, pulled the brush through my hair and looked at his reflection again.

"I mean it." The twinkle had gone. He was serious.

"Oh, Henry." I put down the brush. I did not know what to say. After all my hard thoughts of Henry. I now had power. My father had given me that and Henry had just acknowledged it. "Oh, Henry. I do love you for that."

"I love you too, Anna." He cleared his throat, looked into my eyes for one brief moment and then moved towards the door. I put out my hand, but he had gone.

I knew I must go and talk to Felix and Elene.

In my mother's room, Felix stood by the window. "Don't worry, Mama," he was saying as I came through the door.

"But what can we do? What can we do?" My mother looked up from the bed as I came into room and sat down in the blue satin chair. What was my mother doing in bed? It was not like her. "It's really too bad of Gerthe." She picked fretfully at the ties of her wool comforter, then groped for a missing handkerchief. Finally, she wiped her eyes with the back of her hand. "And keeping his wishes secret." She sat up straighter as if she was a queen, sniffed a few times and looked at me accusingly. "If I had only known; Gerthe never did understand Conrad." She buried her face in her covers as if she could not stand the sight of us.

"Now stop worrying, Mama. We'll look after things." Felix said soothingly and motioned to me.

"I'll be right back, Mama," I said and followed him from the room, closing the door behind me.

"Elene's coming down," Felix said, "and we can talk." He was still in his dark suit but had loosened his tie.

"Why don't we sit in the living room so we don't disturb Mama." My mother could hear through walls. Felix and I walked the few steps down the hall. I heard Elene on the stairs.

"We're here, Elene, in the living room," I called. I moved to draw the heavy olive-green velvet drapes. Except for the white lace doilies on the mohair sofa and chairs that my father routinely removed, my mother had not been able to change this one room. It was much as the Siemens had left it, with the pattern in the Oriental rug fading gracefully away like a medieval tapestry. Elene appeared in the doorway in a dark green velour robe, her hair tied back into a ponytail. Without a word she sat down at the farthest end of the sofa.

Felix took a deep breath, stopped his pacing and sat down in my father's old armchair. "I have an idea how we can do this." He crossed his legs, one foot jiggling to some tune that no one else could hear. "What if we each give Conrad one share so that he legally has control?" He paused and looked at both of us in turn. "It would be... a gesture of confidence, of good will. If we do that...if we do that," he repeated, "we're really no worse off."

He was younger, had his whole life to live. For me that one share meant so much more. That one share meant my boys could have a future here in Millbach. That one share acknowledged my years away from home at the Strachans, all the hours I had spent helping Conrad edit the Millbach News. Was I willing to give that up?

"What's the matter with you, Felix?" Elene burst out angrily. "Why do you want to change everything? Papa knew what he was doing. He had a reason." She looked defiantly at him. "Conrad always was your big hero, wasn't he? So keep him happy. I don't care. What's a few shares in the Millbach News? I won't be coming back here, anyway." She folded her arms across her chest, and then looked at me. "Anna, have you really thought about this? You could be the editor of the News if you wanted. Why would you give that up? If we do as Felix says, give Conrad the control, we're just giving in to his ego." She stood up, her long thin fingers twisting at the knot of her dressing gown.

"But Elene, he's worked hard. He needs..." I stroked the worn mohair on the arms of my chair. I still felt warm and glowing after my encounter with Henry. "And Conrad is a fine editor," I said emphatically as if to convince myself. In fact, the years working beside Conrad had shown me that my editorial skills were as accomplished as his. In my heart I was beginning to relinquish what I always knew I would relinquish. "Millbach is just not ready for a female editor."

Elene and Felix were both silent, then Felix pressed a single key on the open piano, then the full chord with his right hand spanning the octave. "You don't understand, Elene. Conrad and I are a team. We'll have the biggest newspaper chain in the province before too long, just watch us." He leaned over the keyboard and absent-mindedly played several bars of "In the Mood" with one hand. "We need each other, but I know him. He's always been that way. He has to be in charge. I can live with that."

"You're very sure, Felix. Have you asked Conrad if that is what he wants, too?" Elene countered. "I can't understand you.

If you're so ambitious, why would you stay? This is no place for you, Felix. Can't you see?" Elene folded her arms impatiently.

"But Elene," I interrupted, "Felix is right. We do need each other."

"You should have gone into politics, Felix." She paid me no attention. "That's where the power is. People here think only about religion and cars."

Elene had never liked Millbach, she thought it rigid and set in its ways. She was still young, I thought, and just as intolerant in her own way.

Felix said nothing but turned from the piano and lit a cigarette. "In a family we have to compromise, Elene," he said simply.

"Alright, alright. I agreed, didn't I? Conrad's ego will be protected. Just get Ernest over here first thing in the morning. I'll sign. Now, I have exams to think about." She left. I heard her slippers almost soundless going up the stairs.

"I'd like for us all to get along." I said resignedly to Felix. "I'll sign, too." Felix smiled gratefully and I was reminded of him as a child. That smile when I brought home his favourite comic books.

When he left, I stood up from my father's chair and felt my father's absence all around me. I missed the low murmur of his short-wave radio, his comforting footfalls coming through the doorway from the printery, the smell of his tobacco smoke. It was too painful to be in this room alone. I left.

Through the doorway leading to the front hall I could see the hem of Elene's robe and her slippered feet at the top of the stairs. "I suppose power does matter for a man like Conrad," she mused from her perch. "He's the insecure one...but I can't believe you're doing this only for Conrad's sake."

"I do care very much about our family, Elene," I said moving to the bottom of the stairs.

"Speaking of that.... I didn't want to tell you until I was sure." Elene's face had lit up. "There's this man, Max Weber, an assistant history professor. We've been seeing each other. At first I paid no attention, then after a while he grew on me."

I nodded invitingly. We had never shared confidences the way Zena and I did. I always attributed it to the fifteen-year difference in our age but I think it was more than that, what exactly I didn't know.

"Well, Max is..." Elene hesitated. "I wasn't sure if I should I tell you or not." She stopped as if she had said too much. "He's well...we've been...we've become very close. He's not free to marry, Anna. Do you understand what I'm saying?" Elene looked at me beseechingly and it all came out in a rush. "I know you won't like it, but I love him, no matter what anyone will say."

"Oh Elene, what do you mean? Why would I not like him? I want you to be happy. Look at Felix. Have I ever said anything against Alice? So from where is this wonderful man, Elene, this Weber - Max Weber?"

"He's divorced, Anna, but Mama doesn't have to know that, does she?"

"We wouldn't tell her, at least for now," I said. I had always suspected that Elene would not settle for some ordinary somebody. What understanding there was between them, I did not need to know either. Elene wasn't a child.

"So tell me, this Weber, Max you say - Max Weber? A German name. What does he look like? Where did you meet? Was he teaching one of your classes?"

"Elene?" my mother called from the bedroom. Could she hear us? There was nothing wrong with her hearing.

Elene looked down the stairs in the direction of my mother's room. "She'll have to know soon enough, Anna. Max is Jewish. From the North End." Elene's fair skin flushed, her eyes brightened. "Mama won't like it, but I love him. He's a rebel too, like me. And I didn't pick him for his looks. He's an inch shorter but who cares. I've always been taller then everybody else." She shrugged. "He's funny and sweet and very smart. He knows about mothers. He has one, too."

"I want you to be happy Elene," I said swallowing the shock I felt. My sister. A Jewish brother-in-law? We were barely coping with Alice! I met her halfway up the stairs and reached up to put my hand on her shoulder. "Papa would want you to be happy. Oh Elene! If he was only here, now."

Elene embraced me and we stood so in spite of the awkwardness of the stairs, for a long while.

"Come, we'll tell mama, now. It won't be so bad." I said and led the way down the stairs and into my mother's room.

Inside the shades were still drawn but my mother sat now in the chair in the corner.

"Elene has something wonderful to tell you," I said, willing my mother to be glad. Then Elene repeated what she had told me.

"Sarah's met this Max Weber? He comes for you at her place?" My mother's voice rose in disbelief. She had arranged for Elene to live with my aunt Sarah in Redwin, hoping that her sister would keep Elene out of trouble. I had no illusions about trying to control Elene. "You took him to my sister's?" she asked again. "I live there, Mama," Elene said, patient for once. "And Aunt Sarah approves of him. She thinks the world of him, " Elene said. She might as well have waved a red flag.

"What does Sarah know about men?" My mother's voice was scathing. "My sister has lived in a refugee camp for too long. She's obviously a bad influence on you, Elene." My mother groped for her glasses on the table beside her. "Sarah and her Poles and Slovaks. And after all Gerthe did for her, too. She did not even stay after the funeral, but had to rush right back to Redwin and her rooming house, her besotted friends."

"Mama. Stop it. I wouldn't have stayed here in this house either," I said sharply. "You picked and picked on her while she lived here. After all the Soviet Terror, and then barely out of a refugee camp, Mama, you can't do this."

I had watched silently as my mother had first welcomed her sister, and then over the months, literally driven her away. I would not watch while she did the same to Elene. "I don't blame Sarah for marrying a Pole. In the camps those Poles and Slovaks kept her alive."

"Smoking and drinking Schnapps! Now she turns my own daughter against me - with a Jew and from the North End! Oh child, Elene, you cause me such grief! Why didn't you find a nice Mennonite boy?" My mother put her face in her hands.

I pulled her hands away. "Mama, can't you see what you're doing?" I did not care if she had just lost my father; she needed to hear the truth for once. "It's not the first time you've driven someone away. Remember Hedwig? I heard all about it from Sophie, although, Sophie never blames you for it and I know you did it for me, then, but now, not your own daughter, not Elene. This will be your one chance to be generous. You will not drive Elene away, too. I won't have it." I dropped her hands and turned to follow Elene from the room.

"Don't go, Anna. I don't want to be alone," my mother said, reaching her arms out to me.

Chapter Twelve

In the five years that followed my father's death, Millbach and the Millbach News flourished. Felix and Conrad made a good team - at least from what I could see - Felix experimenting with photo-engraving while Conrad worked to improve his editorial skills. Every New Year they would divide the spoils of their efforts in healthy bonuses for themselves.

The cottage at Sparrow Lake remained in the family as my father had stipulated. It became a haven for our family. We varnished the pine-panelled walls, painted the window frames, and when the Hydro was brought to our side of the lake, plumbing was installed. We added a front porch running all around the front and one side of the building. From the beach the cottage took on a friendly and welcoming look.

It was the summer of one of those golden years and the entire family, except for Elene's Max, was gathered at the cottage for the Labour Day weekend. Every bed was taken and the bigger kids had spread out their sleeping bags on the screened-in porch. My mother was in her glory presiding over the stove, cooking pancakes for breakfast and frying jackfish for supper. Richard and Harry were the perfect age for water-skiing. There was a boat with a motor powerful enough to pull them across the blue waters of Sparrow Lake, their orange life jackets two spots of colour in the distance.

On Saturday night there was no moon, and only the stars hung over the blackness of the empty lake. The loons had fallen silent. It was a perfect northern evening with not a breath of wind. From the screen porch where the four of us - Elene, Alice,

Nettie and I - were sitting we could hear mosquitoes buzzing and the muted voices of the children playing Scrabble at the kitchen table. My mother had already gone to bed and Henry had gone for a walk.

And then suddenly we heard Felix's voice, raised, then Conrad's. Unusual for him; unusual for them both. Only a half-hour before, they had got up from the supper table, half-empty whiskey glasses in hand and gone off into the night, laughing, talking happily enough, to check the boat that thumped quietly against the dock.

I heard more angry words, then the sounds of a scuffle on the dock. Beside me, Alice too, was listening with alarm. At the sound of the scuffle she sprang from her chair and charged down the slope towards the beach. But before she reached the water, there was the sharp roar of the out-board, its motor gunning to a high pitched whine as the boat veered away from the dock and in seconds the sound was fading in the distance.

"What is going on, for pity's sake?" Elene said as she got up from the porch swing where she had been rocking. Nettie had also gotten to her feet but seemed frozen to the spot.

"Oh no," she whispered more to herself than to anyone else. "Not this, not this."

I could just see Conrad's white shirt where he stood at the end of the dock. I could see his shoulders heaving. Alice was pacing back and forth on the sand, crying helplessly. "Wait, oh Felix, wait, wait."

I got up and walked anxiously down the hill to where Alice stood. The lake was calm. Only the wash of the boat's wake lapped against the shoreline a few times and then the water was still again.

"What happened?" I asked urgently, Nettie close behind me. "Alice? Conrad? What's going on?"

Alice was up on the dock now, I could see the whiteness of her face and then she was into the small rowboat.

"It's too dark, Alice," I called. "Conrad stop her. Tell me. What's happened?" By this time Elene had joined us and my mother was calling from the porch.

Elene waded into the shallow water in her jeans and somehow got Alice, who was still crying, out of the little boat and up to the dock.

"Felix will come back, Alice," I said trying to reassure her. Then I turned on Conrad. "What's going on, both of you shouting?"

Conrad muttered something unintelligible.

Nettie came from behind me to stand beside Conrad. "It's nothing. We just had a disagreement. Nothing at all," he said dismissively. But I saw his hand grip Nettie's arm. The two of them began to move towards the walk up the slope, the lights from the cottage illuminating them.

Elene and I waited, not speaking, on the narrow strip of sand, straining our ears for the sound of the outboard motor. Alice moaned to herself on the dock. After what seemed like hours but was really only a few minutes, I saw with relief the figure of Henry coming down the slope.

"Thank God, you're here," I said in a grateful voice moving forward to grasp his arm.

"What's happening? What is going on here? Conrad and Nettie look terrible. And where's Felix?"

I explained the little I had seen and heard.

"I wondered when something like this would happen." Henry's voice grim. "You should go up to the cottage, it's warm there. You'll catch a cold," he said to Elene and I. "I'll bring Alice." He moved toward the dock.

Elene and I turned and walked up to the cottage. Behind us I could hear Henry coaxing Alice to leave the dock.

"Let me stay, let me stay. You have no right - you and Anna always take Conrad's side," she sobbed on and on. It was unbearable. "Felix is the one I want. We should never have come to Millbach, never have stayed here."

An hour passed but there was still no sign of Felix. After a while Henry and Alice appeared. Alice, a little calmer now, went to her children. I watched through the open doorway of the nearby bedroom as she leaned over them where they slept in their parents' big bed. We all sat on the porch, ears straining to hear the returning boat. Conrad did not speak. Nettie offered false assurances when the silence grew unbearable. She rattled on and on until I wished she would stop, although I wanted to believe her reassurances. My mother was unusually silent. Conrad and Felix had fought which was terrible enough, whatever was said. Mennonites did not raise fists against each other and certainly not brothers against brothers.

"Gott Im Himmel, Lieber Heiland," my mother shuddered and prayed in a half-whisper. The hours ticked by. She rocked in the old rocking chair she had given me to nurse both my children. Elene went to kitchen to make coffee, something I usually did but somehow that night I could not.

When the light finally returned to the sky, around six o'clock, Conrad and Henry got in the car and drove to the police station at the far end of Sparrow Lake. We women continued to wait while the children slept on.

Henry returned an hour later in a blue and white police cruiser. I went to the back door to meet him. "They found the boat," Henry whispered to me, "hung up on the rocks quite near the police dock."

Alice came from the bedroom. She had heard the car drive up.

"Felix? Felix?" she said shaking Henry's arm. "I want Felix. Where is he? What has happened?"

"I'm so sorry. Alice. They've found the boat. It does not look good." Henry's face was as pale as I had ever seen it. Elene was suddenly there too.

We tried to eat breakfast. "What's the matter, Mama?" Alice's three year old queried.

"There, there," my mother said and tried to take Lily on her lap, but Lily would not have it and wriggled free. It was very quiet in the cottage. The older children were subdued. They knew by our faces that something was terribly wrong. It hurt me to breathe.

Mid-morning the police cruiser returned with Conrad. I watched him climb from the cruiser and walk towards the cottage with a bowed head. The news could not be good.

"Flung from the boat. It was dark. He must have forgotten about that pile of rocks sticking up out of the water," Conrad said from the doorway of the kitchen.

Alice did not scream or cry out. She turned away from Conrad and ran to her room. I looked at Conrad long and hard, but his face showed nothing. Nettie was sobbing, looking for comfort from my mother where she had never found it before. My mother tottered back to the rocker. The younger children began to whimper while the older ones looked bewildered. I looked at Elene - she seemed frozen into immobility. Henry took my hand. I turned to him and buried my face in his chest.

We could do nothing but lock up the cottage, get in our cars and go to our separate homes in Millbach. Elene volunteered to drive Alice and her children home.

The trip home along that long stretch of highway - through East Braintree, Whitemouth, and then Ste. Anne where the road leaves the bush and opens up to the expanse of prairie - was endless. Elene told me later how bewildered Alice's children seemed. And Alice too.

It had always looked to me like Alice and Felix had the perfect life. Alice did not know yet what she had lost, would not know for many days and nights - none of us would. I still could not believe it. Everything had been normal, Conrad and Felix laughing, talking. And then just like that. You could not blame that on a glass of whiskey, a few sharp words. How could God allow such a thing? There was really nothing to say. All the facile words of comfort had fled from our tongues. Who of us could comfort Alice? And Conrad?

"It was an accident, an awful accident." I said repeatedly to Conrad. But he grew quieter and more withdrawn. Felix's death, which might have brought us all closer together, was only driving us further apart.

I dreamt of a police cruiser, lights flashing, siren screaming, come to tell us it was all a mistake. Felix was fine. No broken skull, just a few bruises. I awoke in my bed, my face awash with tears.

Elene stayed with Alice. "She's finally crying, letting the tears out, Anna," she said over the telephone when I called just before the funeral.

"Shall I come?" This was what it was like to be an only child and a motherless one, too. Alice's mother had died the previous year after a long illness.

"Better wait," she said. "She's had the priest from Redwin come. He's here now," Elene whispered. "I've kept the children occupied so far." She paused, then went on. "The police came again - there has to be an inquest."

When I went over to see Alice later, she was dry-eyed but

looked ravaged. We sat on the couch in her living room. I tried to talk but I could only cry.

"This is the worst," she said. "This is the worst. Nothing worse can happen." Her voice was lifeless, her eyes dark with pain. I had not seen a woman so bereft.

Then she said suddenly, "Your mother had better stop it. She's insisting that I have the funeral in a church in Millbach. I won't have it. Felix will have an Anglican funeral in Clear Springs. I don't care if there won't be room for everybody. That's too bad." She was adamant.

I saw her hardening almost before my eyes. She moved to the big window facing into their garden where Felix had planted row upon row of blue spruce, then walked over to the bookshelf and picked out a prayer book. "Baptism, Solemnization of Matrimony," she shook her head as she read, "Ministry to the sick - I won't need that for Felix," she said bitterly. Then she found what she was looking for. "The Burial of the Dead," she read aloud.

And so my brother was buried with those ancient words from the Book of Common Prayer. "We brought nothing into this world..."

We made a very small procession as a family. Alice entered first, dressed in a plain black sheath dress. She was pale, with hollow eyes and grief thin, but walked with a straight back. She wore a wisp of black veil on her head. Bradford held one gloved hand, while Lily clung to the other. Conrad followed with Mama on one side and Nettie on the other, then Henry and I and our children. Elene and Max brought up the rear.

The little church was packed. Felix had been well known as a photographer and a journalist.

"Out of the Deep, I cry to Thee, Oh Lord," the priest in a black cassock and white surplice read from an unfamiliar prayer book. I had steeled myself not to cry. If Alice could contain her tears, so would I.

"The Eternal God is our Refuge and our Strength."

I felt the press of people behind me, the slight coughs immediately suppressed. Bradford and Lily leaned closer to their mother, their two blonde silky heads shone bright against the black of their mother's dress. The air was lead heavy with the scent of flowers.

"Rest eternal grant unto him, Oh Lord, and may light perpetual shine upon him," the priest prayed.

Perpetual Light. Durch nacht zum licht. I thought of the German hymn, Eternal light, from darkness into light. Seit Still, the Elteste had intoned at my father's funeral. Be still and know that I am God.

That was all. I could not think beyond that. I could not think about that senseless quarrel between two brothers which had brought us to this awful day, could not fathom that one single moment in time could bear such terrible consequences. I knew that one day I would have to. But not today. Today I would believe in heaven and in Felix, my brother, his life not cut short but going on and on to a life beyond my limited imagination.

I heard the benediction, but I could not bear to look at the solemn procession out of the church moving into the sacrilege of a warm summer day. Almost without knowing how, I found myself among the black-clad mourners outside the door of the chapel. Clear Springs had grown into a small hamlet over the years and children on bicycles stopped to stare. Across the road a man was cutting his grass with a hand mower. Only the week before we had been sunning ourselves at Sparrow Lake, complaining about mosquitoes, watching the water-skiers tumble into the cool blue waters.

The long procession of cars moved slowly along the highway to the cemetery. Alice had chosen not to drive past the Millbach News. Thank God for that, I thought to myself. The cars lined up along the driveway in the cemetery. They glittered and shone like huge black beads strung together.

At the gravesite the raw earth was covered with glaring green artificial grass. We gathered round where the coffin stood on a canvas sling, ready for its descent into earth. I shivered and moved closer to my two boys. Like two young saplings, they were. Philip sobbed and kicked at a clod of earth at the edge of the ghastly green carpet. He was the soft-hearted one, the one who could not cover up his feelings as well. Henry reached out and put his hand on Philip's shoulder. My mother with Conrad and Nettie on either side, was weeping unashamedly. What must it feel like to bury your own child? It was unnatural. I thought of Phillip and Harry, heedless in their exuberant rush to manhood.

I looked at Conrad, stalwart Conrad, who stood now, between his wife and his mother, his hair lifting slightly in the breeze. I was reminded of that photo of long ago, the one taken just before I had left to work for the Strachans. Conrad's hair had lifted in the same way then. So much had happened since that time. He had survived a younger brother. How did that feel? Did he hear that last bitter exchange of words played over and over in his head? Life had not left him unmarked. He was no unformed youth with an idealistic look in his eyes. Today, he had withdrawn almost completely into himself, his hands folded in front of him as if he were about to pray.

Elene stood across from me, her eyes hidden by dark glasses, Alice and her children between her and Max. Alice looked haunted, her eyes tearless, her face rigid as a mask. Her gloved hand brushed a stray strand of streaked blonde hair. Brad stood tall. When he filled out he would resemble his father. Lily clung to her mother's hand. I saw the scabs on her knobby knees and was brought to tears. We had all been witness to Lily's jump from the dock into the boat only a week before. Turn back, turn back, I cried inside myself. But time would not turn back. It moved inexorably forward as behind us a line of Legionaries in navy blue blazers and berets moved forward to drop red poppies on the coffin.

We did not linger. It was as though I was in a waking dream. Felix was really gone. I had only gone a few steps when it hit me like a blow to the heart. I turned back. The men in black suits had already begun to lower the coffin. I reached over and picked one red rose from the spray on top of the coffin and I brought it to my lips. The fragrance held all the sorrow, all the joy of life itself. I breathed it in deeply.

Epilogue

It's done. Lily has waved one more time and is gone, back into a life I know little about, the trunk and back seat of her small blue sports car stuffed with cartons of notebooks. Her graceful movements reminded me of Alice, her mother who came as an exotic bloom into our staid Mennonite fastness.

Last night I paged through the notebooks until late. Should I remove some parts, black out names? No, I decided I would not change or delete anything. So much sorrow, so much joy. This morning, looking into Lily's eyes, clear and sparkling like her father's, I knew I could trust her with the notebooks, knew it beyond a shadow of a doubt.

Ach Welt, but still, it's a good life. Outside the April sky is blue - the very blue that Mennonite folklore claims keeps the devil away. We Russlender, newcomers to Millbach, have snickered at such an old wives' tales. They tried to keep their flock isolated and walled off, milking their cows, hoeing their potatoes, never looking beyond their noses. If being isolated was so good, what about the endless squabbles over the length of a woman's hair or the amount of chrome on a car? I laugh to myself. The culture wars in Millbach are long over. For good or ill nobody seems to care much about such things anymore.

Certainly not my children. Neither Harry nor Philip go to church but that is the poorest way to judge a person's goodness. They come with their wives to visit regularly, bring daffodils in the dead of winter and new books, often magazines that I would not buy for myself.

Elene comes once a year with Max to visit. They have no

children, just as Elene vowed. Max reminds me of my mother with some of the sharp corners rubbed off. He grew up in the North End of Redwin not far from the Madchenheim where I went as a girl and where I first met Henry. Jews and Mennonites have more in common than they might like to admit. But it's hard to be close to Elene. She's so extremely educated we barely speak the same language, although one thing I like - she never talks down to me. With Max she's rolled across the prairies, like tumbleweed in a dry year, from one university to the next - Brandon, Saskatoon, Edmonton and finally to Victoria, putting a range of mountains and the Straits of Georgia between her and her past.

When Elene comes we go together to the cemetery and plant flowers on the family graves: for Papa and Mama and for Felix. Papa's grave, off by itself and lonely once now has Mama's beside and is surrounded by many the graves of fellow townspeople - Nicholas and Sophie, Ben's father, Machine Unger, Mrs. Peddlar-Braun. No matter what we might have believed about the hereafter or what branch of the faith we belong to, we will all end up here. I believe we will all be saved together, or all lost.

I plant poppies for Felix and remember how his Legion comrades dropped poppies onto his coffin. Next time Lily comes I will bring her to her father's grave. After she has been through the notebooks it will mean so much more to her.

I have planted a hardy rose bush for Henry who lies not far away in another corner of the cemetery. That's where I'll be too. I feel settled about that. It will mean that when our descendants come to visit they have a sense of belonging. Our family graves in Russia are lost to us. The Soviets built a huge dam on the Dnieper River and many of the Mennonite villages disappeared under the water. I will not go back to the old places, as Conrad did. He wanted me to come along with him, but I am still afraid. The ghosts of the old Bolsheviks must still haunt that land.

Conrad and I have become quite close again, much as we were in our childhood. It seemed natural after Henry died and Nettie, too, not long after. When Conrad retired Richard became the editor, but not for long. Like everything else, the Millbach News is now part of a big chain. Felix's dream of an empire the likes of the Thompson chain died with him.

Almost every afternoon Conrad comes to the Home in his sleek Cadillac and takes me for a drive. We talk easily but not about some things. Not about my fathers' will, not ever. Conrad doesn't know it was Felix who engineered the plan to give him the controlling interest in the Millbach Post. I wonder sometimes if Felix ever regretted that decision. I tried once to talk about Felix and his tragic death, but Conrad cut me off. "What happened, happened. I can't talk about any of it, Anna. Please leave it." He was almost begging. His eyes, so blue like Mama's, stared into mine. I did not try again.

The driveway in front of the retirement home is empty now and suddenly, I feel old. I dread going back to my own room and the empty hall closet, loose scraps of paper and grey kittens of dust on its floor. Down the long corridor the little Korean girl in a pink uniform is busy washing and polishing the floor. The odours from the kitchen smell of home - Mennonite-aniseed in the chicken soup, borscht flavoured with dill, yeasty bread dough, rising.

Copies of this book are available for
$25 including postage if mailed in Canada.
Email: deliztel@shaw.ca
Call: 778-433-1864